The Stripper

L J Light

LP Publishing Ltd

LP Publishing LTD
UK

Published by LP Publishing LTD 2022

ISBN 978-1-3999-4303-1

Dedicated to my ever supporting family,
success means nothing without you all.

Chapter One

The evening sky was turning a deep shade of pink as Jess indicated off the main road and turned into the driveway. The gravel crunched loudly under her car wheels as she swung around quickly to the side of the property so as not to be seen.

The house looked much like the others she would visit on a weekend. Characterless, hostel like places in the middle of a quiet lane on the outskirts of a town or city, with tired front doors and cheap roller blinds that could be easily wiped down.

They seemed to be the only places that allowed stag parties these days.

As she climbed out of her little car she could hear the

noise of several drunken men, causing havoc, laughing and joking from inside. The sound of a glass smashing, followed by a loud roar of voices over the music came through the open windows.

The feel of shame and regret was creeping up on her already as she hoisted up her stockings and swapped her trainers for her black high heels. Nevertheless, she needed the money, and this work was very lucrative considering her whole shift took her less than an hour.

Looking down, she straightened her skirt and popped open one extra button of her tight fitting shirt before leaning inside her car to grab her handcuffs and police hat. Pulling her phone from her bag she sent a quick message to whoever it was that had booked her, letting them know she was outside.

Moments later the front door opened and out stumbled a short, stout little man. Jess guessed he was around mid-thirties, with his extra weight and fiercely receding hairline trying to suggest otherwise.

She watched as he peered around before spotting her, a disturbing smile lighting up his face as he began staggering across the driveway. Stumbling slightly, he spilt his pint of what looked like cider down the front of his protruding stomach. He didn't seem to notice as he ran his eyes hungrily over her.

"Cor, we've done alright! He'll be dead chuffed with you," he exclaimed, with a grin that sent a wave of shivers down her spine.

He wasn't wrong to be fair. Men that were completely sober and far more attractive would often have the same response, but generally more subtle and polite. Even in her everyday jeans and polo neck her figure seemed to draw attention.

"Are you all ready for me?" she asked, trying to distract him from staring at her chest any longer.

"Yes love, we're raring to go," he said, raising his glass to her as his eyes moved back down to her cleavage.

"Is there anything specific you would like? All it said on the request was a lap dance."

He hesitated for a moment, the corners of his mouth twitching.

"Are you offering anything else?" he asked, raising his eyebrows as he spoke.

Jess's stomach tightened unpleasantly. She knew precisely what he was suggesting, it's what most men, most weekends suggest.

It was a line she had to tread very carefully when dealing with large groups of drunken men. She needed to give them enough to keep them happy, to feel like they'd got their money's worth, but not let them think there's a chance of anything more. She knew some women who would happily oblige if they were offered the right amount of cash, but that was absolutely not on her agenda, no matter how financially challenged she was.

"I can handcuff him if you like? Or blindfold him?" she suggested, pulling her skirt down slightly as his eyeline moved to her legs.

"Oh, I hardly think that's fair," he smiled, "he'll want to look and touch I should think. Right, I'll go in now, you knock on the door in about one minute," he said, holding up his index finger in case she hadn't understood.

"Of course."

Jess faked a smile, rolling her eyes to herself once he had turned and scurried off through the front door.

She checked her phone one last time, the lit up screen distracting her from the surrounding darkness before chucking it back in her bag. Staring down at her reflection in the car window, she fluffed up her long dark hair and took a deep breath before carefully tottering in her heels across the gravel to the front door.

Closing her eyes for a second, telling herself to think of the money she was about to earn, she gave three loud raps of the cheap brass knocker.

"I've been called about a noise disturbance!" she yelled as she entered the house.

The men all turned, cheering and shouting. A few of them smacked one particular man on the back making him spit some of his drink on the floor.

That would be the stag, Jess thought to herself.

He was tall, lanky even, with a mop of brown hair that flopped down over one side of his pimpled face. He looked young, mid-twenties maybe, so did many of the others. It was clear to her that the small, fat man that booked her was the leader of the event, most likely an older brother trying to relive his youth.

The stag looked embarrassed, his face turning a shade of crimson as he awkwardly laughed with his friends, his eyes darting everywhere except in her direction.

The entire ground floor of the house appeared to be one large open plan room. Quickly glancing around Jess noted the cheap furnishings, all of which were looking a bit worn out and tired. At one end three tatty sofas covered in historic stains surrounded a television that looked at least fifteen years old. At the other end was a small open plan kitchen compromising of a microwave, a kettle, a toaster and a worktop covered in more spirits than the local off license. A few chairs were scattered around the sofas, they'd been removed from the dining table that was currently being used for a beer pong tournament. Jess pulled up the sturdiest one she could see and placed it in the middle of the three sofas.

"I hear you sir, have been a very bad boy," she said loudly as she meandered slowly across the room, swinging her handcuffs around in her hand, swaying her hips so her skirt flicked up around her long tanned legs. Taking hold of the stag by his hand, she walked carefully backwards, peeling the soles of her shoes from the sticky floor with each step.

Directing him to the chair, she put both hands on his shoulders and sat him firmly down.

He winced slightly as his backside hit the hard plastic.

"Do you have anything to say for yourself?" she asked aggressively as she grabbed him by the chin, forcing him to look up at her.

“Erm," the boy said through an uncomfortable laugh, his eyes struggling to meet hers.

She pulled out her handcuffs, even though the fat man said not to, she liked to be in control, knowing no unexpected hands were going to try to get places they weren't welcome.

Standing over him she leant forwards, so he had a full

view of her cleavage and black lace bra before clipping the flimsy handcuffs around his wrists. Then, taking a step back she began unbuttoning her shirt, looking only at the stag. It was easier that way. She wanted to forget about the eight other men staring at her. Some of them had moved to the sofas to get a better view, sitting transfixed on her body with their mouths open, like a pack of dogs begging for treats.

Dropping her shirt to the floor, she paused for a moment as all the men cheered before slowly reaching behind her and undoing the zip on her short, black skirt. In her well-rehearsed routine, she wiggled her hips twice and with that the skirt slid down her thighs, over her knees and dropped to the floor, revealing a lace thong to match her bra.

She stood still for a moment, locking eyes with the stag who was looking more uncomfortable by the second before taking a step forward, making sure not to catch her heels on her skirt as she did. Removing her police hat, she leant forwards, straightening her back to stop her breasts from making an early appearance and placed it on the head of the stag.

A lot of cheering came from the other men as she began her routine. The stag however sat very quietly, his knees clasped together so tightly in front of him they were shaking slightly, his eyes glancing nervously down to his lap every so often. She guessed this was probably the first time he had seen a real life stripper, let alone had a lap dance from one.

This awkward behaviour was great for her. No touching, no weird requests, he was barely even looking at her. Studying his face for a moment, she guessed he probably wanted this portion of the evening to be over nearly as much as she did.

A few minutes went by, Jess continued her routine, so well-practised that she didn't even have to think about it anymore. In her mind she was deciding what to watch on Netflix when she got home as she turned around and squatted down so her backside was just rubbing on his lap. From there she bent forwards and ran her hands down both of his skinny legs, pausing as she reached his ankles before running them back up again. Standing up and turning herself around, she braced herself over him, wrapping her hands around the back of his neck.

The chair he was sat on didn't look that sturdy, although she was light, Jess didn't want to put all her weight on top of him and end up in a pile on the floor, so she stayed poised in the air, hovering just above him, her quads on fire. Reaching slowly behind her back, taking a deep breath in as she silently said goodbye to her dignity for the evening, she unhooked her bra.

There was an almighty roar from the rest of the group as she sent it flying across the room at them. Still keeping her eyes firmly on the stag, she continued to dance for him, the music helping her keep a rhythm as the burn in the legs went to another level.

After a couple of minutes she noticed him discreetly try to cross his legs in front of him, his cheeks turning a deeper shade of red as a flash of fear and shame went across his face. He was pre-empting the hounding he was going to receive from his rowdy friends when they saw him sat on a chair, handcuffed with an erection. Glancing around she saw a couple of others also looking slightly uncomfortable.

Reading his mind she leant over him, her bare breasts pushing against his chest and unlocked the handcuffs, releasing his hands which quickly make their way to his lap.

She smiled and winked at him. That's probably enough for tonight she decided, they had only paid for the express package anyway. With that, she began to her closing routine.

"Well, I certainly hope you have learnt your lesson sir," she said as she took back her hat and placed it upon her own head.

There was a low cry and a couple of boos from the group as they realised the entertainment was over for the evening.

"Come on love, let's have a bit more, how about I have a go?" the short, fat man shouted as he pinged her bra back at her.

She smiled at him, silently hoping she would never come across him again in her lifetime, before turning around and slowly bending over to pick up her discarded clothes, flexing only at her hips.

Just as she had planned all the men cheered and whistled, feeling their request had been mostly satisfied.

Fumbling with her shirt which was now inside out, she began getting dressed as quickly as she could. As she frantically pulled her skirt up over her hips the stag stood up, now with his manhood more under control and thanked her.

"I'm sorry about my friends," he said quietly.

This was the first time she had heard him properly speak. His voice was soft, with a slight northern accent and a pitch that didn't quite match his age.

"Don't be silly, it was my pleasure," she lied with a smile as she secured her skirt zip, "enjoy the rest of your evening."

With that she waved half-heartedly at the rest of the group, most of which were now playing a game of banging beer bottles on top of each other to see who could make the most mess on the floor.

Jess raised her eyebrows to herself as they ignored her, thankful that the agency always got the money upfront, once she had put her clothes on again it was like she had never existed.

Outside she wrapped her arms around herself and made a quick dash to her car before the security light on the side of the house went off. In the short fifteen minutes since she had arrived the last of the sunlight had disappeared from the sky and had been replaced with a bitterly cold darkness.

Once in the comfort of her car she locked the doors and took a deep breath. Leaning behind her seat she dug out a hoody, tracksuit bottoms and trainers and quickly climbed into them over the top of her shirt and skirt.

She was pretty well practiced when it came to changing outfits in the front seat of her car now. She had been pulled over once, a random drink driving check the police had said as they breathalysed her, stood on the side of a very busy road dressed as a sexy nurse with six inch heels on.

Ever since that incident she always kept spare clothes in her car ready.

Cringing to herself at the memory she started the engine, her car feebly chugged to life as she turned the heating up full blast.

Wheel spinning off the gravel, she glanced at the house

in her rear view mirror as it disappeared into the darkness, glad to see the back of another weekend shift.

As she drove home, she noted how the roads around Oxfordshire were surprisingly quiet for a Friday evening. Everyone was perhaps already well indulged in their evening plans, she thought to herself.

The drive wasn't long, only twenty minutes on the A40 before she headed down into Witney, through the middle of the town, past the new Tesco and the McDonald's which had cars queued up for the drive thru right out on to the main road.

She whizzed down the high street towards the old cinema which seemed lifeless, even more so since the pandemic. Three young lads sat on the pavement outside the big glass doors, all of them smoking. Jess watched as a young blonde woman walked past them, one of them shouted something at her and slowly got to his feet. The woman picked up her pace, keeping her head down as he shouted again, cupping his hands around his mouth. Jess slowed right down and watched in her mirror until the woman made it safely into a house further down the street.

As she headed towards the south side of the town, Jess's little Volkswagen Polo was now a suitably tropical temperature. Turning the heater right down, she glanced around as she passed the pet shop that she worked at Monday to Friday.

It was a little independent store, owned by a man called Jeremy who was in his sixties. It was a far cry from her dream career, but she didn't have a lot of choice when she tipped up for the interview nine years ago having lost her job in a local café. She was just grateful for anything to help her pay the rent.

It never felt like she had been working there for that long, it was always meant to be a stop gap, just something to tide her over whilst she looked for something more challenging, more ambitious. But time had quietly sailed by and before she knew it, nearly a decade had passed and she was yet to achieve anything.

A few minutes later she pulled up into her street, a small quiet road in the suburbs of Witney with little cul-de-sacs of houses on either side. Turning in towards her house she swung the car around to the back of the building. Both her neighbour's cars were there, as they often were at this time of night.

It was dark outside the house, Jess noticed the security light on the side of the building still hadn't been fixed as she took extra care reversing her car into the little parking space in the corner.

On the face of it her building looked like a generously sized family home, but was in fact four very small, but cosy one bedroom flats.

Climbing out of her car she saw the familiar twitch of the net curtain on the first floor window. Janet, her neighbour was doing her evening watch. Jess smiled, that woman didn't miss anything, she thought to herself.

Her legs ached as she made her way up the one flight of stairs, lap dancing wasn't for the faint hearted or the unfit she thought, making a mental note to try and do some sort of exercise this week to prepare herself for her next booking.

As she closed her front door on the world outside, she sighed and breathed in the familiar smell of her little safe haven. Her flat was a place just for her, away from her worries and responsibilities, away from the past memories that still haunt her in this town.

Chapter Two

The sunlight shining brightly through the bedroom window made Jess stir from her sleep, she must have forgotten to close the curtains last night. Lying in bed with her eyes still closed, she relished in that lovely state of semi unconsciousness, before you've properly woken up, before your brain has remembered what real life has in store for you.

Her neighbours were arguing already, she could hear them so clearly through the thin walls, it was like they were there in the room with her.

To anyone that didn't know them, you wouldn't think they had been happily married for nearly four decades. For the last three years all Jess had heard them doing was shout at each other. There was a particularly animated row a few months ago when she was sure she heard a plate smash against a wall. Jess smiled to herself. She was incredibly fond of them really and Janet had always looked out for her, it was comforting knowing she was just next door.

Today the argument was about the remote control, it seemed Janet had hidden it somewhere and Paul couldn't find it. Jess, still lying in bed, but now fully awake from all the noise, listened to Janet tell Paul not so politely that she had better things to do with her time and to get off his lazy backside and find it himself.

After listening to Paul's equally rude reply, Jess forced herself out of bed, stepping over the police uniform she had kicked off on her bedroom floor last night and made her way to the kitchen.

Gazing out of the tiny window, she looked down at the row of gardens that stretched out on the next street behind her flat. Each one was different. Some were plastered in children's toys which were already in use this morning. Some were used as a dog pen, with a well-trodden track around the edge where someone's pet had spent the whole day on its own, mindlessly running around in circles. Some had fences so high you couldn't see what was going on in there at all. Perhaps that was the idea, Jess thought to herself.

Yawning, she clicked the kettle on. It was like an automated reaction, the first thing she did when she woke up and went into the kitchen. Sometimes she would find herself sat with a cup of tea and have no recollection of even making it.

Still in her pyjamas, she settled down on the sofa with a cup of earl grey and a slice of buttery toast. Glancing at her phone she checked the time, it was only half past nine, she had three hours before she needed to leave to visit her mum, so she flicked on the television and put an episode of The Kardashians on, cranking the volume up enough to drown out the noise of her neighbours.

Before she knew it two episodes had been and gone. Glancing at the time on her phone she jumped up, brushing the toast crumbs off her lap before dashing to the kitchen and chucking her plate and mug in the sink.

In the bathroom she had a very brief shower, being careful not to wet her long hair, she didn't have time to blow dry it today. Drying herself off and slapping some moisturiser on her legs, she studied her face in the mirror before giving her long lashes a light covering of mascara.

Naked, she made her way back into her bedroom which took three short steps across the hallway. Picking up her police uniform she threw it in the washing basket. It wasn't dirty, she had only worn it for two hours start to finish but she washed it every week, it just felt like she should after what she had done in it.

Opening her wardrobe, being careful not to open the door too far that the half broken hinge fell off again, she pulled out a white roll neck top and some denim skinny jeans.

At the front door she slipped on a pair of trainers, grabbed her keys and her purse and made her way down the one flight of stairs.

The hallway smelt again today, suspiciously like

marijuana, which she knew must be the young couple that didn't seem to go to work. They had been living in the flat below Jess for the last six months but she had only laid eyes on them four times. She only knew they were still alive because of the continued stream of parcels and Deliveroo arriving at their door.

Making her way outside, shutting the door behind her, Jess glanced up and saw Janet leaning out of her window watering her box plants.

"Morning Janet, how are you?" Jess asked, shielding her eyes from the sun with her hand.

"Oh, morning Jess love, I'm fine thank you, apart from that old git giving me grief already."

"I could hear," Jess laughed, "can I get you anything from the shop?"

"Oh no, we're fine thanks love. Off to see your mum are you?"

"Yeah, I didn't manage to get there last weekend so I need to go today."

Janet smiled down at her.

"Of course love, see you later."

Jess waved up at her as she got in her car.

The drive to Audrey's care home went quickly. It always did when she spent the whole journey thinking about her mum, reminding herself how she was before the Alzheimer's took hold of her.

Jess remembered back to her childhood, coming out of the school gates at pick up time with all the other kids and feeling so proud seeing her mum stood there waiting for her. She shone brighter than any other parent, you couldn't miss her, with her big smile, glittering green eyes and long wavy hair. All the dads would come over and talk to her, the mums seemed to stay away, which Jess thought was odd at the time but now she understood perhaps why they did.

Audrey had raised Jess on her own, her father was never around, she said he disappeared when she found out she was pregnant, but that she had preferred it that way, preferred it being just the two of them.

Audrey was thirty eight when Jess was born, she worked as a freelance masseuse so there wasn't an issue with childcare as Jess grew older. Audrey had a massage room set up in the back of their house where she would take clients, Jess would sit and play with her toys or watch TV until they had gone. Then her and Audrey would go for walks together down to the duck pond or go and see the horses along the footpath by the farm, taking treats for them in their bags, even though the sign on the gate said not to feed them.

As Audrey approached her mid-sixties, she started to become forgetful and disorientated, it wasn’t too bad to begin with, but as the years went by it became worse. Some days she struggled to express her thoughts, to remember who people were or where she was.

At the time Jess was living with her in the house she had grown up in, trying to take care of her in between working two jobs. But the situation became more difficult as her condition worsened. Jess would go to work and come home to find she was missing, to discover after a lot of frantic searching that she had made her way down to the local shop, the park or the duck pond, wandering around asking people where she was and how she got there. The final straw was when Jess found her in the duck pond, still in her nightdress, up to her waist in dirty water insisting she needed to speak to a man called Bert.

To Jess's horror several passers-by were stood watching, a mixture of amusement and disgust on their faces. On the far side of the pond a gang of teenagers had their phones out filming her, sniggering at her helplessness.

She remembered sitting in the doctor's office after that incident, wailing uncontrollably as he told her Audrey was a threat to herself, that she required professional care and observation and needed to be placed in a care home.

Once they had found a suitable place and Audrey had settled in, the guilt Jess was feeling was replaced with an almighty sense of relief, the dread of not knowing where her mum would be when she arrived home from work wasn't a feeling that she missed.

Turning off the busy main road and down a quieter street, Jess saw the care home getting closer in the distance. It was a nice enough building, a bit tired and rough around the edges, she liked to think it added character, she thought it was much nicer than the brand new, clinical looking homes she had visited in the past.

At the front of the building there was a small garden full of colourful flowers. It looked glorious on a summers day when they were all in full bloom and the birds were singing loudly, although she had never seen any residents out enjoying it, they always seemed to be sat in their rooms or in the lounge watching television.

Audrey had been here for three years now. The cost was

exceptional, although all the fully funded places Jess had looked around had made her want to cry, at least this one the doctors said they could get the local authority to part fund. Jess just needed to come up with the remainder of the bill, which with her two income streams she just about managed each month.

Letting herself in the door she applied the mandatory hand sanitiser from the stand that sat right in the middle of the hallway. Making her way to the front desk she breathed in the familiar smell of disinfectant, mixed with old perfume and a hint of whatever was being served up for lunch. Whatever it was today didn't smell that appetising.

As she approached the reception desk Jess was greeted by Mrs Brown. She didn't know her first name, that was how she introduced herself initially and had never offered another name in the years since.

She looked different today, it was her hair Jess decided. Her already short grey locks had been cropped even shorter, making her look more efficient than usual.

"Hello Jessica, you managed to make it here this weekend?" she asked, peering over the top of her little round glasses with raised eyebrows.

This wasn't really a question, more of a statement and a slight dig that she was a no-show last weekend.

"Yes, sorry about that, it was a work thing I couldn't get out of," Jess replied, looking awkwardly down at her feet.

This was strictly true. Last Saturday the agency had three girls call in sick, so she had been given a last minute booking down in Kent. It was a life drawing class which she found even more awkward than giving someone a lap dance. Sitting there completely naked, in sobering broad daylight for two hours whilst a group of wannabe artists stared intently at her most private areas. However, it did deliver an exceptional bit of cash for her extra time and required very minimal effort on her part, plus she was able to spend her Saturday evening watching Netflix in her pyjamas with a bottle of wine.

Ever since the pandemic she's only allowed to visit Audrey from one until three on a Saturday, that's her slot. The painfully slow drive to Kent took her three hours each way which meant she had missed her weekend visit.

"Your mother has been a bit below par this week."

Mrs Brown brought Jess back from her thoughts with a bump.

"Oh, how so?" she asked with a frown.

"She is regressing I'm afraid."

Mrs Brown shook her head as she rearranged some files on her desk.

"She's been very disorientated, more so than usual and her memory of recent events is worsening. She continually talks about things that happened over a decade ago as if they were yesterday," she paused exhaling, "but anyway, maybe seeing you will pick her up a bit, she's in her room at the moment."

Mrs Brown forced a quick smile through her furrowed brow as she passed Jess the sign in form and a pen.

Signing her name next to her mother's, along with the time and date, Jess noticed only one other resident had received a visitor today out of the twenty or so. Handing the form back to Mrs Brown who gave her a brief smile, she hoped more were coming later.

Making her way along the sterile corridor, Jess walked the brown track of the well-trodden carpet. Around her the beige walls were flaking with age, along them hung odd pictures of flowerpots and random people dancing in the street, nearly all of them had slid down in their frames leaving a wonky gap at the top.

Turning right at the end of the corridor, Jess passed the lounge where the majority of the residents were sitting watching a day time game show on the small television in the corner. Glancing quickly around the room, she saw a few that she recognised. There was the old boy, Tom, who must have been here over ten years now, the staff joked that he had become part of the furniture. He was sat front and centre, holding court among the other residents, shouting answers at the television. Another lady, Brenda, Jess thought her name was, she was sat knitting in the armchair by the window, her eyes also locked on the screen whilst her hands worked away in her lap, almost as if they had a mind of their own.

Coming to a halt in front of her mother's room Jess knocked lightly on the door. There was no answer which was normal, but Jess always liked to knock. Her mother had always drummed it into her as a child that she should knock on doors before she came in, especially the one to her massage room.

Opening the door quietly Jess saw Audrey, sat up on her bed, her hands together in her lap, swaying ever so slightly back and forth, the sheets laid perfectly flat over her thin legs as she stared at the wall in front of her.

Jess's heart sank, it always did when she first saw her here on a weekend. Audrey's ever weakening body always seemed more shocking having spent the entire car journey relishing in the memories of the charismatic woman from her childhood.

"Hello mum," Jess said softly as she closed the door behind her, "how are you today?"

Audrey turned her head to meet her gaze, her eyes wide as if she had never heard her come in.

"Oh, hello Jessie," she said with surprise in her voice.

Jess sat down on the horribly uncomfortable plastic chair next to the bed, she always forgot to bring a cushion along with her.

"My goodness hasn't your hair grown, it was so short," Audrey exclaimed as she gazed at her daughter, reaching a frail hand up to touch her hair.

Jess sighed, it hadn't grown at all in the last two weeks since she had been here, but she managed to smile at her mother anyway.

"How are you mum? What have you been up to this week?"

Jess noted how the sparkle in Audrey's green eyes had faded even more, like a candle slowly reaching the end of its wick.

"Well not much Jessie, I went to feed the ducks on Wednesday with Bert, but he found it a bit boring really."

Audrey often mentioned this Bert man, even more so since her condition had worsened, Jess wondered if he was a past relationship that her mum still held a flame for. There were a few of those when she was younger, men that appeared and stuck around for a few weeks. They would take them out on nice day trips and buy Jess ice cream, have a few sleep overs at their house only to disappear again a few weeks later.

"How are you Jessie?" Audrey asked reaching across and patting the top of her hand.

"How are you're A levels going? You must nearly be done with exams now. Let's hope you get the grades you need for university."

Jess's heart sank for the second time in the last two minutes. Audrey had been asking this question more and more frequently over the past year.

Jess had been all set to study medicine at university, it was the only thing she had dreamt of since she was a little girl, performing lifesaving surgery on her Barbies. She had some impressive GCSE results, all A* and A's and had spent the summer before her final year doing everything she could to increase her chances of acceptance. She spent six weeks volunteering at the local care home, which basically used her as a free cleaning service, and two weeks shadowing nurses and doctors in the hospital on the other side of town, getting herself up at five thirty every morning to cycle there.

Her final year had begun well, she was happily on target for three A's in her A levels, the final piece to her application which would have been gladly accepted by several medical schools in the country.

But those grades never materialised.

That's when her mother asked a question which sent a disturbing chill down her spine.

"And how is Katie? Such a lovely girl, you must bring her to see me Jessie."

Jess felt the blood quickly drain from her face.

Her mother hadn't mentioned Katie to her in over ten years.

Chapter Three

Katie was Jess's best friend, they had met at secondary school when they were both twelve.

Katie was five years old when she moved to Witney with her adoptive parents. Her birth parents had apparently been caught up in all sorts of issues with drugs and two children had been found alone in the house with a loaf of bread and a carton of orange juice.

Jess never asked what happened to the other sibling, but Katie had been adopted by a lovely couple, John and Annie. They lived in a big, detached house on the outskirts of town, in a quiet street where Katie could ride a bike, where the ice cream truck would tootle down, playing its tune and all the children would happily be let out on to the street to buy their favourite ice lolly.

Katie and Jess would spend hours playing in the treehouse John had built for her in the back garden. They would make up games, talk about boys and when they were fifteen, they sat up there and drank their first bottle of wine that Jess had snuck in her bag from the local Tesco. Needless to say, they were both violently ill and to this day Jess has never touched another Zinfandel rosé.

Although she was quiet and until you got to know her properly she barely looked you in the eye, Katie was sweet, kind and had a wicked sense of humour when she'd had a glass of wine. She was also unmistakably beautiful in an innocent sort of way, which didn't go unnoticed by the boys in their year. She was made even more attractive by the fact she had absolutely no interest in them at all.

Jess had her share of boyfriends, like any normal teenage girl trying to find her way in the new world of sexual relationships, but Katie never did.

There was a line of hormone riddled, nervous looking lads hoping for her to accept their invitation to the local cinema, or an early evening meal deal at Frankie and Bennys. But she always managed to divert them away so nicely, they never even realised she had given them the cold shoulder.

It just didn't seem like boys were her thing.

That was until sixth form.

It was 2008, the year everyone was turning eighteen, there were parties every weekend, sometimes two.

Each Saturday night the whole school year would descend upon some poor parent's house. The parents in question would either be sent out or banished to their bedroom by the birthday girl or boy. They would then be greeted the following day by a house stinking of cheap alcohol, vomit in their bathrooms, stains on their carpets and other kinds of stains on their guest room sheets.

Looking back Jess thought there was no way she would entertain that sort of chaos and disrespect in her little flat, no matter how much she loved her child.

There was one particularly rowdy party at Harry Soloman's house where they were all thrown out early after some of the boys got into a fight over a girl and one guy put his fist straight through the plasterboard in the pool house.

These parties weren't just attended by the pupils from their school, it was a free for all for anyone in the area between the age of sixteen and twenty five, as long as you had some loose connection to someone that was actually invited.

It was at one of these parties, Jess thought, that Katie must have met him, this mystery man that changed her.

It was a couple of weekends before the Christmas holidays, they were at Courtney Goodall's eighteenth birthday party just down Katie's road in a huge house with a pool in the back garden.

Jess was in the kitchen, which was rammed with drunken teens, all necking cheap sugary alcohol as quickly as they could before the limited supply Courtney's parents had left her ran out. As a particularly hectic song began to play through the speaker system, two girls climbed up on the large marble island and began dancing very provocatively in their drunken state. As they did a gang of boys from their year quickly gathered below them, cheering them on.

Jess was stood by the big glass doors that led out to the decking, trying to talk to some of the other girls from their year over the blaring music when she realised she hadn't seen Katie for a little while, she was normally never far away.

She began wandering back through the house looking for her, stepping over vomit and avoiding advances from some very ambitious, drunken year eleven boys.

She searched the whole house to the point where she opened the master bedroom door to find Courtney's parents sat like a pair of rabbits in the headlights watching television in bed. They looked utterly terrified, they probably should have been given the mess that was being created downstairs. Courtney had always struck her as a girl that got her way with her parents, Jess didn't think it would be her on her hands and knees scrubbing the living room carpet the next day.

Making her way down the stairs, she saw Katie appear through the front door, her face a deep shade of crimson, her jacket pulled tightly around her. She looked wired, her eyes wide, turning her head sharply as Jess spoke.

"Where did you go?"

"Oh, the bathrooms were all busy so I popped home to use mine," Katie replied, not looking up at her as she grabbed a half drunk bottle of wine from the console table by the door and took a swig.

"Oh, I was worried."

"Well, you shouldn't be, I can take care of myself," Katie snapped as she strode off into the lounge, tightly gripping the bottle of wine as she went.

Jess stopped in her tracks at the bottom of the stairs, shocked at how she had just been spoken to, Katie was never short or fractious.

The night rolled on with the music getting louder and the cheap alcohol getting nastier. Katie didn't speak to anyone for the rest of the evening except for the one boy who tried his luck. Jess glanced over to see her sat on the sofa, cradling the nearly empty bottle of red wine as she gave him a shove in the chest, her drunk eyes heavy and irritated as she told him to get lost.

Jess kept her distance, annoyed at Katie's outburst. She chatted and laughed as loudly as she could with her other friends, glancing over from the kitchen a couple of times to make sure she was still within earshot.

When Courtney's father finally came downstairs and kicked everyone out at midnight, the forty or so teenagers piled out into the street and began dispersing down the road. Some lucky kids had parents there in warm cars waiting to pick them up, others began the cold, sobering walk home.

Katie strode on ahead of Jess down the road towards her house, staring at her phone, her blonde curls swinging at the base of her neck. Jess had to jog to catch up with her, which wasn't easy in the enormous heels she was wearing.

"Are you okay?" Jess asked cautiously. She was beginning to sober up and her annoyance was turning to concern.

"Yes, I'm fine," she replied, more softly than earlier, "I'm just tired."

They stopped in front of Katie's house. They had got

ready there together earlier but there was no suggestion now that Jess could stay over. She usually did. Katie would normally suggest they make some popcorn in the microwave, hunker down together in the snug and watch a film which they would both fall asleep in front of.

But Katie seemed guarded as she looked down at her feet, shuffling from one to the other.

"I'll see you on Monday, have a safe walk home," she said, managing a little smile, her arms wrapped tightly around her. With that she turned and walked up the path, round the side of the house and to the gate which led to the garden and the back door.

A feeling of sadness washed over Jess as she wondered what on earth she had done to upset her. Replaying the nights events as she walked slowly home, she was sure she hadn't done anything, she seemed fine when they were getting ready. They had shared a six pack of beer and a bottle of pinot grigio whilst Katie curled Jess's hair and Jess did Katie's eyeshadow. They laughed and chatted like they always had. Something had happened at the party, Jess was sure of it.

The Christmas holidays came and went, but they weren't as enjoyable as usual. January mock exams were looming, both Katie and Jess were on the road to straight A's so their revision schedule was packed.

They had both been applying to universities, Jess to study Medicine, Katie to study Psychology. She wanted to become a therapist, to help people that were having problems she said.

Given her recent volatile behaviour Jess couldn't help

but think she should be the one sat on a therapist's sofa.

Some days she was fine, others she barely spoke. Jess found herself treading on eggshells around her, hoping she didn't say the wrong thing and get snapped at, or worse, flat out ignored for the rest of the week.

Katie avoided spending any time with her unless she had to. When Jess suggested going shopping together or watching a film at the cinema, she would instantly give her an excuse. The most common one was that she had to save money for university. Jess would roll her eyes whenever she came out with that one, she knew John and Annie were loaded.

What she didn't know was why Katie was trying so hard to avoid her.

Chapter Four

2nd of February 2009

It was the night of Jade Groves' post-mock party, it was much needed after the stress of the last month. In pure desperation to try and save their friendship Jess had asked Katie to come to her house to get ready, she also asked if she wanted to stay over, an invitation that she had loosely accepted saying that she needed to check with her parent's first.

She arrived fifteen minutes later than they had planned and came empty handed, with not so much as a warm tin of beer for them to share. Slightly annoyed, Jess cracked open a half drunk bottle of gin she had hidden under her bed, although she didn't really need to hide it, her mum had never cared what she got up to. Rummaging in the kitchen cupboard she found a flat bottle of lemonade and mixed them two very strong drinks.

Two gin and lemonades down and Katie began to loosen up. They spent an hour talking about the exams they had taken and how they felt they went. They joked and laughed about some of the teachers, indulging in some school gossip about the science teacher who was married with two kids, being seen kissing the maths teacher in the exam hall after all the pupils had supposedly left.

Jess told her about the boy she had hooked up with at the party before the Christmas holidays, how he made four failed attempts at unhooking her bra as they made out in the utility room and ended up trying to pull it off over her head.

Katie had laughed, like properly laughed, her blue eyes sparkling as she threw her head back, her blonde curls bouncing around her shoulders.

Once they had dressed themselves up in less clothes than they started with and inexpertly applied far too much makeup and hair spray to complete their look, they headed out to the road to wait for their taxi. Jade's house was at least a mile outside of town, down past the river along some quiet country lanes. It was too far for them to walk, especially in the outrageous heels they were wearing.

Jade lived with her mum and her younger sister, her parents had separated when she was young. Her dad had a very successful job in London managing some sort of finance company, so her mum had ended up with a pretty healthy lump of cash from the divorce. They lived in a beautiful house with an enormous garden, surrounded by acres of fields, most of which were used as grazing paddocks for Jades mum's horses. Whenever Jess had visited Jade's house before she would gaze in awe at the newly built stable yard, the big sand school which was lined with mirrors and floodlights and the five gorgeous creatures that resided there. A money pit was what Jade called it, horses weren't her thing, she said her mum would rather spend her dad's money on them than her.

The taxi's headlights shone brightly down the dark lane as it slowly pulled up beside the large wooden gates at the front of the property. Katie was still going on about saving money, so before they left Jess had managed to frantically scrape together enough change lying around the house to pay the driver.

Climbing out of the car they tottered gingerly up the gravel driveway in their heels, the gin and lemonade not assisting with their balance, their teeth chattering as the freezing cold air surrounded them in their small skirts and strappy crop tops.

It didn't take long for them to realise the party wasn't being held in the house. Jade's mum isn't silly, Jess thought to herself as they looked down at the field beyond the garden where dozens of awkward teenagers were gathered.

"Oh my god," Katie laughed, "we're going to freeze!"

"We'll have to get our beer jackets on then wont we," laughed Jess in return, looping her arm through Katie's as they set off down to the field.

In the centre of the gathering was a huge iron firepit surrounded by little straw bales laid on their side for people to sit on. Next to it was a trestle table set up with drinks, plastic cups and some crisps in big bowls. Drum and bass music was playing a little too quietly for its genre out of a pair of small speakers connected to an iPod on the table.

The floodlights from the sand school were on full beam, sending just enough light across the field so people could see what they were doing. There were around thirty kids there already Jess guessed, all mostly from her school, some others she didn't recognise.

Katie sat herself down on a straw bale with some of their friends whilst Jess went to get some drinks. She poured two extra-large Malibu and cokes in some flimsy plastic cups and made her way over to join Katie and the others.

"I don't know what you're talking about," Katie said defensively, staring up at Harry from her straw seat.

"Yeah," he nodded, stumbling slightly as his cup of beer spilt on his trainers, "I swear it was you, that night at Courtney's, you were stood outside on the street cuddling some random bloke."

Jess glanced over at Katie whose face had turned a deep shade of red.

"Take you behind the bushes did he?" Harry laughed loudly.

"Shut up Harry, leave her alone!" Jess snapped, jumping to her defence.

Katie glared at Jess, her expression cold.

"Jess, I'm not a fucking child, you don't have to stick up for me all the time. I can look after myself!"

Jess watched her desperately blink back the tears that had gathered in the corner of her eyes.

With that she got up, marched to the drinks table and snatched the bottle of Malibu before disappearing to the other side of the fire pit and slumping herself down on a straw bale.

This time it was Jess's turn to look embarrassed.

Harry gave her a sly smile.

"Touched a nerve there, didn't we?" he laughed as he wandered off in the opposite direction to see what other trouble he could stir up.

As far as Jess was aware Katie had never been with a boy, she had not so much as kissed one for all she knew. They had talked about Jess's sex life frequently and at length in the past, laughing over all the embarrassing details of awkward teenage love making; about how he kept his socks on during sex, or dribbled on her face when he came. Jess had always been so open with her, so she couldn't understand why she wouldn't have told her about this boy.

It kind of all made sense to her now, that night at Courtney's party was when Katie started behaving weirdly. Given her reaction to Harry's comment, Jess could put every penny that she owned on the fact that this bloke had something to do with it.

Wanting Katie to cool off before they spoke again, Jess went to find the bathroom, which turned out to be something that resembled a cupboard next to the tack room in the stable block, with a smelly toilet, no mirror and a light that didn't work.

A few minutes later she made her way back down the slope to the field, her heels sinking into the grass with every step. Warily, she walked over and sat down quietly next to

Katie who was swaying very slightly, staring into the firepit with glassy eyes and a blank expression, the Malibu bottle lying empty on the grass next to her.

"Are you okay?" Jess asked cautiously.

Katie exhaled loudly.

"Yes, I'm fine, like always, I'm fine," she said quietly, her gaze not leaving the fire.

"You didn't need to get so defensive. If you've met someone then that's great, I just don't understand why you haven't told me about him?"

Suddenly it was like a switch had been flicked.

Katie jumped up, towering over Jess, her eyes ablaze.

"Because I don't have to tell you fucking everything! Just because *you* can't keep your big fat mouth shut about the countless men in your life!"

Now it was Jess's turn to get angry. The other kids there were starting to notice as a quiet hush spread through the gathering, people nudging each other and pointing, ready to watch the drama unfold.

"You don't have to tell me everything!" Jess stood up to match her height, "but I think I deserve to know why you've been such a miserable bitch lately, *I'm* the one that's had to put up with it!"

She was on a roll now, all her pent-up feelings were ready to come tumbling out.

"You've barely spoken to me since that party, I don't know what the fuck is wrong with you? You're meant to be my friend and this is how you treat me!" Jess shouted, throwing her arms in the air.

"Oh yes, that's what everyone thinks of me," Katie

narrowed her eyes, her voice full of venom, "Jess's little friend that follows her around, doing whatever Jess tells her to do. Well, you know what, I don't want to be your fucking friend anymore!" she spat the words as she lunged forward and pushed Jess who stumbled backwards, narrowly missing the straw bale she was just sat on.

Rage soared through Jess's veins, it was a split second reaction, the alcohol, the arguing, it all blurred her judgement.

As she regained her balance she threw her arms back at Katie, pushing both her shoulders hard with her hands.

Katie had drunk more than Jess, at least a whole bottle of Malibu more, one push sent her sailing backwards.

In that moment all Jess could see was Katie falling, her eyes rolling slightly as the fire pit roared behind her.

She wished she could stop time, freeze her in mid-air and grab hold of her, but she couldn't, she just kept soaring backwards.

She hit the ground hard, the noise of her skull connecting with the burning metal edge echoing across the field.

With her heart in her mouth Jess leapt forwards, grabbing Katie's hand and pulling her away from the heat, a couple of other lads had run over too, lifting her up by her arms.

An awful smell of burning hair quickly filled the air between them.

"I'm so sorry Katie, it was an accident, are you alright?" she pleaded, still holding her hand, trying to get a look at the side of her head.

Once she had steadied herself, Katie snatched her hand

from Jess's grip and put it up to where she had been hit.

"You did that on purpose," she said quietly, shooting her a glare.

"What? No, it was accident!" Jess repeated taking a step towards her.

"You did that on purpose you bitch!"

This time Katie was shouting at her, backing herself away. As she brought her hand back down from her head, she opened up her palm to reveal a smear of dark red blood.

"You tried to push me in the fire!" she yelled, pointing her finger at the flames which were roaring away in their iron container, spitting and sparking as if to prove how reckless Jess had been.

"No, Katie, please! I would never do that!" Jess wailed, close to tears as she tried to reach out for her, at a total loss as to how the situation in the short space of two minutes had got completely out of hand.

"Just stay the fuck away from me, leave me alone!"

Katie turned, snatching up her bag, still holding her other hand tightly against the side of her head as she set off into the darkness towards the driveway.

It wasn't until now that Jess realised several of her peers had their phones out, the bright light on the back of them telling her the camera was on and they had been filming the commotion as it unfolded.

In a final desperate plea Jess shouted at them, turning around, addressing each device as she spoke.

"It was an accident! I didn't mean to!"

No one said anything to her. There were a few quiet judgemental whispers, but nothing that Jess could make out.

They all just stood there, surrounding her, hands poised mid-air videoing her wailing defence.

Bursting into tears, she ran, following the same route as Katie. Once she reached the gates she began shouting Katie's name, she needed to make sure she was alright, Jess knew how serious a hit to the head could be. She decided to run the route home, she didn't call a taxi, if Katie had stayed on foot she knew she needed to find her.

Running down the lane to the main street Jess stopped and kicked off her shoes, gathering them in her arms as she set off again, her bare feet burning against the tarmac.

The dimly lit road at the end of the lane was a welcome sight after the darkness. She could hear some cars in the distance, but the road ahead of her and the pavement that ran alongside it was empty.

She carried on running, following the road until she hit the river, her heart pounding in her chest, the alcoholic contents of her stomach sloshing around so much she could hear it.

Crossing to other side of the road, she leapt down the steps to the footpath that ran under the bridge, trying to ignore the darkness that had suddenly surrounded her again. From there she followed the path along the river all the way to Witney.

There was still no sign of Katie, just an elderly lady out walking her dog and a lad in a hood, skateboarding down the path behind her, he whizzed past without so much as a look in her direction.

"Excuse me," Jess panted to the lady, dropping her bag and shoes and leaning her hands down on her knees to try and catch her breath, "have you seen a girl walking along here? Blonde hair, wearing a black skirt and a white crop top?"

The lady frowned at her with confusion.

"Oh no, I haven't seen a girl," she said quietly, "are you okay love?"

Jess realised she must look a state, with bare feet and smeared mascara running in black lines down her bright red cheeks.

"Yes, I'm fine, I'm just worried about my friend," she replied, looking hastily back up the path ahead of her before picking up her bag and shoes and setting off again.

Walking up her road twenty minutes later, the bottoms of her feet aching and sore, Jess concluded Katie must have got a taxi home, she would have seen her otherwise.

Letting herself in her front door, she felt sweat suddenly prickle up on her skin, the house was at least thirty degrees and Jess felt like she had just run a marathon. Glancing at the clock in the hallway she saw it was only quarter past ten, their big night out had been very short lived.

Her mother was still awake, sitting cross legged on the sofa, the haze of smoke from her joint wafting around her as classical music played through the speaker system.

"Hi mum," Jess said, still trying to catch her breath.

"Hello Jessie, did you have a nice evening?" she replied, not bothering to look round at her.

"Not really. Katie and I had a big fight and I pushed her mum," she could feel her voice beginning to wobble again, "I didn't mean to, but she was saying some horrible things to me."

Audrey looked round at her.

"Oh Jessie, look at the state of you!" she exclaimed taking in her appearance, "don't worry love, she's a troubled one that girl, look at the life she's come from."

Audrey took another long drag of her joint.

"That girl was bound to have issues, don't worry about it. I'm sure you'll both sort it out on Monday, everything will feel better in the morning I promise."

Chapter Five

3rd of February 2009

A phone call from Annie on Sunday morning sent Jess's world into darkness.

Katie never made it home last night.

She had told her mum that she would be home in time for breakfast with them on Sunday morning.

It got to nine 'o'clock and Annie called Jess, she had tried Katie's phone but it was dead, she assumed they'd had too much fun last night and were sleeping off a hangover.

Jess could hear the panic rise in Annie's voice when she told her what had happened. She was shouting for John who wanted Jess to explain why on earth Katie wasn't with her.

Jess didn't fill in all the details, it was such a blur. She knew it was important to tell them she had hit her head, but she wasn't entirely forthcoming about how it happened. She told them they'd had an argument and Katie stormed off home. She told them how she ran the footpath back to Witney but there was no sign of her.

Annie had heard enough, she shouted to John to call the police and hung up the phone. The worry in her voice was making Jess feel sick. Where was she? Where did she go if she didn't go home? These were the questions whirring around her brain as she thought maybe she should have told Annie about the man Katie had been seeing. Although Jess knew nothing about him anyway, so she wasn't sure how that would that have helped.

A sudden sense of relief washed over her as she realised Katie must be with him, he must have picked her up and taken her to his house, wherever that was.

As long as Katie was safe, that was all that mattered.

The police found the body within twenty four hours, they hadn't even been looking. They hadn't filed a missing person's report, Katie hadn't been gone long enough.

After John and Annie alerted them, they came to see Jess, it was basic protocol they said.

Jess sat willingly on the sofa, her mother beside her, wrapped in a big wool jumper and jogging bottoms, her hair in one long plait down her back. This morning she looked nothing like the tart Katie had accused her of being last night.

Jess explained everything, the argument, the mystery

man Katie had been seen with and how she was convinced they must be together somewhere. They seemed very casual about the whole thing, they said girls disappear with boyfriends all the time, usually ones that the parents don't approve of, then reappear a few days later.

Her body was spotted in the river by a man out jogging along the footpath on Sunday lunchtime.

Jess was sat on the sofa watching the EastEnders's omnibus when the phone rang, her mother answered it in her usual casual manner. Jess watched the colour drain from Audrey's face as she turned to look at her, her eyes brimming with tears.

"What's happened mum?"

Jess scrambled across the sofa to meet her gaze.

Audrey took the phone slowly from her ear and covered the mouth piece with her other hand.

"It's Katie," she paused, "I'm so sorry Jessie, they've found her body."

Frozen on the arm of the sofa, Jess stared desperately into her mother's eyes, silently pleading for her to take back the words she had just spoken.

Her stomach suddenly spasmed.

Vomit, charged with acid and last night's alcohol came sailing up her throat as she doubled over the back of the sofa. The smell was nauseating. In between each heave and wretch were tears and wails of despair and grief.

She couldn't keep anything in anymore.

All she wanted to do was see Katie.

To close her eyes and wish this nightmare away.

The days and weeks that followed that afternoon were hell. As if dealing with the grief of losing her best friend wasn't painful enough, a police investigation was launched into Katie's death and Jess was their prime suspect.

Video footage of what looked like Jess attempting to push Katie into a firepit the night before they found her body wasn't only just released to the police, it was also leaked onto social media which led to a frenzy of abuse from some locals and her peers at school.

The stories which hit the headlines were, *'School girl fight leads to concussion induced drowning,'* and *'Did she kill fellow pupil on second attempt?'*

Jess had wished *she* was the one that was dead.

Her days were spent sat in her room, curled up on her bed staring at the wall in front of her, flinching every time the phone rang or there was a knock at the door.

It was around eleven 'o' clock on Thursday evening, a couple of days or so after the video had been released online. Jess was lying in her bed, wide awake in the dark when the sound of glass shattering made her sit bolt upright.

On the living room floor sat two red bricks amongst a pile of shattered glass. Written on them in white were the words, 'MURDERING' 'SCUM'.

Audrey's attempts at getting Jess to eat anything were continually unsuccessful, she was holding on to the hunger, it was the only thing she could control. She wanted to punish herself for how she had behaved. Food was the only thing her body longed for that she could give it, so she took it away. Plates of untouched sandwiches and bags of snacks sat on the desk in her room amongst the files, papers and books that had once been so important to her.

Jess must have been called into the police station half a dozen times in the week that followed Katie's death. Her house had been searched from top to bottom for any evidence, her most personal belongings inspected before being thrown to one side when it was decided they were insignificant. Katie was found without her mobile phone, it wasn't in her bag that was still wrapped across her body when they found her, they couldn't find it anywhere assuming it must have washed away in the river.

The police wanted to know every word spoken between them in the last six months, they wanted access to text messages, emails, shared pictures sent to each other, you name it, they wanted it.

But all the messages, all the witness statements from other classmates, even the one from the old lady she had spoken to by the river that evening supported the fact that Jess was her friend, that she did care about her, it was all just a horrible accident.

It was going to be difficult to tell whether concussion was what caused Katie to fall into the river that night. Unless another explanation came forth, it was quite possible no one would ever know.

Chapter Six

Monday the 11th of February

A week following Katie's death the post mortem was released. Jess was sat on the chair in the corner of the living room with her knees tucked up under her chin, her long arms wrapped around her thinning legs, staring out of the window at the empty street.

Taking a long blink, she realised how heavy and swollen her eyes were. You think a person would run out of tears eventually, but they don't, they just keep coming. The ends of her long hair had become dry and brittle, whilst her scalp was becoming greasier with every day that went by. The hairs under her armpits and on her legs were gaining some growth now too, and she smelt, from her head to her feet.

Staring down at the paint on her chipped toe nails, she reminded herself again that she didn't deserve to be clean.

Chewing at her fingernails, Jess flinched as the phone rang. Her eyes darted up to look for her mother entering from the kitchen to answer it.

Jess studied her quietly. She could see the turmoil they were going through was taking its toll on Audrey too, not only physically, her eyes were tired and bloodshot, her skin was pale and she'd lost at least five pounds off her already lean frame, but financially as well.

It's amazing how quickly word spreads. Every client Audrey had booked in for the next month had cancelled. Suddenly they didn't want to be touched by a woman whose daughter was the prime suspect in a very public investigation. Audrey told her not to worry, that it would pick up again when everything blew over.

"Hello?" her mother answered the phone with caution, turning her back to Jess as she did.

She paused for a moment.

"Yes, of course, we'll come straight down."

Placing the phone back in the receiver she turned to face Jess.

"The post mortem has come back," Audrey stared into her eyes, "they want us to come in, they said the findings are significant."

The only time Jess had left the house in the last week was to go to the police station. She sat low in the car seat, the hood of her jumper pulled well up over her head, covering her face from anyone that might see her.

Under the peak of her hood, she watched the road pass alongside the car out of the passenger window. She watched the double yellow lines disappear, reappear, transform into one yellow line, then a white line and then back to double yellows.

She counted the number of streetlights on each road, fifteen on Ralegh Crescent, twelve on Deer Park Road and twenty seven on the stretch of A40. The world continued to whizz by as she sat still, trapped in a chasm of grief and sadness.

They sat in silence for the entire journey, Audrey nervously twiddling the ends of her long hair with her left hand, leaving it only to change gear when she had to.

The car park at Witney police station was situated just off the main road at the back of the building, Audrey swung her old Vauxhall Corsa round and reversed into a spot right in the corner.

There weren't many other cars there, just a couple of police vans lined up on the opposite side next to the building, next to them were two other cars, one shiny new Audi SUV and smaller BMW hatchback.

They both climbed out, Jess kept the hood of her jumper pulled low over her head, her hands rammed in the pocket on her front. They walked quickly, side by side across the car park, Audrey placing a hand around Jess's shoulder as they went.

Once inside they made their way towards the front desk, a large plastic screen shielding them from the person sat on the other side.

"Hello," Audrey began, "we're here see Detective

Jones."

The man behind the screen was familiar to Jess, he was often the one sat in this spot when they were here. Phil, she thought his name was. He was around sixty she guessed, with a lean physique and a polished bald head that shone brightly under the glaring light above him.

All the lights in the station seemed to have this level of lumens, it added to the intensity of the building, along with the cold white walls and lack of carpets making the noise of doors slamming echo loudly down the hallway.

"He'll come and get you in a minute Miss Taylor, please take a seat," he gestured behind them to the waiting area.

Jess wasn't sure which of them he was addressing, they both went under the surname Taylor, Audrey had never married and had given Jess her last name so it could have been either of them.

They turned and sat back down on the blue plastic chairs to the left of the reception desk.

Jess took a deep breath, trying to calm herself as she studied the room. Two large notice boards hung on the walls opposite them, filled with posters and leaflets, each one offering helplines and advice for victims of certain crimes - rape, theft, assault, domestic violence. She had read the text on all of them so much in the last week that she was confident she could recite each one off by heart.

Turning their heads at the noise, Audrey and Jess heard Detective Jones before they saw him, the familiar squeak of his well-polished black shoes came echoing down the corridor.

Clearing his throat as he came into the waiting room, he

handed a file to Phil across the back of the desk, not looking in his direction as he did. Glancing over at them, he strode across the room, his long legs taking two steps for the average person's four.

"Good afternoon ladies, would you like to follow me?" he looked down at them with his large brown eyes, his mouth twitching underneath his thick moustache.

Jess and Audrey stood up in unison and silently followed Detective Jones towards the corridor, past Phil who was busy filing away whatever it was he had been given into the cabinet behind him.

Quickly glancing around, Jess wondered if she would ever see this room again, what would happen if they found out it was all her fault, would she be put in a cell here, or escorted out the back, stuffed into a police van and taken somewhere else? A wave of nausea suddenly came over her as she grabbed hold of her mother's arm.

Audrey placed a hand over the top of hers and gave it a squeeze, attempting to reassure her. But Jess could see the fear in her eyes at the thought of what might happen to her daughter after this conversation, at the thought of what life might now have in store for her.

Detective Jones led them into a small room on the right-hand side of the corridor. They had been in here before, it was perfectly square with bright white walls and a large mirrored window on one side. The red light of a camera glared down on them from the corner of the ceiling. In the centre of the room sat a small table with four chairs, two on either side.

Jess and Audrey sat down on one side whilst the

detective slapped a paper file down on the table and sat down opposite them.

Jess froze. They said on the phone they had found something significant, the answer was in that file, just in front of her, so close she could touch it.

"Right," Detective Jones began, "we have had a couple of very significant findings over the last twenty four hours. Let's start with the post-mortem."

He spun the file around so it was facing him and opened the flap at the top. Pulling out the contents he squinted, trying to work out which piece of paper her needed.

Jess could hear her heart pounding inside her chest, what felt like a lifetime had gone by, like every second went on forever.

"The post-mortem findings," he began, reading from the page in front of him, "have concluded that Katie sustained minor bruising to the left side of her head, not compatible with that of a typical concussion."

Jess exhaled and closed her eyes for a moment, realising her whole body was shaking. Taking a deep breath she bit the inside of her lip, desperately trying not to cry.

"It also says the cause of death was drowning. Now this doesn't really tell us that much," the detective continued, "however *this* does."

He flicked through some pieces of paper on the table and pulled out what Jess could see through the back was a photograph.

He placed it on the desk and spun it around so they could both see.

Jess stared at the picture, her eyes wide as she quickly

wiped her tears away with her sleeve so she could get a better look.

The photograph was a screen shot from a CCTV camera on the street where Katie lived, Jess recognised the house opposite. The camera was fixed on the front of the house and gave a side view of the pavement and the road.

Walking up the road with her arms crossed and her head down was Katie, her black skirt flicking up behind her, still wearing her red strappy heels.

It was her, it was really her. Jess couldn't believe it. She placed her hands on either side of the picture, leaning her face down to study it. The text in the corner read '9.38pm 02/02/09'.

She was there that evening, she made it back to her street at the same time as Jess was running back along the river looking for her.

"But Annie and John said she never came home?"

Jess looked up at the detective, confused.

"They say she never did to their knowledge. They were out that evening and returned home just after eleven. They said she had told them she was going to stay at your house."

The detective spun the picture around and looked at it, Jess could see the frustration in his face.

"She left the party at 9.27, that's when the video of the both of you was filmed, she then arrived at her road at 9.38, that's eleven minutes to get three miles across town, there's no way she ran that," he continued, "someone gave her a lift, or she got a taxi. Now we've called every taxi company within thirty miles, none of them picked her up," he shook his head.

Audrey and Jess sat in silence for a moment, trying to digest this new information.

"There's more," Detective Jones continued as he pulled a second photograph from the file in front of him and span it around on the table, lining it up next to the first one.

Jess leant forward to study it. It was almost a mirror image of the first photograph, Katie walking along the street in the exact same outfit, her eyes scanning the pavement in front of her, but in the opposite direction to her house. She had her arms wrapped tightly across her chest as if she was concealing something. Jess glanced at the time in the left corner, 10.06pm on the same evening.

"She left again!" Jess exclaimed looking wide eyed at the detective.

"It would appear so," he said, studying her face for any sign that she might have already known this.

"But I don't understand why we're only seeing this evidence now?" Audrey asked, crossing her arms and leaning back in her chair, "Katie was found over a week ago."

"The camera was privately installed by a resident who has been out of town for the last month, they have only just returned and checked the footage. No other properties have cameras on that street Miss Taylor," he continued looking at Audrey, "no other cameras in the area have any sightings of her in a vehicle or of Katie herself."

"Do you think there's a chance it was suicide?" Audrey asked quietly.

Jess glanced over at her mother, the thought hadn't even crossed her mind.

The detective shook his head and frowned.

"It's very unlikely. In all the suicide cases I've seen over the years, none of them started like this. She was a bright girl, working hard to achieve a bright future, that's not the behaviour of someone who was thinking of ending their life. And even if she did want to commit suicide, why go all the way back down to the river she would have passed on the way home."

He paused for a moment, looking down at his hands on the desk as he fiddled with the edge of the photograph.

"Besides, committing suicide by drowning yourself isn't actually that easy, it's amazing how your body's survival instinct kicks in. If she wanted to commit suicide, there were far easier ways of doing it."

Jess sat and thought for a moment.

"So, what do you think happened to her?"

He hesitated, looking down at her, his brown eyes finding hers.

"We don't know right now, all we know is that it was highly unlikely Katie sustained concussion given the post mortem findings and the fact she was seen walking to and from her house. All we know is that she made it to her street, she walked herself down the road and for some reason back again. But without being seen by a single eye witness, ended up drowning in the river that same evening."

He exhaled loudly.

"Which leads me to my next question. I know we've been over this, but I am obligated to ask again," Detective Jones paused, "where were you Miss Taylor, between ten and eleven 'o' clock on the evening of Saturday the Second of February?"

Jess could feel the tears coming thick and fast, she was sick of being asked this. Being accused of manslaughter and assaulting someone was one thing, an unfortunate misunderstanding which led to a horrible accident. But asking where she was at the time Katie drowned, that was them suggesting something very different.

Detective Jones could see her anguish and softened his gaze.

"Look Jess, I can see how much Katie meant to you, it's quite obvious she was your friend. I don't believe you had anything to do with this, but this is a question I have to ask you again. You were filmed hours before having a physical confrontation with Katie, she drowned in the same river you were seen running along that very evening, so please for the record, tell me *again* where you were."

Jess tried to take some deep breathes, she only managed one before the spasm of tears came back.

"I was at home," she said between wails, "I was at home with my mum."

Detective Jones turned to Audrey who had wrapped a protective arm around her daughter.

"You can confirm you have no recollection of Jessica leaving the house after she came home at ten fifteen that evening Miss Taylor?"

Audrey straightened her back.

"No, she was at home with me the whole night," she snapped at him.

Detective Jones took a deep breath and raised his eyebrows.

"And were you intoxicated at all that evening Miss Taylor?"

He continued to look at Audrey who slumped back down in her chair.

"I remember everything," she said quietly, "Jessie was home all night."

Jess could feel her mother's embarrassment, it was like he was reading her mind.

"Ladies, this evidence is conclusive that Katie did not accidently fall into the river on her way home from Jade Groves' party on the evening of the Second of February. Clearly there is more to it than that. Given our findings, we believe we could now be dealing with a murder investigation. Whilst this is all I require from you for now, I must ask that if you remember anything at all or think of anything that might help, please don't hesitate to call me."

He gathered up the papers, tapped the bottom of them on the table and slid them back into the file.

Standing up, he thanked them again before opening the door, allowing them to leave.

Audrey and Jess got up quietly.

Jess held her head low as she walked out the door.

Even though the blame had thankfully been taken from her, the sadness of everything that had happened that night, of how she had spoken to Katie only hours before she died, the agony of not knowing how she ended up in the river, it all continued to weigh her down.

She wasn't sure if she would ever feel happy again.

Chapter Seven

2022

Jess had pondered a lot about Katie since her mother mentioned her on Saturday at the care home. It wasn't like she never thought about her, but very rarely did she let her mind dive deep into the memories of what happened all those years ago, she tried to keep them shut away.

She would sometimes drive down the street where Katie used to live. The house still looked the same from the outside, just with a fresh paint job and a new picket fence along the front. Even the tree house in the back garden was still there. There was a large 'For Sale' sign up outside the last time Jess had driven past, she still sat low in her car seat, worried Annie or John might see her, even though they haven't lived there for twelve years.

One of the worst things about the whole situation was Jess never got the chance to say a proper goodbye to Katie. John and Annie had called Audrey the week before the funeral to say Jess wasn't welcome. They said the post mortem was irrelevant to them, that they had seen the video posted online and they didn't want her anywhere near the funeral after how she had behaved.

That video never did leave her. It hung over her, chained itself to her. Jess could close her eyes and replay it second by second in her mind, seeing so clearly what everyone else had seen.

John and Annie never did speak to Jess again. Maybe they would have done if they had found out exactly how Katie ended up in the river, that it was proven she had absolutely nothing to do with her death.

They had moved away around a year after Katie died, somewhere in Hampshire Jess recalls. They couldn't cope being in this town anymore. The weight of not knowing what happened to their daughter must have been suffocating, something they carried with them every second of every day.

The investigation was technically still open, but 'cold' as Detective Jones would refer to it. It basically meant they had absolutely no leads and no better idea than Jess about how Katie ended up in that river.

The mystery man that she was seen with outside Courtney's house that night never revealed himself, there was absolutely no trace of him, whoever he was. There were no phone records or calls made for a lift home from her number, no other CCTV, no eyewitnesses, absolutely nothing.

For years Jess prayed for the answer, for the mystery of what happened to Katie to be solved, for the gaping wound left inside her to heal, but it never did.

In the years after Katie's death Jess would occasionally receive an email from Detective Jones about a lead that they were going to follow up on. She remembered how optimistic she felt when she read the first one, a ray of hope in the darkness that still consumed her. But time and time again it turned out to be nothing except disappointment.

The emails became fewer and far between as the years went on. The last one she received was three years ago, she couldn't remember even bothering to open it.

It was Monday morning, Jess had woken early as she had the last two days. Lying in bed she stretched out her arms and frowned. Her head ached, probably something to do with the bottle of pinot grigio she had for her supper last night.

She had never really been a big eater, it had never bothered her that much, especially living on her own. She couldn't see the point in washing any more dishes than she had to. She would often just have toast and baked beans, maybe a jacket potato if she was feeling really adventurous. If she had a man in her life, she thought, then maybe she would enjoy cooking for him, waiting at home for him to come back after a long day at the office, greeting him at the door dressed in an apron, glass of red wine in hand and a roast dinner in the oven.

Jess grinned to herself at the thought, she didn't think there was a man alive that would want to come home to her cooking.

Forcing herself out of the warm bedsheets, she pulled back the curtains to allow what little light there was to shine in. It was mid-September, the days were beginning to get shorter and cooler, Jess could see the cold dew that had settled on the grass alongside the road sparkling in the early morning sunshine.

Throwing her dressing gown around her shoulders, she padded down the hall to the kitchen, begrudgingly clicking the thermostat up a notch as she went. Checking the time on her phone she saw it was only twenty past seven, she didn't need to be in work until nine.

Sitting herself down at the little kitchen table she opened up her laptop. With her cup of tea in hand, she logged on to her online banking to see if the money from her August shifts had come it. She breathed a sigh of relief as she saw it had landed in her account on Friday, her rent was due tomorrow and she couldn't be late with it again.

She was always paid right on time from the pet shop, never a day late. However the agency she used for her stripping work weren't quite as reliable, she'd had to chase them for her money on more than one occasion. But in that line of work an agency is necessary, they take the money up front, along with contact details and address of the client, they could also provide a backup girl if she wasn't able to make a booking.

As she sat there an emailed pinged through from the

agency confirming her job for this Friday evening.

Bookings were usually made weeks, even months in advance especially for an occasion like a stag do, but they were only confirmed when the client paid in full the week before.

Taking a big glug of her earl grey, she clicked on the email to go over the information. Scanning the screen, Jess saw it must have been a last minute booking, they hadn't paid a deposit, the whole balance had been paid in full yesterday. Scrolling further down she found the address, somewhere near Bath. Rolling her eyes to herself she plugged the post code in to her phone, staring in dismay at the screen as it read, 'one hour and twenty seven minutes in current traffic'. She was tempted to start putting a bill in for her fuel if the agency was going to keep sending her on jobs half way around the country.

Scanning the rest of the email, she saw under details and requests it simply said, 'birthday party'. That was very vague, Jess thought with a frown, hoping it wasn't a sixtieth birthday party, or an eighteenth, that would be even worse. She didn't like it when clients gave her very little detail, she liked to know what she was walking in to.

Pulling up outside the pet shop, Jess looked at the little clock on her dashboard, it read 8.50, which was actually 8.45, she hated being late.

Pulling her large bunch of work keys out of her little rucksack which contained her lunch; a banana and a packet of crisps, along with a jumper and a copy of OK magazine for some lunchtime entertainment, Jess unlocked the door, hearing the familiar ring of the bell as it opened.

The shop was small, but had shelves stacked top to bottom with various pet foods and accessories. Breathing in the familiar smell of dog biscuit and cat litter, she made her way through to the small break room at the back.

In there was a little kitchenette consisting of a sink, a kettle and a microwave. In the corner there was a two-man sofa which was so old the green corduroy fabric had nearly worn right through on the arms. A two person dining table sat in the far corner, it was one that Jeremy must have picked up for nothing, the white plastic top that covered the plywood underneath was coming off and one of the mismatched chairs was missing an arm. Next to it was a small dusty television that no one ever watched, in this age of Netflix and Now TV terrestrial television and the adverts that came with it seemed unbearable.

As Jess hung up her puffer coat and backpack on the hooks by the little table, she heard the shop bell ring. Peering around the door, down through the main aisle of the shop she saw Jeremy and Charlotte making their way towards her.

Charlotte was Jeremy's niece, she had been working at the pet shop since she was nineteen and was twenty seven now. Charlotte's mother, Jeremy's sister, died of cancer when she was just eleven and although Charlotte's father was still around, from what Jess had heard he spent many years drinking his way through the grief of his wife's death.

Jeremy, wanting to do right by his sister had stepped in to help raise Charlotte. He did everything from lifts to school, helping out with homework and dropping her off at music lessons. Jess sometimes thought Charlotte didn't know quite how lucky she was, she essentially had two dads, Jess didn't even have one.

"Morning guys," Jess said.

"Morning," smiled Charlotte, looking up from her phone briefly, "how are you?" she asked, her eyes darting back to the screen.

"All good thanks, how are you both?" Jess replied, stepping out of the way to let them in.

"Not too bad," Jeremy said as he turned sideways to make his way past Charlotte who had stopped right in the middle of the room, he was clutching two large shopping bags, one in each hand.

"Let me help you with those," Jess said as she grabbed hold of one of the bags which contained what looked like a lifetime supply of tea and coffee. She looked quizzically at Jeremy who read her mind.

"It was on offer at Aldi alright, I know how much you two love a brew and a natter," he said raising his eyebrows at them both.

He set the other bag down on the counter and unpacked three semi skimmed milks and a multipack of Kit Kats.

"Right girls, there's a few deliveries outback to unload this morning and get everything restocked okay," he instructed as he unwrapped a Kit Kat for himself, "I'll see you both at lunchtime."

As he walked back past Charlotte, he gave her a chocolatey kiss on the side of her face, her eyes remained glued to her phone as he patted her on the shoulder and wandered out of the room.

Jess felt a pang of jealously in the pit of her stomach.

She always did when she saw this type of fatherly affection, it was something she had never experienced and something especially as a child she had longed for so badly.

Flashbacks of walking through the local park when she was little, watching the dads playing football with their children or seeing them all line up in the fathers sports day race, their kids stood shrieking on the side lines, it was the same feeling that she had then.

Charlotte and Jess spent the morning unpacking boxes, unstacking shelves and restacking them with the new bags of dog and cat food at the back, the older at the front. They set up the stand for the latest new dog collars and leads, an Argentinian brand, very popular so Jeremy had told them.

There were three customers that had popped into the shop throughout the morning. A man came in first, he was young and short with a shaved head and thick round glasses. He spent half an hour quietly browsing different dog toys before walking out with absolutely nothing. The other two, a very glamourous American couple who had recently moved to the area with their Chihuahua proceeded to buy a dozen different items within ten minutes, from beds to toys and treats, totalling two hundred and fifteen pounds.

Jess gave them her most dazzling smile as she managed to talk them into buying a last minute deal on some nearly out of date dog treats that were on offer by the counter. The lady smiled back at her as she punched in her pin number with a beautifully manicured finger, her three diamond rings glistening every time she moved.

All in all, Jess and Charlotte thought they'd had a very

productive morning and decided midday was a good time to stop for an early lunch.

"So, how was your weekend?" Charlotte asked as she sat down on the sofa, raising her eyebrows at Jess.

Jess knew exactly what she was referring to, it was Charlotte who had put Jess in touch with the agency three years ago when money was getting tight.

Unbeknown to Jeremy, Charlotte had been stripping nearly every weekend since she was twenty two. She was in the fortunate position of still living in her family home that she shared with her dad. She deemed herself even more fortunate by the fact that he travelled a lot with his work and had recently met a new lady, Katherine, who lived in London, so he spent a lot of his free time there, which left Charlotte the sole occupant of a large four bedroom house in the Oxfordshire countryside. Her father still paid all the bills, all she needed to do was stock the fridge, which wouldn't be a problem with what she earnt on the weekend alone, but she said she needed something to do for a couple of days in the week. Jess suspected it was more likely she didn't want Jeremy to cotton on to her alternative income stream.

"Yeah, it was alright, didn't take too long," Jess replied as she opened her packet of crisps, "how about you?"

"Oh, it was awful," Charlotte replied, pulling a face.

"It took ages, they had all sorts of stupid requests. They wanted to play that game where they blindfold the stag and he has to find a piece of Sellotape stuck to me somewhere," she flicked through Jess's magazine as she spoke, "it was taped on my arm, I swear he wasn't even trying to find it."

"Oh god, that sounds dreadful," Jess replied, sitting down next to her.

"Well, it wasn't all bad, he was pretty fit," Charlotte smiled, "although, I don't suppose he'll fancy going on a date with me, not now he knows my line of work."

This was true, Jess thought. As lucrative as the job may be, it wasn't really what an eligible man was looking for in his future wife.

Charlotte had been on a few dates with a guy just last week. He had taken her out for two lunches and a dinner and was even such a gentleman he had refused sex from her, which she said was unheard of. They spent every meal talking about her life at his request, he wanted to know everything about her, but as soon as he found out she did some stripping on the side, he vanished.

"Maybe you should think of a different career path?" Jess suggested pulling her banana from her bag.

"Yeah maybe, it's just such easy money. I can't see myself sitting in an office forty hours a week to try and earn that kind of cash," she replied, still flicking through the magazine, pausing to skim over an article about a soap star who had got married in a ridiculously lavish ceremony on a Greek island.

"Just need to keep going until I find Mr Right," she continued before looking across at Jess, "what about you, any blokes on the scene?"

Jess exhaled, "no, no one."

"What was the last one called again?" Charlotte asked with a frown.

"Jake," Jess replied, rummaging in her bag to try and

avoid the conversation.

"Oh yeah, that was it," Charlotte laughed, "the boy was besotted with you and you just binned him off!"

"That's not fair," Jess shot back, slapping her on the knee, "I just didn't feel the same as he did."

Jess got up and flicked the kettle on.

"Well, you were pretty keen that first night," Charlotte said with a smirk as she leant back on the sofa and began scrolling on her phone.

Opening up her memories, Jess thought back to the day she first met Jake. What started off as a fairly tame evening turned out to be the most physically awakening night of her life.

It was just after the lockdown restrictions had been lifted, Jake was part of a crowd of young farmers that had descended upon the local pub. Jess had been having an after work drink with Charlotte which had turned into two bottles of wine and a dance on the table. It was their first night out in a long time and there was a definite feeling of loose inhibitions in the air, people ready to make some bad decisions having been locked in their houses for a year.

She remembered spotting Jake across the makeshift dancefloor. He was stood leaning against the bar talking to a fellow young farmer, his brown arms crossed revealing a white tan line just above where his t-shirt ended. She remembered watching him laugh, his eyes creasing in the corners as a broad white smile lit up his tanned face.

With very little encouragement from Charlotte, who had already laid claim on her own young farmer on the other side of the pub, Jess had sashayed through the crowd and grabbed hold of his hand.

"Will you come and dance with me?" she whispered in his ear.

She remembered the look on his face as he paused for a second, subtly running his eyes over her.

They danced for the next half an hour, their bodies sweating as more people joined in around them.

Jess remembered the fire in her groin as their lips met, his tongue finding hers, his hand moving to the back of her head to grab her hair.

She remembered in that moment how much she wanted him, how much her body was responding to him.

As if reading each other's minds, they made their way through the crowds and to the door that led outside.

"Where do you live?" Jake asked, looking around hopefully, "is it far?"

"Yeah, it's too far," Jess said grabbing his hand, flashing him a mischievous smile as she breathed in the smell of the late summer air, revelling in the rare feeling of being carefree for the evening.

She led him around the back of the pub, past the smoking area and through a small gate which opened into a large grass field. It was farmland with a footpath running around the edge, no other houses or streets where they could be seen from.

As they made their way into the field Jake spun her around and kissed her. Bending his knees, he grabbed her by her thighs, lifting her up with ease and pulling her legs around him.

Once he had walked far enough that they were out of

sight, he gently he laid her down on the grass, pushing her legs apart as he lowered his body on top of her.

His eyes found hers, just for a second.

Jess remembered how they glistened in the darkness.

He kissed her neck, making her body tingle with anticipation, something she had rarely experienced in any of her previous sexual encounters.

Running his hand up under her top, he pulled down one cup of her bra as his fingers found her nipple.

She gasped in response, trying to remember the last time a man had touched her there.

Fumbling drunkenly in the darkness they undressed each other. Jess laid back on the grass, watching him watch her. She remembered the look in his eyes, the sound he made as his hand went straight to her, feeling how wet she had become.

He didn't mess around, the foreplay was minimal and within seconds he was inside her, moving with ease, holding the back of her head, his face mirroring hers, their foreheads resting together.

After a few minutes Jess could feel the climax building, it was something she had never managed to achieve during penetrative sex. In excitement she angled her hips up as he began to move faster, pushing harder inside her.

The heat began to rise to her cheeks, she shut her eyes as she focused, allowing her body's senses to heighten.

The orgasm came magnificently.

She let out a loud moan, her body tingling from her groin to her chest as she flexed forwards before falling back on the grass.

Jake groaned deeply as his hips stopped moving, holding himself steady before slowly lowering his body down on top of hers. He was panting as he rolled over on the grass, wiping his hair back off his face.

They laid there for a few minutes, Jess remembered gazing up at the stars as she began to feel the elation of their encounter wear off very quickly. It was suddenly then very obvious to her that she was completely naked. She sat up and began fumbling for her underwear, pulling her top quickly down over her head. The familiar feeling of shame was beginning to lay itself on her, the same one she got when she took her clothes off for random men on a Saturday night.

"Are you okay?" Jake asked as he sat up on his elbows beside her.

"Yeah, I'm fine," Jess replied, pulling on her jeans.

"Hey," he gently grabbed her arm.

She stopped and looked at him, glancing warily down at his hand on her.

"That was a lot of fun. Why don't we go back inside and have a drink?"

Jess was suddenly brought back to reality from her sex daydream by the ring of the shop doorbell. She was so engrossed in her memory of Jake that she hadn't even realised Charlotte had left the room. She was still stood by the kettle, stirring her now lukewarm coffee, her cheeks flushing in embarrassment at the thoughts she was having at work at one in the afternoon.

Jake was a great guy. They had a physical connection

that was on another level, there was no doubt about it, but Jess could never really let herself get past that sort of relationship, she wanted to, but something inside her would just shut him out.

Was she protecting herself? Or did she not believe she deserved a chance at happiness? She wasn't sure.

They went on a few dates. Jess forced herself to see him again, told herself he would be good for her. He was sweet and attentive, but she didn't find that very appealing. All she wanted to do was take him home, roll around in the sheets for a bit and then see if she could make an excuse to get him to leave.

He was more the type that wanted long drawn out phone conversations every evening and pillow talk after sex, and the more he pushed her for that sort of relationship, the more she couldn't stand being around him. The day he suggested she came to his little sister's birthday party to meet his family was the final straw. But instead of taking it on the chin, he got angry and upset, telling her she was making a mistake and they could work it out, shouting up at her flat window, telling her he thought he was falling in love with her and that she was breaking his heart, which only made Jess more convinced she was better off alone.

Chapter Eight

Jess was busy in the pet shop unpacking bags of Harrington dog biscuit, looking with horror at the price tag, realising she spent far less on her own weekly shop.

Charlotte wasn't in on Thursdays, or Tuesdays as it happens, Jess quite enjoyed the peace and quiet, there was only so much pointless chit chat she could put up with.

She had just unloaded the last bag from the storeroom and placed it carefully on the top shelf, which was so full she was sure that one knock would send the whole lot flying. She always worried when children came running in and charged around the aisles, that they would end up trapped in an avalanche of cat biscuit and dog treats.

Sitting herself down on the sofa in the break room, Jess was about to enjoy her third cup of tea of the day when the doorbell rang. Rolling her eyes to herself, she placed down her cup and heaved herself up off the sofa.

As she walked through to the till she saw a tall man wearing a leather bomber jacket, his sandy hair covering one side of his face as he looked up at the dog biscuit she had just finished restocking. She left him for a moment, she hated when shop assistants jumped on you, asking if you needed help the moment you walked in.

With that the tall man grabbed two bags of dog biscuit, one in each hand and began walking towards her.

Jess smiled politely at him, wondering if she could talk him into buying some out of date dog treats when suddenly her stomach twisted.

She felt the colour quickly drain from her face.

"Jess?" the man asked, "Jess Taylor?"

Jess froze, staring at him for what felt like a lifetime.

"Harry?" she manged once the air had made its way back into her lungs.

"Bloody hell, it is you!" he laughed, "are you alright? You look like you've seen a ghost."

Jess hadn't seen Harry since that night at Jade Groves' party.

The night she had that awful row with Katie.

The night Katie had drowned in the river.

She never did return to school that year. No one ever contacted her, none of her other friends even acted like she existed after that night.

Harry had been to the funeral, she was sure of it. She had

always suspected it was him that had thrown the bricks through her living room window all those years ago. He always did have a bit of side to him.

Jess had never crossed paths with any friends from her childhood, which seemed bizarre as she had never left the town that they had all grown up in. She had seen parents of the pupils she used to know occasionally, drinking at the pub or queueing up in the post office. None of them ever spoke to her, she hoped maybe they couldn't remember who she was. All their own children had left the town, gone with big ambitions to get themselves a well-paid job or go to university in one of the big cities and make a new life for themselves. Jess had stayed in Witney, working two dead end jobs that just about made ends meet.

"How are you?" Harry asked enthusiastically, plonking the two bags of dog biscuit on the counter in front of her, "I haven't seen you in years."

He gazed right at her making her inwardly shudder.

Jess took note of his floppy blonde hair and bright green eyes. He used to wear glasses at school, long rectangular ones that went dark in the sunshine. His face had changed in the years since she had last seen him, he had a strong jaw lined with stubble, quite an improvement she thought to herself.

"I'm well," Jess said cautiously as she scanned the bags of dog food, "how are you?"

"Yeah, good thanks, I'm living in London now, working for an architectural firm."

He paused for her reaction.

She purposely didn't give him one as she kept her eyes

locked on the till, pointlessly pushing a few buttons.

"I'm back visiting mum and dad for a few weeks, mum broke her leg last month and has just come home so I thought I would come back and help out a bit. Oh, and their true love child, the bloody spaniel has run out of biscuit, so I've been sent out on a mission," he laughed, gesturing towards the bags on the counter, "swear they love those dogs more than me," he said as he pulled a wallet out of his back pocket and drew out a credit card.

"Forty-three fifty," Jess said looking up at him.

Harry held the card up against the contactless machine and waited for a beep before tucking it back in his wallet.

"So, what are you up to?" he asked plainly.

Jess glanced around her, thinking it was fairly obvious what she was up to.

"Well, I work here," she said quietly, "would you like a receipt?"

"No thanks," he replied as he pulled the bags off the counter and dropped them on the floor by his feet.

"Listen," he began, "I'm in town for a few weeks, would you like to catch up properly?"

He looked right into her eyes as he spoke.

"We could go for a drink early next week?" he suggested.

Jess didn't really know what to say. She wasn't particularly social, ever since school the only real friend she had made was Charlotte and that was only because they worked together.

"Erm, sure," she replied with a shrug, struggling to find a reason why not.

His green eyes lit up at her reply.

"Awesome! Give me your number and I'll drop you a message."

Jess reeled her number off by heart which he plugged into his iPhone.

"Right, I'll message you over the weekend and we can get something organised," he smiled as he put his phone in the front pocket of his jeans. Bending down, he picked up the dog food, one bag under each arm and smiled at her.

Something inside Jess squirmed and not in a good way.

"Could you get the door for me?" he asked, gesturing down at his occupied arms.

"Oh, of course," Jess said quickly, hurrying past him to open the door, aware of his eyes on her.

"Thanks," he smiled as he strode past.

Jess watched him through the window as he put the bags in the boot of a very fancy looking dark grey Mercedes. As she watched him drive off, she exhaled loudly, it felt like she'd been holding her breath for their whole encounter. Suddenly she felt nervous, why had she agreed to meet him, what good could possibly come from that conversation, she asked herself.

Wandering back into the break room, she topped up her now cold cup of tea with extra hot water and a teaspoon of sugar. Leaning back against the kitchen counter she reluctantly let her mind open up the memories from her school days.

Harry was one of those people that liked to be everyone's friend, he moved between cliques, keeping tabs on all of them and he was always the first to start a drama.

Jess thought back to the time Courtney began dating Freddie, an eligible boy from the other school in town. Harry had loudly announced during a school trip on the bus home that he'd heard Freddie had been telling all his friends she had put out on the first date. Courtney spent the entire journey in tears and proceeded to text Freddie, dumping him on the spot. Jess never believed he had said anything, Harry had just made a lucky guess.

She remembered looking down the aisle to the back of the bus, watching him sat with his friends, gleefully enjoying the pain he was causing, like it was just the result he was hoping for.

Chapter Nine

"So where are you off to tonight?" Charlotte asked as she tipped the remains of her crisp packet straight in her mouth.

"Somewhere near Bath," Jess replied as she threw some damaged dog collars in the bin of the storeroom.

Charlotte leant back against the door frame, still chewing her shards of crisps.

"Blimey, they must really have wanted you, that's an absolute trek," she frowned as she peered with one eye into the bottom of the packet to make sure she'd got every last crumb.

"I know, especially with Friday traffic," Jess sighed as she wiped her forehead with the sleeve of her jumper. It was hot in the storeroom and she had been sorting reject deliveries for over an hour.

"Are you okay if I leave at four thirty? I don't want to be late."

Charlotte scrunched up the crisp packet and threw it perfectly in the bin.

"Yeah of course, I'm not working tonight anyway," her eyes sparkled as she smirked, "I've got myself a date."

Jess had to bite her tongue when it came to Charlotte's love life. It wasn't like she could give her advice on a successful one, but lately Charlotte had been on the hunt for a specific sort of man. A more mature one with a big house, a big bank account to match and a nice car he could drive her around in. The only problem was this sort of man usually came with a ring on his fourth finger and a child seat in the back of his posh car.

One of her most recent conquests had ended in absolute disaster after his wife had come home early from her yoga retreat to find Charlotte naked in the hot tub, being fed chocolate covered strawberries by her equally naked husband. Needless to say, he did not come running after her when she legged it, clothes in hand out of the front gates to avoid being drowned by his very angry wife.

"Oh yeah? What's this one's story?" Jess asked, raising her eyebrows at her as she made her way to the break room.

"Oi!" Charlotte read her mind and smacked her backside as she went past, "this one isn't married I'll have you know."

Following Jess into the break room she sat herself down on the sofa, her legs resting on the coffee table in front of her.

Charlotte was short, about five foot three Jess guessed, with big brown eyes and dark hair to match. She was curvy, with huge boobs that stuck out so far in front of her it was a wonder she didn't fall over. Her hourglass figure, beautiful features and flirtatious personality made it difficult for even the most happily married men to not want to tumble her into bed.

"He's a junior doctor, I met him on Hinge," she continued as she pulled up his profile on her phone.

Turning it around, she flashed an image to Jess of him sat at a restaurant in what looked like a very exotic country holding a pint of beer.

He looked alright, Jess decided.

"Very nice," she said, "where's he taking you?"

"He didn't say, he's picking me up at nine," Charlotte replied, still flicking through his profile.

"Jesus nine, that's so late!"

"Alright grandma, just because your bedtime is eight thirty," Charlotte laughed back at her.

Jess sighed, only wishing that could be true tonight.

Chapter Ten

Jess had been right, the traffic this afternoon was hateful. She had even managed to leave the shop earlier than planned, get home, shower, do her hair and makeup and get dressed in just over an hour, which was quite an achievement for her. She left her flat at five to six and two hours later she was still sat on the M4.

There had been an accident and two lanes had been shut three miles on from where Jess had originally ground to a halt. Looking around her she could see more frustrated drivers, weary from their long week of work, desperately wanting to get home and begin their weekend.

After crawling along for what felt like a lifetime, the traffic eventually squeezed down into single file, a few drivers deciding to defy any motoring etiquette and dash down the now empty lanes, pushing in right at the last moment.

Jess watched with amusement as one man made a rude gesture out of his window at the driver who had just cut in front of him. The driver in question leant straight back out of his window and gave him an even ruder one back.

Feeling herself begin to sweat under all her clothes, her outfit with her mandatory tracksuit over the top, she turned down the heater and opened the window a fraction.

You can request a place to change, a bathroom or a bedroom, but it wasn't that long ago she'd had an unpleasant experience whilst getting herself ready. She was in a bedroom in a skanky house in Oxford, squeezing herself into a horribly uncomfortable bustier when one of the men quietly let himself in, thinking he should be allowed a preview of her performance.

It made her feel sick thinking back to how vulnerable she was, shut in a room, her only exit blocked by a man fuelled with drunken determination.

Never again did she want to feel like that. Now she always travelled prepared, pulling over in a layby near the venue to whip off her tracksuit and change her shoes. She had already scouted this house, there were some quiet lanes nearby where she could stop and get ready.

The traffic was still crawling at an unbearable pace. Jess pulled out her phone and sent a quick voice note to the number of the client she had been given by the agency, explaining the situation and that she would be there as soon as she could.

Almost immediately a reply pinged through.

No problem, I know how awful Friday traffic can be!

Jess let out a sigh of relief, grateful for their understanding.

It was nearly nine 'o' clock and getting very dark as Jess cautiously drove the last couple of miles to the property. There were no streetlights and hardly any houses, it didn't feel safe to stop and get changed but she didn't really have a choice.

Pulling up quickly in a field gateway off the side of a narrow road, Jess locked her doors and took off her tracksuit.

As there was no specific request, she took the opportunity to don her nicest lingerie and her least ridiculous outfit, a plain white fitted shirt and a tight black skirt, which could have still passed as a sexy secretary if she was challenged about her profession.

She tucked in her shirt and pulled down her skirt which had made its way up around her waist after three hours in the car. Flipping open the mirror above her head, she applied a generous layer of dark red lipstick and put on her glasses which had cost her exactly six pounds from Accessorize.

Cautiously she followed her sat nav up the winding lanes into what looked like the middle of nowhere, passing countless fields and muddy farm gateways as she went. Eventually she turned round a corner to the property entrance, glad to see her car meet the little finish line flag on the screen in front of her.

Grinding to a halt, Jess leant forwards and peered up through her windscreen. Towering over her little car were two huge cast iron gates, to the left of them was a long piece of granite built into a red brick wall that appeared to line the property, carved into it were the words, 'The Old Manor'.

After a moment the gates slowly began to edge their way back, jolting slightly, their hinges squeaking under the weight.

Not one to enjoy the unknown, Jess suddenly felt quite nervous. This place couldn't be more different to the houses she would normally visit on a weekend, which meant the people that were staying here were probably very different too.

In the distance she could see the house, lit up like Blackpool, with at least twenty windows glowing brightly across the front. Cautiously she made her way up the long winding driveway, lined from start to finish with chestnut fencing and identical looking trees.

The house was enormous, it wasn't until Jess drove right up to it that she realised the scale of the building itself.

On either side of the front door stood a pair of tall concrete pillars, the same width as a well-aged tree trunk. Above them was a stone balcony, Jess could see two large glass doors set further back, a dim light shining through them into the darkness.

Gazing around she noted the manicured lawn and the row of professionally pruned hydrangea bushes that lined the front of the driveway, sitting in perfectly measured unison in their finely weeded beds. Wisteria, planted many decades ago had grown happily up the whole face of the house, winding its way around the tall sash windows.

Parking her little Polo in the furthest corner of the driveway, next to a long line of shiny sports cars and huge four by fours, all costing at least five times what her car did, Jess pulled out her phone and pinged a WhatsApp message to the client. Within a minute the little ticks turned blue letting her know whoever it was had read her message.

A few moments later the front door opened. Jess could see a figure scan the driveway from right to left before spotting her car in the corner. Hopping down the two large front steps he strode towards her with a playful grin on his face.

She studied him as he approached. He was mid-thirties she guessed, quite a slim build, with floppy brown hair and bright blue eyes.

She rolled down her window rather than getting out, her nerves still getting the better of her.

"Hello," he said enthusiastically, flinging his hand out to shake hers through the window, "you must be Jessica, it's a pleasure to meet you, I'm Adam."

Jess had never been greeted with a handshake on her stripping jobs before.

"Nice to meet you Adam, sorry I'm a bit late."

"Oh, not at all," he said in a very middle class accent.

Jess opened the door and climbed out, catching him run his eyes over her figure as she did.

"Gosh you must be freezing," he said with a sympathetic smile, "please come on in before you catch a cold."

Jess felt her shoulders drop as she began to relax, it was refreshing, she thought to herself as she followed him across the driveway to the front door, to be treated with some respect by someone who had paid for her to take her clothes off.

"My goodness, this is quite a place," she said following Adam into the house, taking in the beautiful sweeping staircase that ran up the left side of the entrance hall. In the middle of the room was a large round marble table. On it stood an extravagant display of white roses in a tall blue vase, underneath that sat a guestbook and a posh looking pen.

"So, have you rented this place for the weekend?" Jess asked.

Adam followed her eyeline.

"Oh no, this is William's family home, they just love a guestbook! It's actually very entertaining reading what people have written after a drunken dinner party," he laughed as he strode across the hallway, gesturing for her to follow him.

Adam led her through a huge oak door and into the kitchen. Jess stopped in her tracks and gazed around in awe, she had never seen anything like it in real life.

To the right hand side of the room was an island the size of her entire lounge, surrounding it was every appliance anyone could possibly need moulded into hand crafted cabinets. To the left of the island was an oval pedestal table that could seat ten people. Jess imagined the family breakfasts on a Sunday morning that might have taken place here.

Under the window was a beautifully upholstered bench seat with shelves on either side, stacked with novels and well-read books about cooking and gardening.

A door opened on the other side of the kitchen into what Jess could only assume was the dining room, releasing an ear piercing amount of laughter and shouting from a lot of male voices. A lady, wearing a black dress and a white apron appeared through the door carrying a tray of empty wine glasses, looking very hot and flustered. She looked warily over at Jess before scurrying off to the dishwasher on the other side of the island.

"Would you like a drink of anything?" Adam asked.

"Oh no, I'm fine thank you," Jess said with a smile as she pulled a little mirror from her bag and quickly checked her lipstick, "so, what exactly would you like? There were no requests on the booking."

"Well, I'm not too sure, just your usual routine I suppose. You see, William has just turned thirty five and we discovered only the other day that he's never had a performance from someone like yourself!"

Jess looked down and smiled to herself as she placed the mirror back in her bag, he was too polite to even say the word stripper.

"So, we all thought we would give him a birthday treat," he said as he clapped his hands together with a broad grin.

"Of course, as it's his first time I'll be gentle with him," Jess said with a wink, hoping that his lack of comparison might mean she could do the shortened version of her routine and be out of here and on her way home within the next ten minutes.

"So, which one is William?" she asked, placing her bag down on the island before straightening her skirt and pulling up her collar.

"He's sat at the head of the table at this end, he'll have his back to you. So, I thought I would go in first and say we had a surprise for him, then you come in."

His eyes were dancing with excitement.

"Sounds great," Jess replied with a smile.

Quietly Adam slunk back into the dining room.

Jess positioned herself just behind the door so she could hear what was being said.

And there was her cue, Adam gleefully declaring they had all organised a special surprise for William.

Heaving the door open, which was a lot heavier than she imagined, she slowly walked her way into the dining room, her glasses sitting low on her nose so she could peer over the top of them, her hips swaying, stepping purposefully with one foot in front of the other.

The dining room was vast to say the least, with a dozen men sat around one long rectangular table. Large portraits and landscape oil paintings hung from the dark panelled walls. In the corner sat a grand piano, its well-polished surface gleaming under the light of the chandeliers.

Adam had sat himself down next to a very large man halfway along the table and was smiling gleefully from ear to ear.

The other men all cheered and began banging their glasses on the table as they saw her come through the door. The big man sat next to Adam smacked him on the back so hard in appreciation it sent his tumbler of whisky flying across the table.

William still had his back to her, his shoulders so broad

they nearly didn't fit in the carver he was sat in.

Jess walked behind him slowly, her heels echoing on the wooden floorboards. Placing her fingertips gently on his right shoulder, she ran them slowly across his back, feeling him flinch slightly under her touch.

He tilted his head fractionally as she moved around into his eyeline.

If Jess thought the kitchen was breath taking, it had nothing on this man.

He gazed up at her, his elbows resting on the wooden arms of his chair as he pushed it back slightly, allowing her to move in front of him.

Jess couldn't read his face, his dark eyes were giving nothing away. He wasn't laughing or shouting or smiling, it was like he was looking through her eyes, right into her soul.

She reached for his hand, still holding his gaze as he reached up for hers almost in symmetry. Pulling his arms around her waist, she moved herself on to his lap.

This wasn't her normal routine, she normally undressed first, but there was something in his eyes telling her what he wanted.

Slowly his hands made their way to her lower back and down to her legs, grazing over the thighs.

It was electric.

Jess felt every nerve in her body come to life and stand to attention.

Studying his face, she ran her hands through his dark hair before gently clasping the back of his neck. Leaning forward so her cheek just brushed the side of his, the heat from his skin radiating against hers, she whispered in his ear, "would you like me to take my clothes off?"

He paused, just for a moment.

"Not here," he replied, breathing into her neck as all her senses went into overdrive.

Standing up, still holding his gaze she took his hand, more heat surging through her body with every touch of his skin.

He got to his feet, standing around six inches taller than her, his broad frame making him seem bigger. Holding her gaze, he let her lead him towards the kitchen.

The other men behind him were roaring, Jess couldn't work out if they were angry or happy.

"A private dance is it?" she heard one of them shout from the far end of the table.

Once in the kitchen William took charge. Leading her back through the main entrance hall, he stepped up to a wall panel on the far side of the room and pushed it gently.

Jess watched as it silently swung open.

On the other side was an office, beautifully decorated in dark patterned wallpaper with an entire wall of mahogany bookcases and a large desk to match. On the left side of the room was a navy sofa, a table covered in various spirits sat to the side of it.

William released her hand, she watched as he turned and locked the door behind them.

Jess noted how this would have normally set alarm bells ringing, but right now, here in this room, with this man, was exactly where she wanted to be.

Catching her eye briefly, William turned and walked

past her, his scent lingering in the air between them.

"Would you like a drink?" he asked as he stopped by the little table and poured himself a whiskey.

Jess took this opportunity to take off her cheap glasses and quickly dab away a couple of layers of lipstick.

"I shouldn't really if I'm working," she replied.

Drinking his whiskey in one mouthful, he turned around and looked at her.

"Of course," he said as he sat himself down on the sofa, stretching his arms out over the back.

He studied her for a moment as she stood in front of him, his eyes running over her body, taking in every inch of her that was on display. Leaning forward, he rested his elbows on his knees and looked deep into her eyes.

"Can I undress you?" he asked, his own eyes darkening as he spoke.

Jess's whole body trembled in response as her heart began to race. This was fast becoming the most erotic encounter of her life and they had barely even touched each other.

Taking a deep breath, she concentrated on trying to stand up straight as her knees threatened to give way.

It felt like a lifetime before she eventually found her voice.

"If you like," she manged through a small whisper.

She watched as his jaw tensed slightly, his cheeks becoming more angular as he rose to his feet.

Jess could hear her heart beating inside her chest like it was about to explode out of her ears. Her breathing quickened again as he walked a slow circle around her, his gaze burning into her skin.

She closed her eyes as she heard his footsteps stop, sensing him just behind her, feeling his breath hit the back of her neck.

Gently she leant her head back, every cell in her skin on high alert, waiting in anticipation as the side of her face touched his neck.

Reaching both his arms around her, he began slowly unbuttoning her shirt, his chest pressing lightly against her back. Taking a small step away from her, he gently slid her shirt off her shoulders and let it drop to the floor.

Holding her breath, Jess felt him find the zip on the back of her skirt, her whole body quivering with arousal as he slowly slid it down over her hips.

Her knees were visibly shaking. For so many years she had been completely confident about her body, that or she hadn't really cared what anyone thought about her before. But this was the first time someone had looked at her like this, in every way, from every angle, and there was something inside her that desperately wanted him to like what he saw.

"What's your name?" he asked as his fingers found her bra clasp.

Her back arched in response to his touch.

"Jess, Jess Taylor."

She didn't know why she added her surname, maybe because it made her sound less like a stripper.

"Well, it's very nice to meet you, Jess Taylor. My name is William Archer," he whispered in her ear as her bra pinged open.

Jess trembled as his breath hit the side of her face, slowly she dropped her shoulders, letting her bra fall to the floor.

William walked around her again, his hands in his pockets, keeping his eyes locked on hers, coming to a stop just in front of her.

He was wearing dark navy trousers and a crisp white shirt with no jewellery, no rings more importantly Jess had noted earlier, just a watch on his left hand. The desperate need to undress him, to rip every button off his shirt was becoming unbearable, but she was unsure what was happening right now. Everything was telling her this was heading in that direction, but she needed him to make the first move.

Slowly he took a step towards her, Jess shut her eyes and held her breath as he leant his head down, his stubble just brushing the side of her cheek.

"You, Jess Taylor, might just be the most beautiful thing I have ever seen," he whispered quietly in her ear.

Jess took a sharp breath as he began to move around her again, running his fingers gently along her collar bone and round to the nape of her neck.

Her body was responding to him.

Glancing down she could see her nipples had hardened. Leaning her head back, relishing in his touch, she felt the wetness begin to gather in her knickers.

Jess closed her eyes, heightening her other senses, waiting for his next move.

Another surge of heat went from her groin right up to her cheeks as his fingers reached for her knickers, a black lace thong that matched her discarded bra.

Slowly he slid them down her thighs, letting them drop to the floor. She wanted to step out of them, but she didn't dare move her legs in case they gave way.

He walked around her once more, stopping just in front of her again, a little closer this time.

Jess suddenly felt like she wanted to cry. The desire to touch him and to have him touch her, properly, was completely overwhelming.

As she battled with the feeling of frustration that was building up inside her William stepped forward, as if reading her mind and took her face in his hands.

Their lips met in an explosion of sensations.

Jess let out a noise, a mixture of a whimper and a groan of satisfaction.

Her hands reached for his hair, his fingers found her breasts, cupping them, squeezing them, rolling her nipples in his fingertips. It had been such a build-up, Jess thought she might orgasm right there and then.

He picked her up as she wrapped her thighs around his waist and kicked off her heels, their mouths not wanting to leave each other.

Blindly she fumbled for his shirt buttons as he placed her down on the edge of the desk.

Stepping back, he gazed into her eyes as he undid the remaining buttons and pulled his shirt down over his arms.

Jess paused for a moment to take in his body, running her hands from his shoulders down to his elbows, his muscles flexing underneath her touch.

Pushing her hands gently away, he dropped to his knees.

Jess exhaled loudly, she knew what was coming as she

leant back, her arms supporting herself on the far side of the desk. Letting her head fall backwards she closed her eyes as she waited for him to find her.

A shiver made its way through her body as his lips met her inner thighs, just above her knees.

Moving between her legs he took his time, kissing, licking, letting her arousal climb to a whole new level.

Excitement radiated through her as she felt him closing in, the anticipation was too much.

She moaned in satisfaction as his tongue found her. She could feel his stubble rubbing against her skin as he pushed her knees even further apart.

She was getting close, she could feel the heat rising in her face.

Again, as if he had read her mind, he stood up, pulling her forward by the back of her neck and kissing her, the taste of her still on his tongue.

Frantically she began undoing his belt. After a few seconds she felt his hands take over from her as he hastily pulled his trousers down, their mouths still locked.

In one swift movement he was inside her.

She gasped as he filled her, arching her back, his hips moving gently back and forth as she matched his motion. Their bodies were in-sync, with every movement hitting the spot they both needed.

William began moving harder, their breathing getting heavier with every minute that went by.

Grabbing her left knee, he held it up under his arm. Watching his face Jess could see he was close, as much as she wanted to prolong this moment with him, she stopped fighting it. Angling her hips upwards she allowed him to move right where she needed him. Seconds was all it took.

She orgasmed spectacularly, letting out a cry as her body fell back on the desk.

William quickened his pace again, his breathing getting faster as he did.

Jess watched him close his eyes, concentrating on finding his sweet spot. Moving her right leg above his other arm, she tilted her hips up further.

Grabbing hold of both her thighs William released, groaning loudly as he did. Beads of sweat were gathering on his forehead as he lowered her legs down, his eyes still closed under his furrowed brow.

They stayed there for a minute, only their laboured breathing breaking the silence before William slowly slid his arms under her back, picking her up, his head buried in her neck. Walking carefully over to the sofa he laid himself down, gently holding her on top of him.

They stayed there, stretched out, their bodies and limbs intertwined. Pulling a large fur throw from the back of the sofa he placed it over their naked bodies, encasing their radiating heat.

Jess stayed perfectly still, her head resting on his chest as she listened to his heart still racing beneath her.

Chapter Eleven

Jess wasn't sure what time it was, she was still half asleep when she noticed the movement and the echoing footsteps of William quietly making his way up the staircase in the hallway, carrying her close to his chest, still wrapped in the throw from the sofa.

Making his was along the upstairs corridor, Jess felt him push a door open with his foot, hearing it creak as it swung back, breaking the silence in the house. Lying her down in the middle of a bed Jess heard the door creak again as it shut. Moments later she felt William climb in behind her, his body fitting perfectly into the shape of hers, his arm wrapped around her.

She kept her eyes closed, she didn't want to open them

and find she'd been dreaming.

Pushing his face gently into hers, he kissed her neck once more before he settled.

She lay quietly and listened for a few minutes as his breathing became slower and heavier before she also fell back into a deep, blissful sleep.

Voices coming through the open window woke Jess, she listened, confused for moment before realising they were coming from the driveway below.

William was still sleeping, his right arm laid up above his head, his face tilted slightly in her direction. Rolling over she studied him for a moment, he really was impossibly handsome she thought to herself as she smiled.

Looking around she took in the details of the room. It was beautiful but simple, most definitely a room inhabited by a man. There were no pictures or throws or cushions indicating a female had anything to do with the décor. The huge curtains that covered the sash window dropped right down to the original oak floorboards, their dark colour breaking up the cream walls. White sheets with an off the scale thread count covered what could only be an emperor sized oak framed bed. On the far side of the room were two freestanding French style wardrobes and a chair harbouring a small pile of discarded clothes.

Trying not to wake William, Jess slipped carefully out of the bed and tip toed into the bathroom, slowly pushing the door closed behind her.

When she returned and got quietly back into the sheets, she noticed the voices outside had grown louder, she could clearly make out what they were saying.

"Look, her car is still here so they must have had a good night together!" one of them exclaimed.

"He clearly got our money's worth then," another laughed in response.

Jess's heart sank to the pit of her stomach.

She had never even considered that William might have just thought he had bought her for the evening.

Sitting herself up against the headboard she pulled the covers up over her naked breasts.

"They're wrong," William said, still lying next to her with his eyes closed.

Jess jumped slightly at sound of his voice.

"That's not what last night was," he opened his eyes slightly and looked across at her.

They could hear farewells being made between his friends outside, the slamming of car doors and the roar of expensive engines coming to life as some of them began to make their way home.

"Don't you want to go and say goodbye to your friends?" Jess asked, gesturing to the noise coming through the window.

"Are you mad? Why would I go down there when I have you up here," he said with a mischievous smile as he swiftly pulled her whole body back down the bed and braced himself over her.

Jess couldn't help but laugh as she ran her hands through his hair and gazed into his eyes, quickly forgetting about her worries.

He kissed her, long and hard, her body responding to him

the same way it did last night.

She could feel him smiling through their kiss.

"Ready for round two are we?" he murmured.

Jess gave every part of her body to him, in a way she had never done with any man before, it was like she belonged to him. They moved together in perfect harmony, like their bodies knew what the other needed. Every touch, every kiss was exhilarating.

Similar to the night before, they climaxed together, their bodies sweating under the sheets, their breath intertwining as they frantically kissed each other, relishing in the wave of endorphins that was surging through their veins.

He remained on top of her as they recovered, his breathing heavy and laboured.

Her hands cradled his face, holding it close to hers as she wondered to herself how she'd ever found sex satisfying before, nothing had ever felt like this.

William rolled over, the sunlight catching the sweat glistening on his chest and shoulders.

"Let's get some breakfast," he said as he picked up the phone on the bedside table. Punching in just one number he held the phone up to his ear.

"Morning Gwen, can Jess and I have two teas in bed please, we'll be down for breakfast shortly," he paused, "great, thank you."

Looking over at Jess, he slapped her playfully on the thigh, "come on, let's have a shower."

Standing up, he made his way to the bathroom.

Jess kept the sheets pulled up around her, discreetly admiring his naked body as he went.

Sitting up on the side of the bed, she peered out of the window at the rolling hills beyond the driveway. The view was extraordinary, made even more beautiful by the blazing sun that was already sitting high up in the cloudless sky.

Suddenly she panicked. She hadn't even looked at the time, her bag with her phone in was still downstairs in the kitchen.

"Have you got the time?" she called through to the bathroom.

William appeared and leant against the door frame.

"It's shower time," he said, flashing her a smile.

Jess gave a small laugh, "no I'm serious, I have to go and visit my mum at lunch time and I have an hour and a half drive ahead of me."

William glanced down at his watch.

"It's not even nine yet, plenty of time," he said as he walked over to her, picked up her hand and led her into the bathroom.

The shower was blissful. A huge cascade of water coming straight out of the ceiling, nothing like the little power shower Jess had in her flat.

William stood in front of her underneath the water, his hands above his head washing his hair, his toned body putting every muscle on display. Once he'd finished, he pulled her towards him, the wonderfully warm water washing over her hair and her face. He kissed her, more gently this time, holding her face in his hands before stepping out of the shower, wrapping a towel around his waist and padding back into the bedroom.

Jess breathed a slight sigh of relief as he left. Wiping her hands under her eyes she could see her makeup from last night was beginning to run down her face.

Having thoroughly washed her hair with some very expensive looking products, she just stood for a while, letting the hot water run over her skin, tipping her head back and feeling it wash over her face.

Eventually she stepped back out through the glass door and wrapped herself up in a huge fluffy towel from the heated rail on the wall. Rubbing a round hole out of the condensation on the mirror she took in her reflection. Her blue eyes looked extra bright today against her tanned skin, her dark hair shining under the bright vanity lights, thankful of some decent treatment for once. Using a flannel, she removed the last bits of mascara from under her eyes.

She didn't have anything with her, she couldn't redo her hair or put on any makeup, she had been totally unprepared for this impromptu overnight stay. Applying some moisturiser from the cabinet below the sink, she pulled her hair up into a bun on the top of her head and dried herself off.

Back in the bedroom William was pouring tea into two large round cups.

"Is earl grey alright?" he asked as he added milk to both of them.

Jess smiled. Earl grey was her favourite, she'd never met anyone else who liked it.

"That's perfect," she replied.

"Are you hungry?" he asked as he handed her a cup and gestured for her to lie on the bed with him. He was topless still, with checked pyjama bottoms on, slung low over his hips.

"Erm, yeah," she said as she scanned the room, "do you know where my clothes are?"

She couldn't exactly pop down to breakfast in her towel.

"I expect Gwen will have put them in the laundry, she's a bugger, as soon as you take something off she's whipped it away to the washing machine."

He took a sip of his tea and winced slightly at the heat.

"Just chuck on one of my shirts," he said, his abdominals tensing as he got up from the bed and opened one of the wardrobe doors. Pulling out a light blue linen shirt he tossed it to her on the bed.

"You'll look great in it," he smiled.

"I've got no knickers!" Jess retorted as she held the shirt up in front of her, still feeling slightly embarrassed that Gwen had been around the house scooping up her discarded stripping clothes.

"What a shame," he replied playfully as he laid back down on the bed.

They finished their tea and made their way down the huge staircase, Jess holding the shirt close to her so no one that might appear below could see that she wasn't wearing any underwear.

"Have all your friends gone?" she asked hopefully.

"Yes, I believe so, they all had things to do today," he said as he held the door open into the kitchen for her. The smell of fresh coffee, bacon and sausages filled the room, Gwen was busy by the cooker preparing two plates for them both.

"Morning Gwen," William said as he made his way over

to the table and pulled out a chair for Jess.

"Good morning William, hello again Jessica," Gwen smiled as she came over and began pouring coffee for them. She seemed a lot more cheerful today, although spending your Friday night clearing up after a dozen rowdy men would be enough to put anyone in a bad mood, Jess thought to herself.

"Thank you," she smiled as Gwen passed her a plate consisting of everything you could want in a full English breakfast. She suddenly realised she was starving, she hadn't eaten since yesterday lunch time at the pet shop and she had built up quite an appetite since then.

"So where does your mum live?" William asked, grinding pepper on to his bacon.

Jess swallowed her mouthful.

"She's in a care home just north of Oxford," she replied as she glanced around at the huge clock hanging above the cooker, "I can only visit from one until three so I really need to get going shortly," she added as she placed her knife and fork down for a moment. She could feel herself getting full already, this breakfast was much heartier than her normal slice of toast.

"Why is she in a home if you don't mind me asking?" William paused, waiting for her reply.

"She has Alzheimer's, I just couldn't look after her at home."

Suddenly Jess felt an unexpected lump form in her throat, she hardly ever spoke out loud about her mum anymore. In an attempt to suppress it she quickly began eating again.

As they finished their breakfasts, Gwen appeared with Jess's clothes, washed, dried and ironed along with her bag and shoes.

"Thank you," Jess said, embarrassed at the outfit she would have to leave the house in.

"My pleasure love," she smiled before heading off to the dishwasher with their plates.

"Will you come back this evening?" William asked, catching her completely off guard.

"Come back here?" Jess exclaimed, not sure if he was being serious. She hadn't thought any further into her day past frantically making it to the care home in time.

"Yeah," he said with a serious expression, "I really want you to."

Chapter Twelve

As she drove her car up the little winding country lanes towards The Old Manor for the second time in the last twenty four hours, Jess reflected on her whirlwind of a day. It had started with such elation and excitement, but the visit to see her mum hadn't gone well.

Audrey had barely recognised her, she kept asking her who she was and why she was in her room, it was the worst Jess had ever seen her. She spent the whole drive back to Witney in hysterics, barely able to focus on the road ahead through blurred, tear filled vision. It was a miracle she didn't have an accident.

Mrs Brown had tried to comfort her, reluctantly patting her on the shoulder from across the reception desk, reiterating it was just the nature of the disease and that sadly nothing could be done.

Her words hadn't brought Jess a huge amount of comfort. It was something she already knew but it still didn't make her mother's deteriorating condition any easier to witness.

At least she had this evening to look forward to, she thought to herself as she came to a stop in front of the large iron gates, her stomach knotted in excited apprehension at the thought of seeing William again.

The invitation was completely unexpected. She wouldn't have been surprised if he had sent her on her way with her clean clothes and a full stomach, thinking he'd been quite the gentleman and never planned to see her again. Jess had asked herself several times over the course of the day how on earth a man like that could possibly still be single at thirty five.

The blue sky was becoming dull, dusk was just beginning to set in as Jess pulled up beside the large black Range Rover parked in front of the house. She had made sure she was dressed much more appropriately tonight, with a camel coloured cashmere jumper she had bought a couple of years ago from a charity shop and white fitted jeans that she had successfully managed to vanish a stain out of earlier this afternoon.

As she studied her appearance in her bedroom mirror before she left, she was satisfied that she looked far more sophisticated than she did the previous evening. Her makeup was subtle but fresh and she had given herself a lengthy blow dry, taming her long hair to fall in sleek waves over her breasts.

Glancing in the rear view mirror Jess checked her appearance for the third time, although considering what she looked like last night and then this morning she wasn't sure why she was so worried, William had seen her in both states and had still invited her back tonight.

Stepping out of her car she decided to leave her overnight bag on the back seat, she didn't want to presume she was staying over and frighten him off. That's how she used to feel when Jake would tip up to her flat on a Friday night with a bag packed for the whole weekend.

As she approached the front door, the large handle turned with a clunk and Gwen appeared, dressed very casually in a striped quarter zip sweatshirt and jeans with little boat shoes poking out of the bottom.

"Hello Jessica," she smiled.

"Hi Gwen, it's nice to see you again, are you off out?" she asked, gesturing to the little duffle bag she was carrying, which wasn't dissimilar to the one Jess had just left in her car.

"Oh yes, William has given me the night off so I'm going to see my sister, I'll be back tomorrow so I might see you then," she winked and squeezed Jess's arm as she went past her down the steps.

"Oh, he's out the back by the orangery love," she called back to Jess with a wave, "and don't worry dear, he's a brilliant cook!"

Jess smiled and waved back at her, wondering to herself what on earth an orangery was.

As she closed the front door behind her, she could hear

William's voice somewhere near the back of the house. Placing her handbag on the table by the roses she followed it down the hallway, past the staircase, past the secret office door no one would know was there and round a corner.

As she wandered through the house, she took in the countless number of family photographs that were hung on the walls. There were so many. Lots of William as a young boy, a little girl sat next to him in staged photographs, there were some more natural ones of them running around a garden, sat on ponies and building sandcastles together on the beach. There were others of what could only be his parents and all of them together. His father, who was handsome and tall with an unmistakeable likeness to his son, and his mother, who radiated a classical, timeless sort of beauty, with long brown hair and a dazzling smile.

Jess continued to follow William's voice to the back of the house, through what she could only describe as a very posh conservatory and out on to the terrace.

Glancing around, she saw him stood over a very professional looking barbeque, tongs in one hand turning something covered in tin foil, the other hand holding his phone to his ear.

Catching sight of her he smiled.

"I've got to go mate, I'll speak to you in the week," he said as he ended the call and put the phone back in his pocket.

"Hello you," he said as she wandered over.

"Hello," Jess said coyly, trying not to look too excited as he pulled her into his arms and kissed her.

"How are you? How was your day?" he asked as he

stepped back and pulled the hood of the barbeque down.

"Yeah, it was okay thanks, how was yours?" she replied, trying not to encourage a conversation about her mother.

"Well, I had a terrific start to my day," he flashed her a smile, "then it's been pretty quiet here to be honest."

Jess looked around at the garden. It was stunning.

The terrace, surrounded by flower filled planters, stretched the whole width of the house. A vine covered pergola stood at the far end next to a swimming pool surrounded by wooden sun loungers and cream parasols.

The garden beyond the terrace stretched back three acres or more. An enormous oak tree stood proudly in the middle of the freshly cut lawn with a large wooden seat hanging from one of its branches, Jess recognised it from one of the pictures she had just seen in the hallway. In the back corner there was an extensive and beautifully kept kitchen garden, lined with rows of vegetables and dozens of fruit bushes.

"I should think a quiet day here is a bit like paradise," Jess said, still taking in the scene around her.

William followed her gaze and smiled.

"Yeah, I am very blessed, it wasn't a bad place to be brought up. Now, what would you like to drink, I've got champagne, wine, gin and tonic?"

Jess guessed she was probably going to be needing that overnight bag.

"Erm, I'll have whatever you're having," she said, confident that whatever type of alcohol William gave to her would be ten times nicer than the bottle of wine she normally bought from the local corner shop on a Saturday night.

"I'm going to make you one of my gin and tonics," he said, "here take a seat, I've put out some snacks." He gestured for her to sit at the table by the pool, it was laid up for two with a bowl of olives and peanuts sat in the middle.

"Thank you," Jess smiled as she sat down and made herself comfortable.

William appeared from the house a couple of minutes later with two gin and tonics in hand. Watching him as he strode towards her, Jess admired how effortlessly handsome he looked, dressed in washed denim jeans and an untucked light blue linen shirt, similar to the one she had worn to breakfast this morning.

"Here, try this," he said as he handed her a beautiful crystal tumbler. Jess held on to it carefully with both hands, confident it probably cost more than her whole kitchen.

"That's delicious," she said after taking a sip, "what gin is this?"

"It's my gin," he replied taking a seat opposite her, his eyes sparkling.

"You make gin?" she asked taking another mouthful.

"Yeah, I have my own distillery not far from here, it's been up and running for around four years now," he said proudly.

"That's amazing, was that something you always wanted to do?" she asked, placing her glass down to listen to him.

"Well, I always wanted to do something of my own you know, build my own business. The gin industry in the UK is booming right now so it's a really great product to be developing."

The ambition that was oozing out of him was making

Jess want to skip dinner altogether and head straight to the bedroom.

"Well, it's delicious," she admitted taking another large mouthful. She could feel the alcohol making its way into her blood stream already.

"A good drink needs to be made well," he said, holding up his tumbler and observing it, "fresh cucumber, juniper berries and crushed ice, the perfect combination."

Jess watched his eyes sparkle as he spoke, thinking how wonderful it must be to have that sort of passion for something.

"Anyway, enough about my career, what do you do aside from your weekend work?"

Jess hesitated for a second.

"I work in a pet store," she replied looking down at her lap, pulling at a thread on the sleeve of her jumper.

She had never felt ashamed of her job before. She had always been happy there, even though she knew it wasn't particularly ambitious or what she had once wanted to do. But hearing how much William had achieved already in his life was starting to make her feel slightly inadequate.

"Oh nice," he replied.

Jess could tell he wasn't sure what to say next, he had probably never been with a woman with such low career prospects.

"When I was at school, I wanted to be a doctor, to study medicine," she blurted out.

Jess was suddenly very aware of where this conversation might lead, the last thing she wanted to do was talk about her past, but she wanted to justify why her career path had become so stagnant, she didn't want him to think she was stupid.

William suddenly glanced at his watch.

"Sorry, would you excuse me, I'm just going to get the rest of the food from the kitchen, I'll be right back."

He raised himself from the table, placing his left hand on her shoulder. Jess looked up at him as he planted a kiss on her lips.

"Would you like anther drink?"

"Yes please," she replied, breathing a sigh of relief as she handed him her tumbler.

William returned minutes later with two fresh glasses, placing them down on the table he went straight back inside and brought out two plates of roasted new potatoes and salad.

"I've done lamb tonight, I hope that's ok?" he asked, placing a plate in front of her.

"Sounds amazing," Jess said taking another large mouthful of her drink.

"I've tried it on the barbeque, so I hope it's alright."

Flipping open the lid, he pulled out a leg of lamb covered in foil and brought it over to the table. As he unwrapped it the smell filled the air between them, it was mouth-watering. Jess could hear her stomach rumbling in response to the spread of food in front of her, she couldn't remember the last time she ate a meal this wholesome.

"This looks amazing, thank you so much," she said as she watched William skilfully carve off the meat and place it on her plate.

"My pleasure, thank you for coming back to spend the

evening with me," he flashed her a smile, his eyes dancing.

They began their meal as the darkness started to fall around them. Above their heads a full moon took centre stage surrounded by thousands of stars lighting up the sky around it.

"Sorry, I interrupted you earlier," William said as he began cutting his final piece of lamb, "why didn't you end up studying medicine? I have heard it's bloody hard, my cousin has been applying for two years now and it seems even three excellent grades aren't enough to get you in anymore."

Pausing for a moment, Jess took a deep breath before placing her knife and fork down.

"My best friend died," she said looking down at her lap, twisting her napkin between her fingers, quietly impressed with herself for being able to say the words out loud, "it was our final lead up to exams, I just couldn't cope with it, so I ended up failing everything. They don't let you study medicine with no A levels," she smiled, trying to make light of herself as she picked up her knife and fork.

It was the first time she had spoken out loud about Katie's death for a long time.

William paused, a fork full of food hovering mid-air.

"I'm so sorry, that must have been awful. Was she sick?" he asked, his dark eyes holding her gaze.

Jess finished her mouthful and took another deep breath.

"No, she wasn't sick. She drowned, or was drowned. We never found out."

She squinted as her eyes brimmed with tears. Desperately blinking them back she stared down at her plate, hoping William wouldn't notice.

"My god, that's terrible," he paused for a moment, unsure how to respond, "well, you still enjoy what you do now at the shop?" he asked, relaying his napkin on his lap.

Jess sniffed slightly, thankful that he had changed the subject.

"Yeah, it's great there, the girl I work with is really nice."

"Well, that's the main thing," he paused, "so, if you don't mind me asking, why do you do your weekend work? Is that for enjoyment?" he looked down at his plate as he finished the last of his salad.

"Oh god no," Jess blurted out before correcting herself, "obviously except for last night," she smiled, briefly placing her hand on his arm before continuing, "no, I hate it, but it's really good money and I have rent and bills and my mum's care to pay for, I don't have many other options."

He nodded slowly as he placed his knife and fork together on his plate.

"Another drink?" he asked as he stood up to clear the table.

Jess could feel the mood had shifted, there was a slight darkness in William's face. It was obvious he didn't approve of her taking her clothes off for groups of random men, but she couldn't work out if that was because he found it a generally unacceptable profession or was it *her* taking her clothes off that he didn't like, she couldn't tell.

"Why not," she smiled, rising from her seat and picking up the two tumblers, "you can teach me how to make a good gin."

Jess led the way into the house, feeling William's eyes on her as he followed. She needed to inject some playfulness into the situation, it was all becoming a bit too serious, she thought to herself.

They sat outside well into the evening, talking about their lives, family and friends. Jess discovered William had a sister, the girl in the pictures was called Matilda, she was five years younger than him and was living in Spain with her new boyfriend. His parents spent most of their time at their family estate in Wales, sometimes flitting back to The Old Manor. William spent most of the week in London, in meetings with potential new suppliers or working on marketing his gin brand.

Before they knew it the darkness had completely surrounded them, even the light from the glowing moon above them wasn't enough to counter it.

William got up and turned the lights on around the pool, Jess watched as the waves of steam made their way from the blue ripples up into the cool night air.

Returning to the table with a blanket, William wrapped it around her shoulders, gently pulling her head back to kiss her, every touch making her body tingle with the prospect of what the rest of the evening had in store.

As he settled back in his chair with yet another gin and tonic, Jess took a deep breath.

"So, if you don't mind me asking, how are *you* still single at thirty five?"

It was a question she wasn't one hundred percent sure she wanted the answer to, but the large volume of gin that was now soaring through her veins had convinced her brain it was a good idea to ask.

He leant back in his chair and smiled at her.

"I could ask you the same question."

"Oi!" she retorted, kicking him playfully under the table, "I'm not thirty five yet."

"Well, I have actually been married," he said once his laughter had subsided.

Jess hadn't been expecting that.

"Oh, what happened?"

"Well, we married young for a start, then we ran into some problems along the way."

William was looking down at the tumbler in his hand, running his fingernail over the edges of the crystal.

"We desperately wanted children," he continued, "we went to the best fertility doctors in the country, had every possible course of treatment, three rounds of IVF. It just didn't happen for us."

Jess's heart reached out to him.

"God I'm sorry, that must have been so difficult for you both."

He nodded, still looking down at the glass in his hand.

"It was. Francesca took it the hardest though, she became completely consumed by it and in the end, it destroyed our marriage."

Jess could hear the pain in his voice as he spoke.

"Where is she now?" she asked.

"She's living in London with her sister. I still see her quite a bit because she's still a partner in my business, she has been since the beginning so I guess it's good we can still get along."

Jess felt an odd pang of jealously hit her out of nowhere, which was ridiculous considering she had only known this man for twenty four hours, still, it was a feeling she had never had to deal with before and not one that she was particularly enjoying.

"That's nice," Jess lied as she gazed up at the star covered sky, "God it's just so beautiful here, I can't imagine you would ever want to leave."

William followed her gaze.

"Yeah, you can't beat a clear night sky, you don't get this in London."

Jess turned her head slightly.

"That pool looks awfully inviting."

William raised his eyebrows and smiled.

"Does it now?"

Jess nodded, playfully biting the corner of her lip.

"Come on then," he said as he stood up, holding her gaze with a serious expression, "put your money where your mouth is."

With that he walked over to the pool, unbuttoning his shirt as he went, pulling it off his toned arms and dropping it down onto one of the sun loungers.

Jess watched intently from the table as he took off his shoes, jeans and boxers, his back muscles moving like ropes underneath his skin as he dived headfirst into the water.

Jess waited for a moment before sinking the last of her drink and slowly getting up, unwrapping herself from the blanket and casually walking over towards the pool. William had emerged from the water, wiping his hair back from his face, his body floating with ease amongst the steaming ripples as he watched her.

She stood above him at the end of the pool, the lights glowing up over her like she was performing on a stage.

Keeping her eyes locked on his, she slowly undressed herself, pulling her jumper over her head and letting it drop to floor, goosebumps erupting on her skin as she slowly slid her jeans down over her long legs.

Floating forwards in the water a fraction, William held her gaze as she removed her bra and knickers, dropping them onto the floor next to her.

Making her way slowly down the sloping stone steps at one end, she paused to gather up her long hair above her head and fasten it in a ponytail, purposely taking her time, aware of William's eyes on her naked body.

Elegantly she slipped into the water, submerging herself. It was wonderfully warm, the contrast with the cool night air making the water feel even hotter. Floating across to the pool edge, she pushed herself up against it and leant her head back against the cold stone, letting the steam flow up over her face.

William swam up to her, his head low in the water like a predator circling its prey.

Jess leant her head back further, deliberately not looking at him as he made his way towards her.

With his dark eyes still locked on her, he wrapped his arms around her back, pulling her legs up around his waist, her wet naked breasts emerging from the water as he lifted her.

He was aroused already, she could feel it.

Tightening his arms around her back, he kissed her, his

intentions unmistakably clear.

Jess could feel his impatience, his sense of longing, she felt it too. Cradling his face in her hands, she matched his passion.

Wasting no time, William gently moved her body down onto him.

Jess gasped as he kissed her neck, gripping hold of his shoulders as their bodies moved together under the water.

"That was quite a performance," he whispered in her ear.

Jess closed her eyes and moaned in response to him.

"I want to be the only man that gets to see that," he continued, moving his head so they were looking straight into each other's eyes, their foreheads touching as he began to move more forcefully.

"Just me, okay?" he breathed, staring deeper into her eyes.

An overwhelming sense of being saved suddenly washed over her. That the feeling of loneliness she had buried deep inside her for so long could finally be gone, a sense of being wanted by someone that she wanted in return.

"Just you," she whispered back.

William kissed her hard, holding her tightly as he picked up the pace, Jess's back rubbing harder against the wall behind her as she felt the climax coming.

She stopped moving and arched her back as she released, her cry of satisfaction echoing into the night air. William was moments behind her, using one hand to brace himself against the pool edge, the other still holding on to her tightly.

She kept her legs wrapped around his waist as he

recovered, his head buried in her neck, his breathing laboured.

Gently she planted a line of kisses along his shoulder, feeling his muscles tense as he held her.

Wrapping his arms even more tightly around her, he smiled, still catching his breath.

"You Jess Taylor, you are pure magic," he whispered.

Chapter Thirteen

Jess woke for the second morning in a row in William's enormous bed at The Old Manor, trying to recall the last time she spent two nights in a row away from her flat.

Listening quietly, she could hear William behind her, his breathing still heavy and calm, his right arm laid over the top of her waist. Carefully she slid out from underneath him and stepped quietly into the bathroom.

After closing the door she observed her appearance in the mirror. Her hair was wild and her makeup was smudged in dark circles under her eyes. They had tumbled into bed shortly after midnight straight from the pool, completely intoxicated with alcohol and lust.

Turning on the shower, hoping she wasn't going to wake

William, she stepped through the large glass door into the gathering steam. At least ten minutes went by, Jess stood under the warm water, enjoying as she had the previous morning the sensation of it running over her skin, it's what she imagined a real life waterfall would feel like, only warmer. Giving her hair a thorough wash and condition, she stepped out of the shower and dried herself off. Today she had come more prepared and had her hairdryer, wash bag and makeup to hand.

Tiptoeing back through the bedroom, she quietly opened the door and stepped out into the hallway, leaving William still sound asleep in bed. Wandering along the corridor, she looked for another room out of earshot that she could blow dry her hair in. Trying her luck a few rooms down, Jess gently pushed a door open. Peering in she saw a pale pink bedroom, a queen sized four poster bed sat at one end made up with white waffle sheets, a few teddy bears were sat up on the pillows looking very pleased with themselves. Jess entered cautiously, quite aware that she was blatantly invading someone else's privacy.

All around the bedroom were little pictures in frames, lots of Matilda, some of her as a child and some when she was older, into her teenage years. There were countless photos of school trips, lots of girls lined up in unison wearing matching blue blazers and tartan skirts. There were some netball team photos, all the girls grinning towards the camera, Matilda sat in the middle of them holding a trophy in her lap. There were others of her playing hockey, her long dark hair flicking up behind her as she ran.

On the dressing table there were some professionally

taken photographs of her with William and their parents, laughing and smiling at each other, most likely staged by the photographer but Jess could see how real the love was in their eyes.

She suddenly felt a spasm of excitement in her stomach, that she could potentially be included in such a wonderfully happy family.

Scanning the photographs along the little mantlepiece Jess picked up the last one. It was a picture of William stood outside a church in a morning suit, looking a fair bit younger than he did now but still just as handsome. He was beaming from ear to ear, his bride Francesca stood next to him looking equally as dazzling in a chic strapless fitted dress, her arm looped through his, her eyes bright and full of happiness.

Jess studied the photograph closely, they did make a handsome looking couple, she thought to herself.

The sound of William's voice traveling down the hallway made her jump, it sounded like he was on the phone. Hastily she returned the frame back to its original place on the mantlepiece and sat herself down in front of the dressing table.

A few minutes later William appeared behind her, topless with a towel wrapped around his waist.

She smiled at him in the mirror.

Standing behind her, he placed his hands on her shoulders and kissed her on the cheek before making his way back to his bedroom.

Jess finished drying her hair and went back to find him.

"Good morning," she smiled as she entered his

bedroom.

William was sat in bed with a cup of tea looking at an iPad.

"Hello you," he looked up at her and smiled.

"Sorry I didn't want to wake you with the hairdryer," she said gesturing to the hallway behind her.

"Don't be silly, make yourself at home here," he said as he threw the iPad down on the bed in front of him and began pouring her a cup of tea.

"So, my friend Tom just called me, he was asking how the rest of my weekend was."

Jess studied him, realising Tom was clearly a friend that was present on Friday night.

"Oh yeah?" she said warily, hoping he hadn't divulged too many details of their weekend to him.

"He was asking if we wanted to join him and a few others for a meal in London next Saturday, what do you think? We could crash at my flat afterwards."

Jess felt her stomach flutter.

"You want to take me with you?" she asked.

After the whirlwind weekend they were having and everything that William had said, she still couldn't quite believe he was serious about her, she just didn't feel good enough somehow, a part of her was still expecting him to say thanks very much and send her on her way.

"Of course I do," he said as he reached forwards and pulled her towards him, her towel falling to the floor as he did, "I would take you everywhere with me if I could."

Jess beamed down at him.

"Well, that sounds lovely," she said, planting a kiss on

the tip of his nose.

"Now how are your skills on the breakfast front?" she pulled away from him and walked across the room, playfully displaying her naked body, "I've tried Gwen's breakfast and she's set the bar pretty high."

Looking over her shoulder she flashed him a mischievous smile.

He was grinning at her, his eyes sparkling.

"Oh, I think mine will be very satisfactory."

Finally, they made their way downstairs. Together they stood over the stove, Jess cooking the bacon, William frying up mushrooms and eggs as they sipped on fresh orange juice. The early morning sun was beaming through the large sash window as Sunday morning radio played loudly through the speaker system.

Looking across at William, his brow furrowed as yet another egg yolk split in his pan, Jess thought this could be the most perfect morning of her life. A sudden realisation of what she had been missing all these years washed over her. The perfect simpleness of happily being in someone's company, whilst quietly performing everyday tasks is something that most people in a relationship would probably take for granted. Silently she made a promise to herself that if she was lucky enough to have more moments like this, that she would savour every single second.

Once they had finished cooking, they sat down together at the table and proudly observed the feast they had created.

"What do you think?" William asked after a few minutes.

"It's good, but Gwen still tops it I think."

"Yeah, she does make a bloody good breakfast," he admitted with a smile.

Once they had both finished Jess cleared away their plates, William was busy washing and drying pans at the sink, very aware that Gwen would not be happy if she returned home later to find a dirty kitchen.

Sitting back down at the table, Jess topped up their coffees as her phone pinged in front of her. Looking down at the screen she saw it was a message from an unknown number.

Hey Jess, good to see you the other day, does tomorrow sound good for a drink? 7pm at the Rose and Crown?

It took Jess a moment to register who it was from, so much had happened since she had seen Harry last week.

"Everything alright?" William asked, looking over at her frowning at her phone.

"Yeah fine, I just forgot I bumped into an old school friend last week and agreed to go for a drink with him. I sort of wish I hadn't now."

"How come?" he asked putting the last pan back in the cupboard.

"Well, he wasn't really that much of a friend, I never heard anything from him after Katie died. I'm just a bit wary of him I guess."

"So don't go," William said with a shrug, "in fact, don't go home at all, come to London with me this week."

Jess laughed as she reread the message on her phone.

"William, I have to go home, I have work," she said, trying to decide what she was going to write back to Harry.

As much as she was loving the time she was spending with William, she was conscious of the promise she had made to him last night to give up a very lucrative income stream. Jess knew that until she found another way to make some more money she was going to need all the work at the pet shop she could get.

"What do you think he wants?" William asked, sitting down opposite her and adding some milk to his coffee.

"I would think just a catch up, I haven't seen him for thirteen years. Although there isn't exactly much to report in my life, I haven't gone anywhere or achieved anything."

"You don't think he might have an ulterior motive?" William asked raising his eyebrows.

Jess looked into his eyes.

"He wouldn't stand a chance even if did," she said sliding her hand across the table to his, their fingers intertwining.

"Good, I'm glad to hear it. And don't put yourself down like that, you had a shit time. You've spent your life being independent and paying to care for your mum, that's an amazing achievement," he replied, his face softening.

Jess suddenly felt tears gathering behind her eyes, it was the first time anyone had acknowledged what she had done to try and help her mum, how hard she worked to give her the best care she possibly could.

"Thank you," she smiled at him, giving his hand an appreciative squeeze.

It was midday before Jess rounded up her things and began her drive back to Witney. William had dinner plans with some family friends in London, he had asked her to join him but she needed to get home. The weekend had been so perfect, just the two of them, she wanted to keep it that way for a little while.

Before she left, he kissed her, on the front steps of the house, his hands holding her face like he never wanted to let it go. He really meant everything he was saying, Jess thought to herself, she could feel it.

On the drive home she relived their weekend a hundred times in her mind. His kisses, his touch, his body, the way he made her feel.

She had agreed to dinner next weekend with his friends in London. He said he would call her in the week, maybe swing by and stay with her in Witney one night.

Her whole body shivered in excitement at the prospect of spending another night with him, after just one weekend together William had taken her sexual expectations to a level she never even knew existed.

Chapter Fourteen

"Here I got you chicken and bacon, is that alright?" Charlotte asked throwing the sandwich to Jess across the break room.

"That's perfect, thanks," Jess replied, ripping open the box, "I'm flipping starving."

Charlotte smirked at her.

"Must be all that sex you've been having," she said, sitting down next to her on the sofa and playfully elbowing her in the ribs, "how many times was it? Three in twenty four hours, that's a bloody record for you," she continued with a grin still etched on her face.

Jess rolled her eyes as she stuffed her sandwich in her mouth. She was beginning to regret telling Charlotte the details of her weekend with William.

"So has he got any fit, eligible friends?" Charlotte asked, resting her legs up on the coffee table in front of her.

Jess swallowed her mouthful, "I don't know, I'm meeting some of them this weekend so I'll let you know."

This was a completely empty promise, there was no way Jess would be introducing her to any of William's friends. With Charlotte's track record Jess was sure any sort of relationship she endeavoured on wouldn't end well and she would then end up feeling the backlash.

"So how was your date on Friday?" Jess asked, chucking her sandwich wrapper in the bin and flicking on the kettle.

"Yeah, it was really fun, he took me out for dinner to that little Italian place on Broad Street, then we ended up back at his," Charlotte said with a mischievous look on her face, "but I haven't really heard from him since."

Pulling out her phone she checked it for the hundredth time that day, as if talking about this guy might have somehow manifested him to message her.

Jess remained quiet, she couldn't exactly preach about why you shouldn't sleep with someone on the first date, but thankfully William's behaviour had been the complete opposite.

He had called her last night after his dinner, Jess smiled at the memory, the excitement she had felt being tucked up in bed, hearing her phone buzz beside her and seeing his name light up on the screen. He sounded a little drunk, he kept threatening to jump in a taxi and come and join her in bed. They had spoken this morning too, a few flirtatious messages, he said he wanted to come down on Wednesday evening, that he would come straight from the office to her flat. Her stomach tightened at the thought, it had only been a day, but she longed for him already.

"You're away with the fairies today," Charlotte said waving a hand in front of her face, "I'll make my own tea," she teased as she knocked Jess's hips with her own.

With that the doorbell rang.

"I'll get it," Jess said, playfully bumping Charlotte back, making her spill the hot water from the kettle all over the counter.

Making her way through to the till Jess stopped abruptly at the sight of Harry, stood looking at her with a silly smile on his face, holding two more bags of dog biscuit.

"Me again," he said, lifting the bags up to support his comment.

"Hello," Jess said cautiously, "more biscuit for the spaniel?"

"Yeah, the lab got into the boot room and devoured a whole bag, so I've been sent out again," he laughed.

Something inside her was telling her not to believe his story as she beeped the bags through the till.

"So, I'll see you at seven?" he asked hopefully as he pulled a credit card out of his wallet.

"Yep, I'll see you then," Jess said trying to minimise their conversation, acutely aware that Charlotte would be listening to every word from the break room.

"Cool, see you later," he smiled, nodding behind her before picking up his dog biscuit and heading for the door.

Jess turned to see Charlotte leant up against the wall behind the till, tea in hand with a huge smirk on her face.

"Miss Taylor," she said raising her eyebrows, "I didn't have you down as a serial dater. Two men in one week!"

"It is not a date," Jess interrupted her quickly, "I went to school with him, he came in last week and asked to go for a catch up, that is all. It is absolutely not a date."

Charlotte walked down the aisle and peered out of the window as Harry drove off in his car.

"Well in that case, ask him if he's single would you?"

The day seemed to drag on forever, there wasn't a whole lot for them to do which Jess hated, she was so much happier when she could keep herself busy. Harry was the only customer they'd had in all day, Jess was very aware that the two bags of dog biscuit he'd bought wouldn't cover even one of their wages. She had been quietly gearing herself up to ask Jeremy if he would consider giving her a pay rise, he usually popped into the shop to do the end of month bills, she was planning on asking him then. Although lately there had been such a lack of customers that she was pretty sure she knew how that conversation was going to go.

Five 'o' clock eventually rolled around. Charlotte had already left to go home, the guy she had spent Friday night with had blocked her on WhatsApp after her barrage of messages all afternoon, which had put her in a particularly foul mood. Jess was glad when she announced she felt poorly and needed to leave early.

Turning on the alarm, she locked up the front door before heading to her car. The evenings were getting cooler, even at this time of day there was a feeling summer was well and truly over and winter was on its way.

Swinging off the road, around her building and into the tiny car park at the back, Jess parked carefully in her usual space next to Janet and Paul's yellow Nissan Micra. She always left the spot closest to the door for them, although neither of them seemed to drive very much these days. Janet would venture out only once a week to the shops and Jess was pretty sure Paul could barely see past the end of his nose, so it was probably good he didn't get behind the wheel any more.

She was about to let herself in the front door when she heard Janet calling to her from the window above.

"Hello Jess love," she said with a smile.

"Hi Janet, how are you?"

"Oh, we're fine thanks dear. We missed you on the weekend, I was a bit worried, were you alright?"

A small spasm of guilt ran over her, she should have told Janet she wouldn't be here on Saturday night. She felt touched though, that she was looking out for her, she was the closest thing to a mother figure she'd had in a long time.

"Oh, I'm so sorry, it was a spontaneous trip away."

"Oh, don't be silly dear, as long as you're alright," she smiled, "were you away with a nice young man by any chance?"

Jess could feel herself blushing at the mention of William.

"I'll take that as a yes," Janet said winking at her, "it's about time you found a nice chap, I can never understand how you haven't been snapped up already. Anyway, I'll let you get on, Mr Grumpy is moaning about wanting his tea." She rolled her eyes and tutted as she shut the window.

Throwing her bag down on the kitchen table Jess opened the fridge. The contents were bleak, she made a mental note to go shopping after work on Wednesday so she had at least half a chance of cooking up something edible for her and William. She was already stressing about what to make for him, she'd spent the afternoon at work googling easy dinner party recipes trying to find some inspiration.

Pulling out a nearly empty bottle of pinot grigio from the door of the fridge, she filled a small wine glass right to the brim, emptying the contents. If she was going to have to sit and talk to Harry this evening, a cup of tea wasn't going to cut the mustard.

The clock read six thirty as she got ready to leave her flat, she had showered and had a slice of toast to try and soak up the wine which had gone straight to her head.

Rifling through her wardrobe, she picked out the least sexy outfit she owned, boyfriend jeans, trainers and a long sleeve, high neck top. She didn't want an inch of flesh on show tonight.

Briefly glancing at her reflection in the mirror, she decided not to top up her makeup and to leave her hair in the same haphazard ponytail it had been in all day.

Charlotte's comment had got to her slightly, she in no way wanted Harry to think they were going on a date.

Positioning herself in the furthest corner of the pub, Jess sat herself down at a little two person table with a pint of diet coke and a packet of peanuts. Checking her phone, she saw it was 7.05, Harry was late already. She was quietly pleased, hoping he might not show up and she could make a beeline home to watch The Kardashians in her pyjamas. As she sat deciding what would be an acceptable time to make a run for it, a hand landed on her shoulder making her jump and spill her drink on her lap.

"Shit, sorry," Harry laughed, "I just wondered if you wanted a drink?"

"No, I'm fine," Jess replied sternly, wiping her jeans with her sleeve.

"Okay, I'll be back in a minute," he said as he made his way to the bar and ordered a lager.

Jess sat watching him, wondering to herself why on earth she had agreed to come this evening after all these years.

Harry made his way back to the table with his pint and sat down opposite her, taking a big gulp of his beer as he did.

"So, how have you been?" he asked, taking his coat off and hanging it on the chair behind him.

"Yeah, fine," said Jess, unaware of what he was really asking.

"How long has it been? Twelve years since we last saw each other?"

"Thirteen," Jess said correcting him, twisting the empty peanut packet through her fingers.

"God that's a long time," he replied, looking up at the ceiling as if he was sifting through some memories in his mind.

"So, you're working at the pet shop, any husband or children on the scene?" he continued.

"I'm seeing someone," Jess blurted out a little too quickly, "it's quite new, but we're very happy. What about you? Do you have a wife or any children?"

"No, I haven't been that fortunate yet," he smiled, running his fingers around the condensation on his glass, "I'm hoping in this case, fortune favours the patient," he laughed.

They chatted for a little while, Jess managed to relax slightly, enjoying Harry's story about his family and the disastrous wedding of his sister and brother-in-law last year that ended in a drunken row between the mothers.

"Would you like another drink?" Jess asked, getting to her feet.

"Yes please, I'd love another Peroni," he said handing her his empty glass.

Jess ordered another beer and a shandy for herself. Whilst she stood waiting for the landlord to pour her pints, she saw a notice hung on the wall behind him.

'BAR STAFF NEEDED.'

"Are you still looking for staff?" she asked hopefully as he finished pouring the second pint.

"We sure are love, finding good staff is a bloody nightmare these days. That's why I'm here pulling pints on a Monday evening," he plonked the drinks in front of her and leant his hands on the bar, "why, you interested?" he asked raising his thick eyebrows, his mouth twitching underneath his handlebar moustache.

"Well, I could only do evenings, would that work?"

"Yeah sure," he said shrugging his shoulders, "anything's better than nothing at the moment. Why don't you come by one night this week and have a go, see what you think?" he suggested as he wiped down the bar in front of her.

"Okay, sure. Would Thursday work?"

"Yeah, that's perfect love, come in for six thirty," he said as he glanced over at some drunken workmen who were demanding more pints from the other end of the bar.

She smiled at him as he rolled his eyes and made his way over to them, flicking his dish cloth over his shoulder as he went.

Walking slowly back to the table, being careful not to spill the drinks, Jess noticed Harry looking at her, his eyes watching her a little too intently.

"So, when exactly did we last see each other?" he said as she sat back down opposite him.

"Upper sixth."

Jess scrambled her brain, trying to think of something to change the subject, desperately wanting to avoid getting into the specifics of their last encounter.

"Jade's party!" Harry declared loudly, slapping his hand on the table, pleased with himself for homing in on the memory.

Jess could feel the blood making its way to her face, her cheeks beginning to tingle.

"Wasn't there an argument or something?" he said with a frown.

Jess watched silently, frozen like a statue as his mind rewound back to that night.

She watched the smile fall slowly from his face as he appeared to piece the memories back together.

"Shit. I'm sorry Jess. That was the night Katie died," he said quietly, sliding his hand just a fraction across the table in her direction.

Jess was still frozen, her arms tightly folded in front of her.

"Did they ever find out what happened to her?" he asked.

Jess remained still, her eyes wide in disbelief.

At the time Katie's death was a national news story, it was public knowledge that the case hadn't been solved.

But then everyone else had moved on with their lives. For the last thirteen years people like Harry had continued living, they had moved away, got new jobs, had families and had never given Katie a second thought, she had become old news.

Jess however had remained stuck in the past, inwardly consumed by the death of her best friend, more so because in a way she felt responsible for it. She hadn't allowed herself a new life, in a new place, with a new career because she didn't feel she deserved it. Katie never got that chance, so why should she?

It was a minute before Jess could find her voice.

She stared glassy eyed at Harry, her mind opening up the old memories she usually kept locked away.

"No, they never found out what happened," she whispered, shaking her head, "she drowned that night in the river, having made it home after the party. It made absolutely no sense."

She had said these words to herself, gone over them in her mind a thousand times. It felt good, she realised, to be saying them out loud to someone after all these years.

"There were no sightings, no eyewitnesses, they never tracked down the guy you saw her with at Courtney's party," she continued.

Harry looked down at his glass.

"Well, that bloke could have been anyone."

"What do you mean?" she asked with a frown, studying his face.

"Well, she was just stood outside talking to some lad, they weren't actually doing anything."

He kept his eyes down as he spoke.

"The truth is I liked her, but she never took any notice of me," he said picking at the coaster under his glass, "I just wanted to wind her up a bit, to get a conversation going and see if there was anyone on the scene, but she just flew off the handle so quickly."

Jess paused for a moment before leaning forward, her eyes narrowing.

"So, you're telling me, you didn't see her getting off with some bloke outside Courtney's house?"

He paused, colour rising in his cheeks.

"No, she was just stood talking to some guy, they weren't even touching," he said, finally managing to look up at her.

Jess couldn't decide if she was angry or not.

"But then why was she so pissed off about it?" she said, thinking back to their argument at Jade's party, the venomous words Katie had spat at her.

"I don't know," Harry replied shaking his head, "but I definitely blew that one out of proportion."

His cheeks turned a deeper shade of red.

"It's something I've always felt bad about, that I caused that row between you both."

Jess took a deep breath, leaning back in her chair as she studied him for a moment. She realised now why he had asked her here. He wanted to repent, to be forgiven, as much as he behaved like he had forgotten, this was something he carried with him also.

Sitting quietly, she began piecing everything together in her mind.

"Do you know what my life was like after that party?" she said, her voice rising a decibel.

Harry didn't look at her, his eyes remained fixed on his hands on the table.

"Because of that argument, I was the prime suspect in her case," she leant forwards, spitting the words across the table at him, "because of that argument, Katie stormed off on her own and ended up drowning in the fucking river, or worse, being drowned by someone in the river!"

Jess watched him recoil, flinching at her words.

Pausing for a minute to calm herself down she took a deep breath, rubbing her forehead with her hands.

"Look Harry, things weren't right between me and Katie, something was troubling her and I never found out what, I think that's what upset me the most. That I failed her somehow."

Jess's eyes brimmed with tears.

"I'm sorry for what I did. For the things I said. I never meant to cause that argument between you both," Harry managed to look up into her eyes, "I know that evening ruined your life, that video was terrible. All the thing's people said about you because of it," he said shaking his head.

Jess looked across at him with tears in her eyes.

"I was the one that pushed her Harry, no one else," she whispered, "I have to live with that."

Driving home, Jess tried to control her thoughts, her mind reeling from the evening she had just had. She couldn't forgive Harry yet for what he had done, this new information, this new betrayal, it was just too fresh. They had said polite goodbyes to each other before they both went their separate ways, Jess silently praying she would never see him again.

The realisation that he had only invited her out tonight to try and clear his own conscience was angering her.

Letting herself into her flat she flicked the kettle on. Pulling her phone from her bag she saw she had a message from William. For the first time all evening she genuinely smiled.

Hey trouble, how was your evening?

She quickly sent a reply back.

Nothing exciting to report, back home now. Can't wait to see you.

Seconds later another message pinged through.

Oh, I can't wait either, it's been too long already.

The thought of being with him again sent a wave of shivers around her body, Wednesday couldn't come soon enough.

Chapter Fifteen

Jess had ventured to the local Tesco on a mission to try and prepare herself for this evening's meal with William. Her usual purchases from the corner shop weren't quite going to create the home making image she was hoping for.

Trawling the aisles, having no idea where anything was, she managed to bump into two different people and knock over a Halloween display because her trolly wheels just wouldn't go where they were supposed to.

It was quite a treat though, she thought to herself as she wheeled down the snack aisle, throwing items into the trolly she never knew existed.

The bright, polished stands in the beauty aisle drew her in like a magpie. Before she could talk herself out of it, she threw two new mascaras, a foundation and a hideously expensive face cream into the trolley.

Once she had finally gathered everything she needed on her list for her evening meal, plus a lot of extras, she joined the long queue for the checkout.

When she finally reached the till the lady greeted her with a half-hearted grunt before quickly pinging through her purchases. Jess watched as the total began racking up on the little screen above the card machine, every beep making her a little more anxious, she was normally so careful with her money. Jabbing in her pin, she silently cursed herself for being so frivolous, yet she wasn't feeling quite brave enough to apologise to the stern looking lady and put it all back.

Jamming half of her shopping in the boot of her car, she threw the rest of it on the passenger seat before returning her badly behaved trolley.

As she pulled out of the car park and on to the main road her stomach rumbled loudly, her fridge contents had been so bleak she hadn't taken any lunch to work with her today. Leaning across she pulled a packet of crisps out of the bag next to her to keep her going.

She had two hours before William was supposed to arrive, he had messaged her an hour ago to say he was heading into his final meeting and should be with her by seven thirty.

Jess organised her thoughts as she clock-watched through the evening traffic, making a mental list of all the things she wanted to get done before he arrived; prep the dinner, hoover the lounge, clean the bathroom and get herself looking presentable, all the things she would never normally bother to do when she got home from work.

It was five to seven, Jess was sweating but it had been a productive hour. She had prepped the chicken pie and vegetables, not completely from scratch, the thought of trying to make her own pastry when she could buy it from the shop seemed ridiculous. She had cleaned the kitchen, bleached the bathroom and hoovered the whole flat. In the lounge she lit some scented candles and put some posh crisps and houmous out in the least chipped bowls she could find.

Walking through her flat she admired her hard work. In her bedroom she had a quick tidy up and threw every discarded bit of clothing in the wash basket, regardless of whether it was dirty or not. Looking around, she wished she had splashed out on some sort of new bedding in the last three years, but other than that she was pleased with her efforts. It was no mansion in the country, but it was her home, one she had made all by herself and she was proud of it.

After a very quick shower she touched up her makeup and straightened her hair, she would have liked to curl it but that wasn't a speedy process.

Working her way through her wardrobe, thinking to herself she really should go clothes shopping soon, she tried to choose an outfit for the evening. Her legs were still tanned from the hot summer months and seeing as it was a special occasion she had cranked up the thermostat, so she decided on a little blue wrap dress and some sandals.

Knots of anticipation spasmed in her stomach at seven twenty when the phone buzzed in the hall.

Jess jumped up and ran to the door, hitting the buzzer in the hallway as she went.

Standing in the doorway, she watched as William appeared below her, looking irresistible in a dark blue suit with a white shirt, unbuttoned at the top.

He beamed at her as he made his way up the stairs.

"Hello trouble," he said as he picked her up and kissed her.

Jess let out a little squeal of delight.

"Hello you," she smiled back at him.

"You look beautiful," he said as he put her down and handed her a chilled bottle of white wine.

"Thank you," she smiled, tucking her hair gingerly behind her ear and gesturing for him to follow her through to the kitchen.

"What a great place," he said, taking his jacket off and hanging it over the back of a chair, "it's so homey".

Jess smiled to herself as she opened the bottle.

"Yeah I like it here, it's my little safe place," she said as she poured the wine into two large glasses.

"Shall we sit next door?" she suggested, feeling very much the hostess as she bent down to check the pie in the oven.

They drank the entire bottle of wine within half an hour, Jess felt a bit wobbly as she dished up her pie, silently praying it wasn't going to taste disgusting.

They sat together at the little kitchen table which Jess had laid up with placemats, napkins and a candle, more of her earlier, impulsive purchases from Tesco. They reminisced about their weekend together, laughing at how awful it would have been if his parents decided to drop back on Saturday evening when they were in the pool. They often came back spontaneously William said. His father was a retired stockbroker and his mother had never had to work.

What a lovely life, Jess thought to herself, to come and go as you please to whichever stately home takes your fancy.

"So how was your catch up with this other man then?" William teased.

"It wasn't great, I was glad to come home," Jess replied pushing her vegetables around her plate.

"Although," she said, "I have got myself another job, which doesn't involve taking my clothes off," she grinned, nudging him with her foot under the table.

"Well, that does please me, as long as it's not working with Harry," he smiled, narrowing his eyes.

"No," she laughed, "it's bar work at the pub we met in, they've said I can have the evening shift," she said as she leant behind her and opened the fridge door to fish out another bottle of wine.

"But you've already got a fulltime job, that's a lot of time spent working," he frowned, gathering their plates and taking them over to the sink.

"Well, I need the money," she said, wanting to remind him that not everyone was as financially equipped as he undoubtedly was.

William took the wine bottle from her and topped up their glasses.

"I have stuff to pay for, mum's care isn't cheap," she said taking a large mouthful of wine.

"Yes, I remember you saying," he replied sitting back down opposite her, "I just don't want you to work too hard, if you're working all day and all night, what time will you have to spend with me."

He paused, holding her gaze as he took a sip of his wine.

Jess felt goose bumps travel up every inch of her body, the hairs on her arms standing to attention.

Did he really just say that? she asked herself.

She couldn't help but smile at him, happiness was oozing out of her, but she also wanted to remain realistic. This was a man that she had met less than a week ago and she had already given up one job for him. She had to remind herself that she still had responsibilities.

"Well, I think there's plenty of time for us after working hours," she said seductively, trying to lighten the mood as she got up, her eyes holding his gaze as she took his hand and led him into the lounge.

The room was dimly lit by a small lamp in the corner and a candle flickering on the coffee table. The wine was making Jess feel playful as she sat William down on the sofa. Placing her glass on the table, she swept her hair over her left shoulder and sat herself on his lap.

Running her fingers slowly across his collar bone and down to the vee in front of his shirt, she brushed her fingertips gently through his chest hair.

His jaw tensed slightly, like it did that first time in the office at The Old Manor.

William kept his eyes on hers as she slowly undid each

button of his shirt, leaning forward so she could pull it down over his arms.

Jess ran her eyes lustfully over his body, thinking how he looked even more toned than he did just three days ago.

Slowly she moved herself round so she was straddling him, her knees resting up on the sofa, her dress falling around her revealing her bare upper thighs.

Holding his gaze, she gently pushed his shoulders so he was leaning against the back of the sofa, his arms stretched out on top of the cushions.

His eyes darkened as she slowly undid her dress, pulling the bow on the side of her waist, letting the material fall open in front of her. Tonight she was wearing white underwear, lace and see through, leaving very little to the imagination.

William let his eyes run down over her body, his breathing getting deeper as he did but his expression remaining unchanged.

Jess let the dress fall from her shoulders as she leant forwards, her face so close to William's she could almost taste him. Looking down at him through her long lashes, she took hold of his chin and gently tilted it up towards her. Slowly she brushed her lips over his, ever so softly, just for a second, watching as his eyes closed in frustration.

Dropping to her knees, she planted kisses down his bare chest as she undid his belt and trousers.

She was commanding the situation tonight, it felt right that in her home she should be the one in control.

Glancing up, she saw him watching her as she pulled down his trousers and boxers, his jaw still locked.

Sweeping her hair to one side of her neck she took him in her mouth as deeply as she could, hearing him quietly gasp above her. She focused as she moved, trying to control her breathing as she gradually picked up the tempo. After a minute or two she stopped, keeping her eyes on his body as she ran her tongue up his torso to his chest, smiling to herself as she placed a kiss gently on his lips.

Standing up in front of him, she slowly removed her knickers and bra, pausing for a moment, letting his eyes run over her before she climbed on to his lap.

Wrapping her arms around his neck, she gazed into his eyes as she slowly flexed her hips down on to him.

William's eyes closed, his mouth opened just a fraction.

She began to move, slowly at first, holding the back of the sofa to steady herself, William's hands gripping around her thighs.

Her hair fell down over his face as the pace quickened, their bodies and breath radiating warmth onto one another, making Jess wish she hadn't been quite so blasé with the heating.

The burn in her thighs went to another level as the momentum increased further. She grabbed hold of William's shoulders as she moved her body back slightly, sweat glistening on her skin as she willed her muscles to keep going.

Feeling the climax building inside her, she closed her eyes and focused on her rhythm, moving herself harder down on top of him, the radiator behind the sofa clanking noisily under the pressure.

Glancing down at William she could tell he was close.

He looked up at her, willing her to reach the same peak with him.

Closing her eyes again, she focused on the feeling that was spreading through her, letting it take over her, leaning her head back as it travelled through her body.

Jess clung to him as she came, her leg muscles finally giving in as she collapsed on top of him.

Just moments later she felt William reach the same point. Burying his head in her chest, muffling his groan, he wrapped his arms around her back, holding onto her like he never wanted to let her go.

Jess kissed him, hard at first, adrenaline still pumping through her veins, then more softly, her lips holding onto his as her body recovered, every inch of her still quivering on top of him.

They stayed there on the sofa for a while, William holding her close to him, kissing her neck, their naked bodies fitting together as one.

"Another glass of wine?" Jess whispered.

"Why not, I'll get them," he said, planting another kiss on her shoulder.

She watched him walk through to the kitchen, admiring his naked body as he went.

"So, what's the plan on the weekend?" she asked as he sat back down next to her with two fresh glasses.

"Well, we have dinner with some of my friends on Saturday, then I'd like to take you out to lunch on Sunday. How does that sound?"

"Wonderful," she smiled, "are they all friends that were there last Friday?" she asked quietly, taking a sip of her wine.

He smiled, recognising her concern.

"Some of them are yes, but don't worry, none of them will say anything."

Jess laughed sarcastically and rolled her eyes.

"Oh please, they're not going to have something to say about you bringing last weekend's stripper to dinner with you?"

It had been playing on her mind slightly, especially given the comment one of them made about her as they were leaving on Saturday morning.

"Trust me, none of them will say anything," he said, his voice hardening as he took a sip of his wine.

Reading his tone, Jess decided to leave the subject alone.

"What time do you have to leave in the morning?" she asked, wrapping her arm around his stomach, her head resting on his chest.

He laid his hand on her hair, smoothing it slowly.

"I'll leave at about eight, I don't have to be in the office until ten."

"That's nice, not too early," Jess said as she tried to suppress a yawn.

Kissing her head, he tapped her gently on the thigh.

"Come on, let's get into bed."

Jess woke the next morning when it was still dark, the wine had left her with a bit of a headache and a very dry mouth. Glancing at her bedside clock she saw it was only quarter to six.

Leaning over she watched William through the darkness,

he looked huge in her double bed, his torso stretching well over onto her side.

Getting back to sleep didn't appear to be an option, so when six thirty rolled around Jess tip toed into the kitchen to make herself a cup of tea.

Flipping her laptop open whilst she waited for the kettle to boil, she tapped into her online banking. Quickly glancing over the screen, she was reminded of the money she spent so effortlessly yesterday. Taking a moment, she mentally totted up next month's bills in her head to see how many hours she would need to work at the pub.

A few new emails pinged through as she stirred the milk into her tea. Flicking through them, sending most of them to the trash bin, she saw one was from the agency asking if she wanted any more bookings. It looked like a generic email that was sent out to most of their employees, especially the ones that had cancelled all their future bookings.

Jess had emailed them on Sunday evening, it was a bold move, the job had earnt her some serious money over the years, but she knew it was important to William. It was very early days, but this was the first man she had wanted to pursue a relationship with, so she needed to give it her best shot.

There was another email, it was from the police department titled, 'New information in the Katie Lockhart case'. Jess clicked on it, it was written from a Detective Hill, she had never met him or her, she assumed Detective Jones had finally retired and the case had been passed on to someone else. It read the same as the others she had received before, saying they wanted to inform her there was some new information in the case.

In the past Jess would have got her hopes up, that this snippet of information they were dangling in front of her might have been the answer to what happened to Katie, but time and time again she was always disappointed. She deleted the email, along with the one from the agency and padded back down the hallway with her cup of tea.

Daylight was seeping through the curtains as Jess slid silently back into bed next to William. She sat and watched him for a minute, sleeping so peacefully, his breathing deep and heavy. Outside she could hear car engines start up on the street beyond her flat as people began their morning commute to work.

William stirred at the noise, rubbing his eyes as they adjusted to the light in the room.

He turned to her and smiled.

"Good morning," he said, pushing himself up on the bed and planting a kiss on her mouth.

"Morning," Jess smiled back at him, "I'll get you a cup of tea," she said without asking, as if they had been together for years and this was their morning routine.

She smiled at the thought as she slipped out of bed again and went to the kitchen.

"I've put some bacon in the oven," she said a few minutes later as she handed him a cup of earl grey and sat down on the edge of the bed.

"Perfect, thanks," he flashed her a smile as he propped himself up on a pillow, "what time do you have to be in work?"

"Not until nine."

"Let's have a shower then," he suggested, tugging on her satin nightdress that she had purchased especially for his visit.

Squeezing into the tiny shower together, they laughed as the water dribbled over them, their damp bodies knocking into each other as they covered one another in soap.

Jess rubbed William's chest, moving her hands in slow circles as the bubbles began foaming in his hair. Moving down to his stomach, she ran her hands over his abdominals before making her way right down to the muscles between his hips.

He was getting hard. She pretended not to notice and continued intently washing him, moving her hands up to his shoulders and down his arms.

William restrained for a minute or so, his breathing getting faster, his chest moving up and down more deeply as she continued to wash him. Suddenly he'd had enough.

Taking hold of her chin, he tilted it up so she was looking right at him, his eyes wild and dark as he kissed her, just for a few seconds.

Wasting no time he turned her around, holding on to her tightly by her hips.

Jess knew what was coming. Bracing herself up against the cold tiled wall, she held herself steady, gasping as he filled her.

Water was still streaming down over them, a cloud of steam building up around them in the little cubicle.

William held on to her as he thrusted, his shoulder banging loudly against the plastic door as he moved.

Jess threw her head back, standing up on her tip toes, trying to find her sweet spot as William increased his pace, moving more forcefully with every second.

His tempo quickly became more frantic, Jess knew he was nearly there.

Closing her eyes, she willed her body to give her the high she so badly craved, like an addict needing a hit, the more she had it, the more she wanted it.

Behind her William moaned loudly. He stopped moving and wrapped his arm around her waist, keeping himself inside her. Still holding on to her, he leant forward, his head next to hers, his breathing heavy. After a moment he turned her around, wrapping her in his arms, holding her so close to his chest all she could hear was his heart beating. Pulling her head back, he pushed the hair from her face, Jess squinted as the water splashed off his chest into her eyes.

He gave her that look, the one where she felt he was looking right into her soul. For a second it looked like he wanted to say something, like it was on the tip of his tongue, but he didn't. Cradling her face, he kissed her once more before stepping out of the shower, the trapped steam billowing out of the door into the small bathroom.

Jess finished washing her hair and did her makeup for the day. Stepping across the hallway to her bedroom she smiled as she caught sight of William in the kitchen, making bacon sandwiches as he happily whistled along to the radio.

A few minutes later they were sat together at the kitchen table, polishing off their sandwiches with another cup of tea.

"So, I'll see you on Saturday?" Jess said picking the last

of the crumbs from her plate. Since spending time with William she had definitely developed more of an appetite, maybe Charlotte was right, she thought to herself, maybe it was all the sex.

"Yeah, come whenever you're ready, I'll text you my address," he said, getting up and clearing away their plates.

Placing the milk back in the fridge, he paused as he closed the door.

"Is this where your mum is?" he asked, pointing at a piece of paper stuck to the fridge with a heart magnet.

"Yeah, I always forget which line to ring for different things, so I just have it there."

"It looks like a nice place," he said, peering down at the photos on the bottom of the contact list.

"Yeah, she seems to like it," Jess said finishing the dregs of her tea.

William pulled his jacket off the back of the chair.

"Right, I had better get off or I'll be late for my first meeting."

They said their goodbyes, Jess walked outside to wave him off. In the car park William's huge shiny Range Rover stuck out like a sore thumb next to the other small, battered cars.

"See you on Saturday," he said planting one last, long kiss on her lips.

"See you then," she smiled back.

Jess waved as she watched him drive off. Turning to go back inside, she caught sight of Janet peering out of her window.

Seeing Jess catch her, she smiled and gave a thumbs up

before disappearing again behind the curtain.

Jess laughed to herself as she closed the door, hoping Janet and Paul hadn't heard her and William through the walls this morning.

Chapter Sixteen

Jess had never driven the roads in central London before. It wasn't long before she discovered it was a small piece of hell right here on earth. Even on a gloomy Saturday afternoon it was hectic, she hated to think what it would be like during actual rush hour. Three times she was nearly run off the road by an Uber driver, as well as being beeped at for crossing a bus lane and sworn at by a cyclist. Everyone else seemed to know what lane they were supposed to be in and where they were going, she didn't have a clue.

Eventually she pulled up outside William's building having done three laps of Kensington before she found the road she needed to head down. Thankfully his street was quieter, just along from his building she found a tiny parking spot and squeezed her little car into it, leaving an inch spare for the van in front.

His building was beautiful, it was four storeys with one almost below the pavement. Bending down, she peered in at the brightly lit room, inside she could see a large rack of weights, treadmills, a line of spinning bikes and a pair of expensive looking rowing machines.

The building was white with two large pillars outside the front door, the number seventeen painted in black on them. Walking up the steps, Jess hit the button for flat number four.

A few moments later William's voice came through the speaker as the door buzzed in front of her.

"Hey trouble, come on up."

Pushing open the door Jess let herself in to the foyer, a single room the size of her entire flat with a huge elevated ceiling and a lift at the opposite end. Walking quickly across the shiny tiled floor, her heeled shoes echoing as she went, she pushed the upwards pointing button on the wall, hailing the lift back down from the third floor.

As the lift glided upwards towards William's flat, Jess checked her reflection in the mirrored wall. She'd had the time to curl her hair this afternoon, her visit to the care home had been brief again.

Audrey's condition had deteriorated even more in the week since Jess had last seen her. For half an hour she sat watching her mother lie in bed, drifting in and out of sleep, her pale, thinning face not registering a word she said to her. In her heart she had hoped that last weekend was an anomaly, a one off, that this week Audrey would be better.

Mrs Brown had sat Jess down in her office after she burst into tears at the reception desk in front of three other visitors. She gave her a stern, yet sympathetic look as she told her Audrey wasn't eating well and they needed to put her on a drip to make sure she was getting the fluids and nutrients that she needed.

The reality of this new development was a difficult one for Jess to come to terms with. She had known it was coming at some point, just not quite yet.

For the second week in a row she left the care home hysterical, feeling totally heartbroken that the woman she once knew and loved was slipping away from her, that she would never have a proper conversation with her again, that now she finally had some happiness to share with her, she wouldn't be able to.

Gracefully the lift came to a halt and moments later the two metal doors slid open revealing a room very similar to the foyer downstairs, only smaller. On the far side was one lone black door with a large brass number four on the front. Before Jess got close enough to the door to knock on it, William pulled it open.

He was topless with a towel around his neck, his bare chest glistening with sweat.

"Hey you," he said planting a kiss on her lips, "sorry I've just come up from the gym."

"I can see that," she said, taking in his appearance.

"Come on in," he smiled, holding the door open for her.

The flat was gorgeous. Having seen his other property Jess should have expected as much but it still managed to take her breath away.

The rooms were huge, with ceilings so tall you could have put another floor in. She gazed in awe at the modern furnishings, the beautiful blend of greys and whites making everything look so clean and fresh. There was a distinct lack of clutter that could only come with a space occupied by a male. Her flat was full of little trinkets, flowers, candles and pictures, it was like a bric-a-brac shop compared to this place.

"Did you do this place up yourself?" she asked as she walked a circuit of the open plan kitchen and living area.

"Oh god no," he replied with a frown, "Matilda did it all for me a couple of years ago when I bought the place. She studied interior design and loves doing stuff like that."

"It's beautiful," Jess said, pausing between the two huge sash windows to admire an abstract painting of a Cornish coastline.

William had a rugby game playing on the television, which was a suitable size for a small cinema. In front of it sat a huge U-shaped sofa, stacked with pillows and throws. A large glass topped coffee table sat in the centre, piled with magazines and books on cocktail making.

"Would you like a drink? We don't have to leave until seven," William asked, making his way to the kitchen and opening up a glass doored fridge full of chilled wine bottles.

"Why not," Jess smiled as she sat herself up on a stool at the island.

"Chablis okay?" he asked, already peeling the casing off the top of the bottle.

"Sure," Jess smiled at him, confident his wine palate was miles more sophisticated than her own.

"How was your day?" she asked, feeling incredibly civilised as he handed her a drink in an expensive looking glass with an unnervingly thin stem.

"It's been good, I managed to get a bit of work done here this morning," he said, gesturing behind him to the hallway, "it's quite nice not having to go into the office. How about you? How did the pub shift go last night?"

Jess could tell William wasn't as enthusiastic as she was about her new career in bartending, especially after he called her on Thursday night to see how her first shift went and she told him how friendly all the local men had been to her.

"Yeah, it was good thank you, I think I'm getting the hang of it," she smiled, taking a sip of her wine.

"You haven't been chatted up too much?" he said, playfully raising his eyebrows, his eyes staying a little serious.

"No, not at all," she lied with a smile.

The truth was she had been chatted up a lot, particularly last night when a group of young lads came in after their shift on the building site next to the pub. But Jess felt this probably wasn't worth mentioning, she hadn't known William that long and already she could sense a protective streak in him.

Making his way around the island, William sat himself up next to her on a stool.

"You look beautiful by the way," he said as he leant forward and kissed her.

Jess felt her cheeks flush.

"Thanks," she said glancing down at her clothes, "I've

brought some more outfits for tonight, I wasn't really sure what to wear," she said with a slight frown.

William laughed at her with affection, "you'll look beautiful whatever you wear."

Taking a large swig of wine, he placed his glass firmly down on the marble island top.

"Right, I'm going to jump in the shower, do you want to join me?" he asked, his eyes dancing playfully.

Jess twirled her freshly curled hair between her fingers.

"As tempting as that is," she smiled, shaking her head, "I am not doing my hair again."

"Fair enough," he replied, accepting defeat.

Slapping her knee gently as he got up, he kissed her again, his lips holding on to hers for just a second longer.

She could feel the tingling in her groin at his touch, her body and her brain telling her two different things. Bringing her hand up to hold the side of his face, she wondered whether she should sacrifice her fresh hair style for a session in the shower.

Pulling away, her eyes locked with his, Jess watched them sparkle mischievously as he smiled at her, creasing in the corners. It was rather unfair, she thought to herself, that men were able to look even more attractive with wrinkles, whilst women spent their whole lives trying to avoid them.

"Make yourself at home," he smiled as he strode across the room to the hallway.

Jess was feeling delightfully relaxed as she wandered slowly around the living room. Gazing out of the windows she could see the buzz of the city below, groups of people walking along the street, all dressed up and laughing together ready for the night ahead. In the distance the magnificent silhouette of the London skyline was glowing, lit up by the setting autumn sun.

Continuing her nose around, Jess glanced along the made to measure bookshelves that fitted so perfectly around the television. Running her fingers along the books lining the middle shelf, she caressed their spines, curious as to what genre William enjoyed. Pulling one out, she studied the blurb on the back. It was some sort of murder mystery, a best-selling thriller. Having not read much since school, Jess made a quiet promise to herself to ditch the Netflix series and go and buy herself some books when she got home.

Walking through into the hallway, wine in hand, she continued exploring.

Next to the front door was an office, the room William had been gesturing at earlier. It was incredibly neat and tidy, no piles of paper or files anywhere, it seemed like the sort of office someone would have as a secondary to their main one. It was large for its purpose, with deep navy walls and a dark wooden floor, there was no other furniture except for a standalone desk positioned in the middle of the room with a huge MacBook sat on the top of it. Jess walked carefully around it, sure that one knock would send the computer toppling over.

On the back wall there were a few wooden shelves sparsely decorated with some photographs. Jess recognised his parents and Matilda from the ones she had seen at The Old Manor. In the middle there was a particularly large photo in a silver-plated frame of all four of them, stood together in front of a large industrial building. William was in the middle of his family, beaming as he held one of his gin bottles proudly in his hands. In the bottom right corner was a handwritten message.

So proud of you son.

Scanning the other photos Jess saw a few more of his family, others with his friends. On the top shelf was a large group shot of him surrounded by twelve other men on what looked like a stag do, Jess knew what they looked like, she had seen a fair few in her time. William was stood front and centre on a street outside a bar, the colourful lights glowing behind them. They all wore white linen shirts, buttoned down to below their chest and shorts in a variety of different colours. William's deep tan was glowing, his wide smile shining brightly in contrast to his skin.

Jess studied the other men in the photograph, trying to sift through her memories to see if she could recognise any of them from last Friday night, although she was only in the dining room for the best part of a minute and she spent most of that completely fixated on William.

Continuing back down the hallway Jess past a spare bedroom, sparsely furnished so as not to distract from the glorious view of the city out of the tall sash window. At the end of the hallway was the master bedroom. Jess wandered in quietly, her feet silently padding on the thick cream carpet. The room, like the rest of the flat was stunning, the walls were simple and bright, tying in tones of grey and dark blue with some of the furnishings. Against the back wall sat a huge sleigh style bed, opposite it was another enormous television with a long bar speaker mounted on the wall below. On the left side of the room, next to the window was a freestanding bath, the modern kind, made from a cream coloured marble with smooth edges and sleek silver taps.

Jess could hear the shower running in the bathroom to her right, hot steam floating out of the open door. On the opposite side of the room was another door, a wardrobe Jess discovered, lined with rails full of suits and shirts, shoes stacked tidily in their handmade cubbies underneath drawers full of neatly folded jumpers and jeans. She looked around in awe, it was like being inside a small clothes store, the kind where a member of staff runs around gathering up expensive items that they think will look good on you.

Making her way back to the kitchen Jess topped up her wine glass again. Noting the bottle was nearly gone already she had a quiet word with herself, conscious that she wanted to arrive at dinner in a sensible state and make the best impression she could on William's friends.

Sitting herself down on the sofa, she made herself comfortable amongst the mountain of cushions, trying to work out what on earth was happening in the rugby game.

"We could grab a drink somewhere before we head to the restaurant?" William suggested as he appeared back in the room, a white towel wrapped around his waist, another smaller one in his hand rubbing his hair dry.

"What do you think?" he asked.

Jess winced as a player got taken out mid-air on the television, his neck taking the brunt of his fall.

"Yeah, that sounds great, what's the time?"

"Quarter past five," he said glancing at his watch, "shall we try and leave at six?"

"Sure, I'll go and start getting ready," Jess said, rising quickly to her feet, glad to not have to watch the two men involved in the illegal tackle have a fight in the middle of the pitch, the tiny referee blowing his whistle loudly, not quite brave enough to push himself in between them.

"I've put your bag in our room, it's the one at the end of the corridor," William said as he turned and made his way to the fridge for more wine.

'Our room' Jess thought to herself with a smile, a week ago they had only just met and now he was referring to his bedroom as theirs.

Four dresses, two pairs of trousers and three different blouses. That was the extent of Jess's outfit options for this evening. Lying them all out on the bed she stood back, trying to work out which one would be most appropriate. Eventually she decided on a midi wrap dress with black boots, she wanted to look as sophisticated as possible after her appearance last Friday, so the longer the skirt the better, she thought.

She dressed herself and reapplied her makeup. Thankfully her hair was still looking good, she had definitely drunk too much wine to be handling hot curling tongs right now. Standing in front of the floor length mirror leant up in the corner of the bedroom, she applied one more layer of lipstick as William appeared in the doorway behind her.

"You look amazing."

"Thank you," she smiled back at him in the mirror.

Still in his towel he moved slowly up behind her and

wrapped his arms around her waist, his chin resting against the side of her face.

"This looks lovely on you," he whispered in her ear, running his fingertips slowly along the waistline of her dress.

Jess inhaled, feeling the familiar tingle in her groin at his touch.

He kissed her neck, his stubble rubbing gently against her skin as his hand travelled down the split of the fabric. She gasped quietly as he touched her thigh, running his hand up her leg, closing in on her inch by inch. Suddenly all her senses were on high alert, every part of her body was focused, waiting for him.

Slowly his fingers brushed over her hip, her stomach muscles tensing in excitement. His eyes were still locked on her face in the mirror as she leant her head back into his chest, her body getting itself ready for him, knowing what was coming next.

Moving his hand slowly across her stomach, he found her knickers and ran his fingers gently across the top of the lace. His other hand moved up to her breasts, her nipples hard beneath her bra, responding to his touch.

Jess let out a quiet moan. Opening her eyes, she saw he was still watching her, his dark eyes finding hers.

Still holding her gaze, he moved his hand slowly down the front of her knickers, inhaling loudly as he felt how wet she had become. Caressing her breasts now with slightly more force, he slowly slid his fingers inside her, his erection pressing up against her back.

Jess moaned, pushing her hips back into him, pulling his

hand gently away from her. She didn't want any more foreplay.

Quickly William moved her around, he didn't need to be asked twice.

Placing her hands down on the bed, Jess heard his towel drop to the floor.

Leaning forward he kissed the side of her neck, his breathing heavy as he pushed her dress up around her hips and pulled down her knickers.

He moved slowly for a minute or two, making sure she was enjoying the pressure. Gripping on to her hips, he kept her steady as he built up speed, holding her tighter as he moved more forcefully, his breathing quickening with his pace.

Jess threw her head back, relishing in the feeling as she braced herself hard against the end of the bed. It didn't take long for her this time, she let out a loud moan as William quickly wrapped his arm around her waist, holding onto her as her knees threatened to give way.

Once she had steadied herself, he carried on, his movement becoming more powerful with every second, his breathing getting more desperate as he tried to reach his moment. A couple of minutes later he did, holding her tightly, keeping her pressed against him.

They both collapsed on the bed. William took hold of her hand as they lay there regaining their breath. After a minute or two he turned to her and kissed the back of her hand, flashing her a smile across the sheets before sitting up and gently pulling her up next to him. Running his hands through her hair he laid it down on the front of her shoulders, grazing her breast as he did.

"Still looking good," he smiled as he kissed her, her body still recovering from the passion that had just erupted between them.

The disappearing sunlight was shining blindly through the bedroom window as they got themselves ready to leave. Jess touched up her lipstick, again, and smoothed down her hair. William disappeared into his wardrobe, reappearing within a couple of minutes dressed in dark blue jeans, a white shirt and Chelsea boots. Jess watched him fiddle with his collar and put on a different watch, a smarter one than he normally wore, with a brown leather strap and round face. His aftershave followed him around the room as he picked up his wallet and phone from the bedside table, checking it briefly before putting it in his pocket.

"Right," he looked up at her sat on the end of the bed, "shall we go?"

They made their way down the lift and out into the cooling autumn air, William holding Jess's hand as they went, his fingers intertwined with hers. Leading her down the street and round the corner, he waved very casually at a black cab parked half way down the road, as if it had just been sat there waiting there for him.

William opened the door for her, greeting the driver as they got in. It seemed they had met before, William said he regularly came across him around this street.

"Where are we going tonight then William?" the driver asked.

Jess took a deep breath, silently pondering how many other women spending the evening with William this taxi driver had driven around London on a Saturday night.

As they moved closer to the centre of the city everything became more intense. The traffic got heavier, the noise of rowdy, already drunk people became louder and the lights surrounding the bars and restaurants got brighter.

"Here's fine," William called through the glass as they joined the line of other cars pulling up on the side of the road.

Holding his phone up to the contactless machine, William waited for the beep before climbing out of the car, pausing by the door to help Jess out behind him.

"Thank you," Jess said smiling at the driver in the mirror.

"Bye love, enjoy your evening," he said, busy staring at his phone.

William kept hold of her hand as he helped her up out of the taxi. Immediately it's orange light pinged on over the cab as it whizzed off down the road. Jess watched as it was hailed by a young woman not twenty meters away, two other men who already looked a bit worse for wear piled in with her as the orange light disappeared and off it went again.

They walked the busy street, William leading the way keeping Jess behind him, protecting her from the riot of drunken people laughing and shouting at each other, walking in big groups off to their evening destination.

There were lots of bars, some with tables out on the street, groups of men and women sat together wrapped up in coats, drinking wine and beer, deep in conversation. Towards the end of the road the crowds grew thinner, the noise grew quieter as William led her into a small bar on the corner of the street.

Walking through the door Jess dropped the collar of her coat as a wall of warm air hit them. The room was large and dimly lit with low mood lighting, emphasising the huge fireplace at the far end, the flames within it crackling away happily. In the corner light jazz music was being played by a young man wearing a very seventies outfit and a pair of small, round sunglasses.

It was busy, looking around William spotted the last empty table in the far corner of the room and strode towards it, straight past the sign saying, 'please wait to be seated'.

Following him through the tables of people, Jess caught sight of a pair of women sat alone in the middle of the bar, staring at William as he walked past, quickly running their eyes over her as she followed.

Pulling out a chair for Jess, William sat himself down opposite her.

"It's so busy here," Jess said glancing around at the tables.

"It's always busy here," he said, opening the drinks menu and turning it around for her to see, "I can't say I'm much of a fan of London anymore, I think you grow out of it you know?" he said as he made eye contact with one of the waiters.

"Yeah, it's not exactly a quiet life here is it," Jess said, studying the menu in front of her.

The waiter appeared at the side of their table, pen and paper in hand.

"What can I get you this evening?" he asked, looking at Jess still perusing the menu.

"I'll have an espresso martini," William said, "and some olives please."

"Of course sir, and for you madam?"

"I'll have the same please," she said handing him back the menu. It had been a long week juggling two jobs, a shot of coffee and vodka sounded like just the ticket.

"Sorry, I forgot to ask earlier how your mum was today?" William said once the waiter had scurried off with their drink order.

Jess looked down at her hands on the table as she fiddled with her napkin.

"She wasn't great in all honesty."

She paused taking a deep breath.

"She didn't recognise me or speak, she just sat there in her bed. It was horrible."

Jess brought her gaze up to meet William's, she could see the compassion in his eyes.

"I'm sorry. Is there anything they can do for her?" he asked, although he knew very well what the answer was.

"No," Jess looked back down at her hands and shook her head, "they can just keep her comfortable, they're going to try her on a drip to make sure she's hydrated, they're struggling to get her to eat or drink anything."

The look on William's face was a lot like the one on Mrs Brown's earlier, they knew the end was coming.

Suddenly the waiter appeared with their drinks in what must have been record time, placing Jess's down first in front of her.

"Thanks," William said keeping his eyes on Jess.

She looked up at him and faked a smile.

"So, what restaurant are we going to tonight?" she asked, suppressing the threatening lump in her throat by taking a huge mouthful of her drink.

"It's a seafood one I believe, Tom's organised it all so I'm not one hundred percent sure."

"I'm excited to meet them all properly," Jess lied. Inwardly she was still worried what they would all think of her.

William took a sip of his drink and smiled at her.

"They're excited to meet you too."

They chatted some more and ordered another round of espresso martinis, Jess began to forget the conversation about her mother and relaxed, the vodka seeping its way into her blood stream.

They had just polished off a second bowl of olives when William glanced at his watch and announced they needed to leave.

Drinking the last of his cocktail in one he waved at the waiter, signalling for him to bring over the cheque. He appeared in a shot, card machine already in hand. Out of the window Jess could see a queue of people on the street, huddled up in little groups, waiting hopefully for a table.

Attempting to down the last of her cocktail, she went to pull her purse out of her bag as William opened the bill. Catching sight of the total at the bottom Jess nearly spat out her drink, it was eyewatering for four espresso martinis and some olives.

"Put that away," William frowned at her as he pulled out a credit card.

"Are you sure?" Jess feebly fought back, thankful for his

generosity.

"Of course, tonight is my treat," he said as he punched in his pin number and handed a ten pound note to the waiter. "Come on, let's go."

He pulled his coat off his chair and stood up. Jess did the same. As he took hold of her hand and led her back through the bar, Jess caught sight of the two women from earlier, still sat at their table, lustfully gazing at William as he approached. As she walked past she flashed them a huge smile.

"Enjoy your evening ladies," she said, sarcasm oozing from her voice as the women hastily averted their gaze back to each other, embarrassed at how obvious they were being.

It was dark outside when they left the bar, Jess pulled her trench coat back up around her chin and rubbed her hands together, wishing she had gone for trousers tonight instead.

William stood on the curb and hailed another taxi that was parked up just down the street, again as if it had been sat there waiting for them.

The restaurant was less than a mile away, but it took them over twenty minutes to drive there, it surely would have been quicker to walk, although glancing down at her heeled boots, Jess thought maybe not. Apart from her short stints on a Saturday night she was not very well practiced at walking in heels, she never seemed to have an occasion to wear them anymore.

The taxi ground to a halt outside the restaurant. Jess gazed up at the enormous building, with blue lights that shone brightly down the walls at the front, guiding you into the large glass doors. Even from the street below it was impossible not to hear the loud buzz of customers out of the windows on the first two floors.

Taking hold of Jess's hand, William led her through the doors where they were greeted by a very efficient looking concierge.

"Good evening," he smiled brightly, "do you have a reservation?" he asked, looking at William with raised eyebrows.

"We're here with the Farrow party."

"Ah, very good sir," the man nodded and gestured for them to follow him.

Making their way quickly through the busy tables, trying to keep up with the concierge who practically jogged along in front of them, they headed up the stairs to the first floor.

Jess was beginning to feel nervous, a feeling of unease churning away in her stomach.

Reading her mind William turned and winked at her, giving her hand a little squeeze.

As they approached the table there was an almighty roar as William's friends spotted them.

"You guys made it!" said the large man sat at the head of the table, Jess recognised him as the one sat next to Adam last weekend at The Old Manor. He stood up, nearly knocking his drink over with his stomach as he did and sidestepped his way around the table to greet them.

"Tom, how are you doing?" William said, shaking his hand, "this is Jess," he said stepping to one side.

"Jess, so lovely to see you again," Tom said with a smile, his big red cheeks squeezing his eyes together as he enveloped her in a hug.

"So nice to meet you," she smiled back.

Glancing around, she saw William had made his way to the other side of the table, shaking hands with the men, kissing the women politely on each cheek.

Looking over, he gestured for her to come and join him.

"Come," Tom said, intercepting her, "sit down and I'll introduce you to everyone."

Tom sat her down next to him, William was sat on the other side, halfway down the table. There were twelve of them all together, seven men and five women.

"Now Jess, this is Felix," Tom said, slapping the man opposite her on the back making him wince slightly.

"Hi Jess, it's nice to meet you," he said with a smile, reaching out to shake her hand.

She smiled back at him, "you too."

"Next to him you have Elizabeth," Tom pointed at a blonde lady who was sipping her cocktail through a straw.

She waved before swallowing her mouthful.

"Hello," she said, flashing her a friendly smile.

"Then next to William is Georgina, that's Adam's girlfriend," he raised his hand to face to cover his mouth, "she's a new one on the scene, we're not too sure about her yet," he whispered quietly.

"And then of course that's Adam at the end," he said back in his normal volume.

Jess looked down the table at Adam who gave her a friendly wave.

Tom reeled off several other names, Jess smiled and nodded, knowing full well she had absolutely no hope of remembering them all.

The buzz in the restaurant was electric, Jess could barely hear herself over the noise of everyone chatting away. Tom had ensured that the drinks were flowing, with nearly everyone on the table double parked with a cocktail and a glass of wine.

"So, Jess, where abouts are you from?" asked the man to her left, Ben, she thought his name was. He was tall, his head towering over hers even when they were sat, with light brown hair and narrow eyes. He spoke slowly and very clearly when he told Tom he didn't want any alcohol, as if Tom didn't understand what he was saying. Jess noticed he was only drinking water, bottled not tap.

"I'm from Witney, near Oxford."

"Oh, that's a nice place," he said with a blank expression, "and what do you do?" he asked as he straightened the knives and forks around his placemat.

"I work at a pet store," she said, watching him as he made sure every piece of cutlery was at ninety degrees.

"How about you, what do you do?" she asked, tactfully steering the conversation away from her career choices.

"I'm in tech, coding specifically."

Of course you are, Jess thought to herself, not sure what her next line of conversation was going to be with this man.

Looking across the table she caught sight of William, he was watching her, next to him Elizabeth was chatting away in his ear, but he was still looking over at her, silently asking if she was okay. She flashed him a smile and took a large mouthful of wine as the waiter arrived to take their orders.

The ordering took a while, with nearly everyone making substitutions and extra requests. The waiter had already used three pieces of paper on his notepad and was getting more impatient by the minute.

Jess went for the sea bass, she hadn't tried a lot of seafood and thought it best to play it safe. Scanning down the menu she saw all kinds of weird and wonderful things listed, the thought of poached octopus was making her feel a bit queasy, thankfully no one else at the table requested it.

Once the waiter had dashed off with their order before anyone else could change their mind, Elizabeth stood up and made her way around the table. Leaning down beside Jess she whispered in her ear.

"Do you want to come to the bathroom with me?"

Jess didn't need the loo, but she did want to make friends, so she excused herself and followed Elizabeth downstairs.

"God, I'm so sorry you're sat next to Ben," she said once they were in the privacy of the bathroom, "he is so bloody boring!"

Jess laughed, "Oh no it's fine, he seems nice."

Elizabeth raised her eyebrows at her in the mirror as she reapplied her lipstick.

"So, I heard how you and William met," she said with a smirk.

Jess felt the blood rush to her cheeks.

"Yeah, I'm sure you all have," she said, stepping up to the mirror and rummaging in her bag for her lipstick.

"Hey, I'm not knocking it," Elizabeth said, "I think its bloody amazing how much you've worked to look after your mum. William's been telling me all about you."

"He has?" Jess asked looking round at her.

"Yeah, he can't stop talking about you, I've not heard him talk about another woman like that since Francesca," she paused, "and that was in the old days, before all the baby stuff."

They finished touching up their makeup and washed their hands.

"Hey, give me a nod if you want me to swap with you," Elizabeth said as they left the bathroom, "I'll take one for the team with Mr Boring."

Jess laughed, "thanks, I'm sure I'll be fine."

They made their way back upstairs, as they approached the table Jess saw Georgina deep in conversation with William, her hand on the back of his shoulder, her face a little too close to his. William was sat as upright as he could get, his arms folded in front of him.

Leaning down on the other side of his face, Jess planted a quick kiss on his cheek as she walked past.

He turned his head, flashing her a smile.

The evening went on nicely. The food when it finally arrived was delicious, an absolute feast laid out down the table. Jess couldn't bear to think what the bill was going to be.

She spoke at length with Tom about his work, he invested in restaurants, that's what they were all doing there apparently, he was scouting it out to see if he wanted to put money into their new seafood restaurant on the other side of the city. He had a wife, although she couldn't make it tonight, Tom explained that she was away visiting her brother with their two twins, Oliver and Jack. Pulling out his phone he produced a picture of them, both embodying their father's characteristics with little round faces and big cheeks.

"Oh, they're gorgeous," Jess said, staring at the photo.

"They're a pair of little hell raisers is what they are," Tom laughed, putting his phone away and tucking into his lobster, which was surrounded by so much garlic butter it was practically floating on his plate.

"Do you have any children Jess?" Felix asked, catching her off guard.

"Oh no," she blurted out a little too loudly, "I haven't got to that stage yet," she laughed, shaking her head.

Felix looked at her with a little smile, not quite sure how to respond. She could guess he was probably thinking that she needed to get on with it, that your early thirties were not too soon to be starting a family. But inside she still felt too young to have children, like she hadn't properly grown up yet. Plus, she knew how William and Francesca had struggled to conceive, the last thing she wanted was him turning down the table to their conversation and hearing her say that she wanted children. If by some miracle they ended up together but never had a child, she would be completely fine with that.

It was ten thirty by the time everyone had finished their meal and had a dessert or a coffee, Jess was nursing a very strong Americano, hoping it was going to keep her awake.

"Right, where are we off to now?" Tom announced, clapping his enormous hands together making Jess jump.

"Let's go to that little bar around the corner," Elizabeth said with excitement in her voice, "I want to dance!"

Once the bill, which was quite literally as long as Jess's

arm, had arrived and was paid for entirely by Tom, they all made their way down the stairs and out onto the street.

"Thank you so much for that Tom," Jess said, tying her coat tightly around her waist, "it was so generous of you."

"Ah, you're welcome Jess, it's all in a day's work for me really," he said, winking at her.

With that William appeared at her side and wrapped his arm around her shoulder.

"Have you behaved with my girlfriend this evening Thomas?" he asked.

Jess could tell he'd had a few wines, the fact that he had just referred to her as his girlfriend was making her heart race. Wrapping her arm around his back she gave him an affectionate squeeze.

"I'm always well behaved my good man," Tom replied giving William a playful jab in the stomach, "are you two going to join us?" he gestured to the rest of the group who were walking down the road, gleefully led by Elizabeth who was demonstrating her slut drop on the pavement.

William looked at Jess who smiled.

"Sure, why not, we'll come for a quick drink."

The bar was rammed. By some miracle Elizabeth had homed in on a large booth at the back just as it was being vacated by a group of women.

"Quick, quick," she gestured, "everyone come and sit down before someone else pinches it!"

All twelve of them squeezed into the booth. A very tired looking waitress reluctantly came over and took Tom's order of twelve gin and tonics and twelve tequila shots, which ended up taking so long to arrive the men all went to the bar to order some more.

Now they had more room the women all shuffled themselves around the booth, Jess found herself sat next to Georgina who was swaying slightly in her seat.

"So, what do you do?" she slurred at Jess through narrowed eyes, "apart from stripping."

She spat the word at her.

Jess paused and wiped her face purposefully with her hand.

"I work at a pet store."

Georgina snorted in response, smiling to herself.

With that Adam appeared at the table.

"Hey G, come and sit next to Elizabeth," he said, giving her a warning look.

Sticking out her bottom lip, she slid around the table, keeping her eyes on him.

Adam sat down on the other side of Jess.

"Sorry about her," he smiled, "she's had too much to drink."

"It's fine," Jess smiled back, "how are you anyway? I didn't get to speak to you at dinner," she said, eager to change the subject.

Adam smiled, crossing his lean legs in front of him.

"I'm very well thanks, work is super busy at the moment."

"What is it you do?" Jess asked.

"I work in the stock market," he shouted over the music which had just cranked up.

Jess heard Elizabeth squeal with glee as a song came on that she wanted to dance to.

"It was actually William's dad that gave me my first job a couple of years ago just before he retired, that's how we became friends," Adam smiled, looking over at William who was stood by the bar with Felix.

"Oh, how lovely," Jess said.

Georgina who had clearly had enough rose to her feet and walked around the table, holding on to it for support.

"Come and dance with me baby," she whined, tugging on Adam's sleeve.

Adam turned to Jess.

"See you in a bit," he smiled as he stood up and followed Georgina to the dance floor, holding on to her as they went.

Jess watched them dancing for a minute, struggling to work out how such a nice man had ended up with such a horrible woman.

The men returned with their drinks from the bar just as the waitress brought over the ones they had originally ordered.

Jess didn't think this was going to be one quick drink as she watched the alcohol being unloaded on to the table.

The shots were mandatory, Tom said as he instructed them all to down theirs.

Jess winced as the tequila slid like petrol down her throat, quickly she grabbed another glass and took a large gulp of gin and tonic to try and wash it down.

Elizabeth had downed her shot and grabbed Tom by the hand, dragging him on to the dancefloor.

Jess watched them for a minute, thinking how oddly majestic he was for a larger man. It didn't take too long before their dancing became a little overly friendly,

Elizabeth turning herself around, grinding her backside into Tom's crotch. Tom without hesitation grabbed her hips, squeezing them with his chubby hands.

Jess raised her eyebrows, she was sure his wife wouldn't be too happy if she saw them right now.

Suddenly her thoughts were interrupted.

"Hello," said a man who had shuffled around the table next to her. He held his hand up to shake hers, "sorry I didn't get to speak to you at dinner."

"Hello," Jess said returning his handshake, trying to remember what on earth his name was.

He was short and completely bald with a little pop belly that hung out over his strained belt. Jess had to mentally tell herself off for staring too much as the colourful disco lights reflected off his shiny head.

"I'm sad I never got to see your performance last weekend," he looked at her, raising his eyebrows.

Jess eyed him warily.

"Yeah, that was just for William," she said, pulling the split of her dress up over her knees.

"That's a shame," he said with a little frown, still staring at her, running his eyes down over her dress.

Jess inwardly shuddered. Looking around in slight desperation for William, she saw he was still stood by the bar in conversation with Felix.

"Where are you from?" the bald man asked, ignoring her glances elsewhere.

"Erm, a town near Oxford," she said, not wanting to reveal any information about herself.

"Oh, I know Oxford, I grew up there. Shame we never

bumped into each other," he said as he placed his hand down on the seat between the two of them, the side of his wrist grazing her thigh.

He continued to stare at her as he moved his hand on to the top of her leg. Before Jess had time to slap it away William appeared at the side of the table.

"Stephen," he said in a stern voice.

The bald man's hand shot back to his lap under the table.

"I hope you're not upsetting Jess," William said, his eyes locked on the man sat in front of him.

Stephen paused, eyeing William.

"Of course not," he said, a sly smile creeping onto his face, "just getting to know the latest one."

Holding William's gaze, he shuffled himself around the table before getting up and wandering off to the bar.

"Are you okay?" William asked placing a hand on Jess's shoulder.

"I'm fine," she replied, her cheeks ablaze.

"Come on, let's go home," he said as he picked up her hand and led her to the group that were occupying the dance floor.

"We're off," he shouted at Tom, "thanks for a great evening."

Tom gave them a thumbs up.

"See you soon," he shouted.

Elizabeth waved at them with a drunken smile as she wrapped her arms around Tom's neck.

Outside a line of taxis sat waiting for intoxicated people to hail them as they stumbled out of the bars, William opened the door and helped Jess into the one nearest them.

Once they were on the move he wrapped his arm around her shoulder, her head resting on his chest, she could feel the hangover coming already.

Back at his flat they made cheese toasties and washed some paracetamol down with two pints of water.

"So, did you have a good evening?" William asked, handing her a plate.

"Yeah, it was nice, most of them are really friendly," she said, pulling the crusts off her bread.

"Yeah, sorry about Stephen, he's not really a friend, he's Tom's brother and always ends up coming out—"

"What did he mean by latest one?" Jess interjected.

William looked up at her.

"Have there been lots of women that you've taken out with your friends, am I just one of them?"

Jess didn't want to get emotional, but the alcohol had hold of her and she couldn't help herself. The feelings she had been developing for William both amazed her and terrified her all at the same time.

William walked around the island until he was standing right in front of her.

"Yes, I have taken other women out with my friends in the past, but you are not just one of them," he paused, looking down into her tear filled eyes, "you are the only one now, you're all I can think about."

He held her face in his hands as hot tears ran down her cheeks.

They stood for a minute, William pulling her in against his chest.

"Come on, let's go to bed," he said as he picked up her

hand and led her down the hallway.

Jess undressed herself, quickly realising how tired she was. In the bathroom she brushed her teeth and removed her smudged makeup before climbing into bed.

William got in beside her, his body moving in behind hers, his arm wrapped around her as if he was protecting her from something.

Jess felt the warmth of his skin, his breath hitting the back of her neck as they drifted off to sleep together.

Chapter Seventeen

The sun was high in the sky and birds were singing outside the open window when Jess woke with a pounding headache on Sunday morning. With bleary eyes she glanced across at the clock on the bedside table, it was nearly half past ten. Looking behind her she saw William was already up, no wonder she thought, it was nearly lunch time.

The faint sound of the television in the living room was coming down the hallway, Jess could hear William clattering some pans in the kitchen. She lay in bed for a minute with her eyes closed, hoping if she stayed still long enough her hangover would go away.

The sound of William's footsteps in the corridor made her open her eyes again.

"Morning," he said smiling at her from the doorway.

"Morning," Jess said as she rubbed her face.

"Would you like a cup of tea?" he asked, coming round to her side of the bed and giving her a kiss.

"Yes please and some paracetamol," she said quietly, sticking her bottom lip out and frowning.

"Oh no," he laughed, "are we a bit hungover?"

"A bit!" she scoffed, "didn't you see how much wine Tom made me drink at dinner, plus those shots."

Jess needed to stop talking or she would end up seeing last night's bad decisions all over again.

"I'll go and get you some," he said as he got up.

"Thanks," Jess mumbled, pulling the duvet back up over her head.

A dose of paracetamol, a cup of earl grey and one hot shower later, Jess was beginning to feel human again, but had sworn off all alcohol for the foreseeable future.

"Something smells good," she said as she walked through to the kitchen and sat herself up on a stool.

"This will sort you out," William said, presenting her with a piping hot bacon sandwich, dripping with butter and ketchup.

Jess inhaled it, William was right, it was just what she needed.

"So where do you fancy going for lunch?" he asked, listing off restaurants on his phone as she cleared away their plates and poured them a fresh cup of tea.

"I don't mind, you know those places better than I do."

"Let's go for a Sunday roast," he said, tapping his phone a few times before announcing they were all booked in at a local pub.

They decided to take advantage of the glorious autumn sunshine and go for a walk before lunch.

Hand in hand, they strolled through the local park. It was filled with people, some out jogging, others out walking their dogs, some sat picnicking under the oak trees that lined the tarmac path. There were a countless number of families out enjoying the weather, the children all riding bikes, trikes or scooters. Jess clung on to William's arm as they watched them whizz around, squealing with glee as they chased each other.

The pub William had booked for lunch was on the corner of a road not far from the park, it was very gastro, beautifully decorated inside with lots of brass and dark coloured furnishings. Jess sat down at their table, her stomach rumbling already. Adjusting her jeans around her waistline, she noted how they felt a little tighter on her today, it was no wonder she thought, considering how much she had eaten and how much wine she had consumed in the last couple of weeks.

Twenty minutes later they were presented with two plates of roast beef with all the trimmings which they both devoured. William managed a couple of glasses of red wine, Jess stuck to lime and lemonade, she still wasn't sure she should be driving after last night let alone drinking more today.

"So, what are your plans this week?" William asked, clearing up the last of his gravy with his Yorkshire pudding.

"Just work, then seeing mum on Saturday. The usual week," she smiled, shrugging her shoulders.

"Well, I'll pop down on Wednesday and see you," he said, placing his knife and fork together on his plate.

"That would be nice," Jess smiled at him, "I'll make sure I'm not doing the evening shift at the pub."

A waitress suddenly appeared at the side of their table.

"Is there anything else I can get you?" she asked, smiling at William as she cleared away their plates.

"Would you like anything?" he nodded at Jess.

Putting her hand on her stomach she shook her head.

"God no, I'm so full."

Jess looked up at the waitress who was still gawking at William before she trotted off to get their bill.

"Thank you for this weekend," she smiled, leaning forward and taking his hand in hers.

"It's been my absolute pleasure," he smiled back, his eyes dancing, "I'm away next weekend on business in America, but the following weekend the gang are doing a couple of nights in a hotel in Buckinghamshire, it's for some charity do that Felix is organising. Will you come with me?"

Jess grinned with excitement.

"Sounds wonderful, although I'll probably join on the Saturday after visiting mum."

"Yeah of course," William said finishing the last of his wine, "just get yourself down there when you can, the drive shouldn't be too far from you."

They walked hand in hand back through the park, which was still full of people out enjoying the autumn sunshine. Back at William's flat Jess began to gather up her belongings which she had managed to spread out over nearly all the rooms in the short twenty four hours that she had been there.

"It's been so nice having you here," William smiled, watching her collect up her shoes and car keys from the living room.

"It's been nice being here, it's such a beautiful place," she looked around the room, "the company's alright too," she added, flashing him a smile.

William smirked at her.

"Here, I'll carry that," he said, picking up her duffle bag and holding the front door open for her.

They stood on the street, kissing for far longer than Jess ever imagined she would have done in public. She could feel the awkward stare of passers-by on the pavement where they stood.

"I'll see you on Wednesday," William reassured her as she got in her car.

Jess watched him disappear from the rear view mirror as she drove off down the street.

Once she had navigated her way out of central London, she allowed her brain to relax and relive the moments between the two of them over the last twenty four hours.

The way his eyes had darkened as he looked at her last night in the bedroom.

The way he kissed her, the way he touched her, the way he moved her.

The way he owned her.

Chapter Eighteen

"So, you've just quit?" Charlotte asked, turning around from the sink to look at her.

Jess had sat herself down on the sofa in the break room, nodding through a mouth full of sandwich.

Charlotte stared at her wide eyed, waiting for an explanation.

Jess winced as she tried to swallow a large piece of bread.

"Yeah, I emailed them last weekend."

She took another bite of her sandwich, trying to avoid the conversation.

"Who does he think he is asking you to stop?" Charlotte asked, throwing her hands in the air.

"Oh, come on," Jess said, "you know first-hand how hard it is to have a relationship when your dancing naked for other men every weekend."

"But you've only known him two weeks!" Charlotte continued, voicing her outrage.

Jess had run out of things to eat to try and avoid talking.

"Yes, I know. But I like him, like, really like him," she said, widening her eyes.

Charlotte paused.

"Well I never thought I'd see the day, the independent Jessica Taylor throwing the towel in for a man." She spun round and began stirring her tea on the countertop.

Jess rolled her eyes to herself.

"I'm still independent, just in another job," she said as she got up and cleared away the remains of her lunch, "make me a tea would you, I'm going to sort out some stock."

"So, are you working at the pub tonight?" Charlotte asked a few minutes later when she delivered Jess her tea.

"Yeah, I think I'll nip home and have some supper, then head there," Jess replied, not looking up from the cat collars she was pricing up.

"Well, I might come along for a drink," she said sheepishly, "I've got nothing better to do."

Jess wasn't happy about this. All she wanted to do was make it through a shift and not smash any glasses or serve anyone the wrong food, she didn't need Charlotte there getting hammered at the bar.

"Sure," she replied, trying to be tactful, "it's pretty quiet though, I'm not sure you'll enjoy it very much."

"I think I'll be the judge of that," she smiled as she turned on her heels and made her way back into the shop.

The day dragged on and finally it was time to lock up and leave. Charlotte had left early to go and get herself ready for the pub, Jess had a bad feeling about this but there wasn't a lot she could do to stop her, once Charlotte had an idea in her head, trying to discourage her usually had the opposite effect.

Swinging into her road, Jess glanced at the clock, she had made it home in record time which was good because she didn't have long before she had to leave again. Running up the stairs to her flat, she let herself in and chucked a pizza in the oven to cook whilst she got changed. Her pub uniform was very informal, plain jeans and a black top, because black didn't show up stains when she inevitably dropped some kind of sauce down her front.

Heartburn raged through her chest as she drove the roads down to the pub. Jess tried to take some deep breaths, silently cursing herself for eating a whole pizza in under five minutes. Heading straight into the bathroom before Gavin saw her, she dug some old heartburn tablets out of the bottom of her bag and downed them with some water from the tap.

Thankfully the pub was quiet this evening, she was tired from the late night on the weekend and a long day at the shop.

There were only two tables booked in for dinner and three men sat at the bar. She had seen the men here before, they were all locals that came in on their own at the same time every day and sat in silence at the bar, one of them read the paper, the other two just sat staring into space.

Leaning on the bar trying to suppress a yawn, Jess watched them all sat there, thinking how bizarre it was that none of them struck up a conversation.

The first of the two tables finally arrived, Jess quickly greeted them and went over to take their order, thinking the faster they were served their food, the faster they would eat and go home. Carefully she wrote down their requests on her notepad, double checking with them at the end, not wanting to make another mistake after she put the wrong meal through the till last week and received a bollocking from the chef when it got sent back to the kitchen.

Standing behind the bar, holding her pad up next to the screen she carefully put the order through, checking it three times before she did.

"Hey Jess."

Glancing over her shoulder, she did a double take at Charlotte strolling towards her, dressed up like she was going to a nightclub in a black strapless top and a leather skirt which were tightly sandwiching a small portion of her midriff.

"Blimey Charlotte, you're a bit overdressed, are you heading somewhere else?" she asked hopefully.

"No," she said plainly as she hopped up on one of the empty stools, "vodka tonic please bar lady."

Jess made up a very weak drink and placed it firmly down on the bar in front of her.

A few minutes later Gavin appeared in the kitchen as Jess was balancing two starters and a bread basket on her arm.

"The other lot have just come in, I've shown them to their table if you can go and get a drink order."

"Sure," Jess replied, concentrating on her armful of food as she walked cautiously past him and out into the restaurant.

A few seconds later she triumphantly placed the starters and bread quickly down on the table, pleased with herself for not dropping anything on the floor.

Turning around, pulling her pen and notepad out of her apron, she smiled at the couple who had just sat down behind her. Pausing for a second, she tried to work out where she recognised them from.

"Would you like some drinks while you wait for the rest of your party?" Jess smiled, gesturing at the empty place laid up opposite them.

The little lady looked up at her, peering wide eyed through her big round glasses. Next to her a pair of crutches stood leant up against the wall.

"Oh no thanks dear, Harry's just gone to get some drinks for us at the bar," she said quietly.

Jess spun around. Sure enough, leaning against the bar in conversation with a gleeful Charlotte was Harry Solomon.

Jess made her way over, walking cautiously around the bar to face the two of them.

"Jess, look who it is!" Charlotte said excitedly, gesturing to Harry in case she had missed him stood right in front of her.

"Hello," Jess said, her voice guarded as she remembered

the last conversation they'd had, right here in this room.

He turned to look at her, his face slightly flushed.

"Hi Jess."

"Can I get you some drinks? Your parents are waiting."

"Oh yeah of course," he said as he began studying the pumps in front of him, "I'll have two pints of Peroni and a small merlot please."

"Sure, I'll bring them to your table."

"Thanks," he smiled, glancing at Charlotte before turning to sit down with his parents.

"God, he's so fit, don't you think?" Charlotte said, her gaze following him.

Jess scoffed loudly, not even bothering to answer her.

"Can I have another vodka tonic?" she asked sliding her empty glass across the bar, her eyes still locked on Harry.

The evening dragged on, Charlotte was on her fourth drink and third packet of crisps by the time Harry came to the bar to pay the tab.

"How was everything?" Jess asked, only because she had to, not because she cared.

"Yeah, everything was great, thanks. Hello again," he said, turning to Charlotte who was smiling at him with a drunken twinkle in her eye.

"Hello, will you join me for a drink?" she asked as she crossed her legs, revealing even more of her upper thigh.

Running his eyes over her, he smiled.

"What an offer."

"We're closing soon," Jess said abruptly as she began placing dried glasses back on the shelf behind her.

"No matter," Charlotte shrugged, "we can have a drink

at my place if you like, it's not far."

Harry flushed slightly at her boldness.

"Well, I need to make sure mum and dad get off okay," he said, turning to look at the table where his father was helping his mother put her coat on, "I'll be back in a minute."

Harry disappeared out of the door, holding on to his mother's arm as he went.

Jess turned to Charlotte.

"What are you doing?" she spat.

"What?" Charlotte said downing the last of her drink.

"Inviting him back to your house, you don't even know him!"

"Oh, calm down," Charlotte said rolling her eyes, "I'm sure he's not a serial killer."

As Jess was trying to find a retort to stop what was about to happen, Harry reappeared through the door.

Picking up her bag, making no indication of paying for her tab, Charlotte hopped down from her stool, wobbling slightly in her heels as she pulled down her skirt.

"Come on Harry, let's go," she said as she turned him around on the spot, looping her arm through his.

"Oh okay, bye Jess," Harry gave her a little wave as he was marched out of the pub.

"Unbelievable," Jess whispered under her breath as she watched them disappear into the night.

It was gone eleven by the time Jess made it home. Slowly she climbed the stairs to her flat, every step feeling like a monumental effort. Heading straight to her bedroom she stripped off her clothes, leaving them in a pile on the floor before she half-heartedly brushed her teeth and collapsed into bed.

The aggressive buzz of her phone on the bedside table woke her with a start the next morning. Panic rose in her chest as she saw sunlight streaming through the curtains. Glancing quickly at the clock, she breathed a sigh of relief as she saw it was only five past eight.

Picking up her phone she smiled seeing William's name flash up on the screen.

"Hello you."

"Good morning," he said cheerfully, "it sounds like I've woken you up?"

Jess rubbed her face.

"You have in all honesty," she yawned.

William paused.

"You sound shattered Jess."

"I'm fine," she cleared her throat and sat herself up, "how are you anyway?"

"Yeah, all good, just heading into the office now."

In the background Jess could hear the noise of London commuters, the rumble of traffic on the street, a few horns blaring in the distance.

"I was going to leave work early and come straight to yours tomorrow, I'll cook us some dinner if you like?" he suggested.

Jess smiled at the thought.

"That sounds wonderful, I'll make sure I'm not back late from the shop," she said, pulling back the duvet and heading to the kitchen.

"Great, well I'm about to get on the tube so I'll lose you in a minute, I'll call you later."

"Okay have a good day," she said, suppressing another yawn as she hung up the phone.

As soon as she put the phone down to fill up the kettle it started ringing again. Glancing at the screen, she felt another wave of panic come over her as she saw it was the care home calling.

"Hello, is that Jessica?" Mrs Brown's unmistakable voice came through the speaker.

"Hi, yes it's me, is everything okay?"

"I just wanted to update you on your mother's condition," she paused, "she's continuing to refuse any food or fluids, so we've had to place her on a drip. We've also organised for a specialist nurse to come in daily and monitor her vitals to make sure she remains stable."

She paused for a moment, Jess knew what was coming.

"I'm sorry Jessica but this is a bit of a one-way street, I'm not sure how much longer she'll carry on if she stays like this."

Jess held her breath, desperately trying to keep it together but it was no use. Tears gathered in her eyes, the combination of this news and her sheer exhaustion was all too much.

"Can I please come and see her?" she sobbed.

"I'm sorry Jessica, we need to continue with limited visiting at the moment to keep our residents safe, I'll see you on Saturday. If she worsens any further, or her condition changes, I'll call you."

Jess kept the phone to her ear as Mrs Brown hung up,

tears gliding down her cheeks, her heart sitting heavy in her chest.

Charlotte wasn't in the shop today. Jess was thankful, she couldn't have coped with listening to her bang on about Harry and whatever they had gotten up to.

She spent the day sorting orders and restocking shelves, trying to keep herself busy. It was lunch time before she realised not one single customer had come in. As she stood reorganising the till, the doorbell rang. Looking up hopefully, she saw it was only Jeremy, here to run through the monthly takings.

He gave her a brief smile before scuttling past her and shutting himself in the break room. Peering through the little gap in the door, Jess watched him staring at his laptop through a furrowed brow, files spread out in front of him on the coffee table, biting his nails as he studied the bank statements. Jess had a feeling her plan to ask him for a pay rise probably wasn't going to go down well.

"Can I make you a tea or coffee?" she asked as she gently pushed the door open.

Jeremy didn't look up from his laptop.

"No, I'm fine thanks Jess."

He continued plugging in numbers, frowning as they totalled up on the screen in front of him.

In an effort to try and look useful, Jess wiped down the kitchenette and washed up some mugs. She was just about to walk back into the shop when Jeremy stopped her.

"Jess, wait a minute."

She turned around, catching him glance at her quickly

before looking back at the screen.

"I just wanted to warn you that the way things are going I'm going to have to make some cut backs."

He leant back on the sofa, looking down at his hands resting on his knees.

"I may have to drop back to just one member of staff."

It took Jess a moment to register what he way saying.

"You mean you might have to get rid of me?" she said, shock radiating through her voice.

He sighed, forcing himself to look up at her.

"Well, you have another job now, Charlotte doesn't have any other income other than this shop, she's totally reliant on this place."

Jess could feel the rage bubbling up inside her.

Charlotte, who has a house and all her bills paid for, who does in fact have another income and who barely pulls her weight in this job as is it.

Taking a deep breath, she tried to calm herself.

"Well do let me know won't you, I do have my own responsibilities and people to look after," she snapped before turning on her heels and heading back into the shop.

The rest of the afternoon dragged on, Jess shut herself in the storeroom, angrily sorting out orders of new dog beds.

Half an hour later the doorbell rang as Jeremy left, Jess peered into the shop and watched out of the window as he drove off, a cloud of black smoke following his old, battered Land Rover as it chugged down the road.

Chapter Nineteen

For some reason Jess woke up on Wednesday with the desire to go for a run. Standing outside in the car park, dressed head to toe in the gym gear she usually only wore to lounge around her flat in, along with two jumpers and a beanie, she did some half-hearted leg stretches before she set off, her breath creating a small cloud of mist in the cold air as she ran.

She made it a mile down the road before her lungs began to hurt. Grinding abruptly to a halt, her face red with sweat, she stripped off two layers of clothing and decided a walk would probably be better. Thirty minutes after leaving her flat she was back again, climbing the stairs slowly, her muscles already aching from her rare attempt at exercise.

At the top she met Paul shuffling through his post.

"Hi Paul," she said, too quietly for him to hear.

"Hi Paul," she tried again, this time louder.

He jumped at the sound of her voice.

"Bloody hell Jessica, don't go creeping up on me," he shouted back at her with a frown.

Jess tried to hide her smile.

"Sorry, how are you?" she asked.

"Fine. Janet's got a cold but other than that we're fine," he said, squinting at an envelope so closely it was almost touching his nose.

"Oh, I'm sorry to hear that," she said sympathetically, "is there anything I can get her?"

"No, we're fine," he said sternly, waving his post at her as he opened his front door. A wall of hot air came billowing out of the flat, it must have been at least thirty degrees in there. Jess wondered to herself what on earth their heating bill must be, she always ended up with frost on the inside of her windows in the winter because she couldn't face spending any more money on electricity.

Thinking of bills, she remembered she needed to do some totting up for the month ahead. Once she had showered and her face had returned to its normal colour, she wrapped herself up in her dressing gown and sat down at the kitchen table to make a plan for the month. After some quick sums she worked out she could just about do it. Audrey's bill was always taken at the very end of the month, which was this Friday, she had enough in her account for that, then she needed to do four shifts at the pub a week plus her normal salary from Jeremy to be alright for the next month, although given their conversation yesterday, she wasn't sure how long she would be able to rely on that income.

Jess leant back in her chair and exhaled, wondering how on earth she was going to keep this up, it wasn't exactly a sustainable lifestyle. Although giving up stripping wasn't initially her decision, it was one she was glad William had encouraged her to make, she was happy that part of her life was behind her. All she needed to do now was find another income stream that required less work than twenty hours a week behind a bar.

Glancing at the time on her phone, she quickly made herself some peanut butter on toast and one more cup of earl grey to set her up for the day. Once she had done her makeup and got dressed for work, she hastily loaded the dishwasher and quickly wiped down the worktop in an effort to leave the flat looking half presentable, just in case William arrived home before she did.

Charlotte was unusually already in work this morning when Jess arrived, she spotted her shiny black golf parked haphazardly outside.

"Morning," Charlotte called through from the break room, "I've just popped the kettle on, would you like a cuppa?"

Jess walked through the shop and chucked her bag down on the sofa.

"Sure," she replied.

She couldn't be angry with Charlotte, it wasn't her fault

the shop was doing so badly and regardless of who worked harder Jeremy was always going to keep her over Jess, she was basically his daughter.

"How are you today?" Charlotte asked, busy making Jess her tea.

"I'm fine," she sighed, joining her bag on the sofa and rubbing her face, "how are you?"

"Yeah, I'm good. Right, I'm going to start sorting the storeroom and restocking," Charlotte said, passing Jess her tea and marching off out the door.

It was unlike Charlotte to be so proactive at work, she normally didn't lift a finger unless she absolutely had to, perhaps Jeremy had mentioned something to her, Jess thought to herself.

Whatever the reason for Charlotte's new work ethic, Jess was pleased to have a quiet morning, why should she work herself silly for someone who might sack her at the drop of a hat? Lounging idly on the sofa finishing her first cup of tea, she got up and made herself another before sitting herself behind the till. As she finished flicking through her second Grazia magazine, the doorbell rang. Looking up she saw a woman and three young children come hurtling through the door, each child disappearing up a separate aisle.

Jess rose to feet, readying herself for the carnage.

"Hi, have you got any cat wormer?" the woman asked as she approached the till.

"Of course," Jess replied reaching behind the counter for a small packet of tablets.

Something that sounded like a metal dog bowl fell off a

shelf down the left aisle making one of the children shriek loudly.

"Erica! That nearly hit me you idiot!"

The woman closed her tired eyes and exhaled.

"Put it back!" she shouted before taking another deep breath, "can I pay by card?"

"Sure."

Jess quickly presented her the machine, as the woman went to tap her card all three children appeared behind her at once.

"Mum, look what we found for Milo," said the eldest one excitedly.

All of them had collected armfuls of various cat toys and treats.

"No, I'm not getting him anything else," the woman said, not looking round at them.

"But mum, he'll love them," the middle child whined as she stamped her foot.

The woman pinged her card, ignoring her children as she picked up the tablets and smiled briefly at Jess.

"Thank you."

Jess smiled back at her as the youngest child began to cry, her face turning red as her eyes scrunched together.

"I want to get this for Milo!" she screamed, holding up a toy fish attached to a bit of string on a stick.

The mother turned, holding her head up, ignoring her youngest child's outburst and walked straight out of the shop. The two older children paused and looked at each other for a moment before admitting defeat and following her, their heads down, dropping the toys they had collected on the floor by the shop door.

The youngest child was now in full flow. She sat herself down on the floor and began banging her heels on the ground, her face turning from red to a disturbing shade of purple.

Frozen to the spot, Jess stared at this little person making the most unbearable noise, praying that her mother was going to come back in for her. After a minute the child got up, still screaming as she threw the toy fish and the stick across the till at Jess, who ducked as it sailed past her and hit the break room door. The child gave her one last venomous stare before stomping out of the shop, kicking the discarded toys as she went.

"What on earth was that?" Charlotte said appearing in the doorway behind the till.

"The child from hell!" Jess exclaimed as she began picking up the discarded items and returning them to their rightful place.

Charlotte walked down the aisle and peered out of the window.

"God, she will not get in the car the little sod, I'd leave her there on the pavement if I was her mother."

"Not if there's a chance she might come back in here, quick lock the door," Jess laughed.

Charlotte smirked, still staring out of the window.

"Oh no hang on, she's bribed her with a snack and now she's getting in the car."

"Well thank god for that," Jess retorted as she put the final toy back on the shelf.

"Right," Charlotte sighed, looking at her watch, "I'm

popping the kettle on."

They sat together on the sofa in the break room, dipping kit kat bars into their coffees, discussing how dreadful children could be.

"Katherine has a kid called Reuben, all I've ever heard him do is whine and I've only met him twice," Charlotte said, getting up and chucking her wrappers in the bin.

"Did you say William has children?" she turned looking at Jess.

"No. He and his wife tried for years but it never happened for them."

"Oh well, at least you won't have to be the evil stepmother," Charlotte joked throwing another Kit Kat at her, "when are you next seeing him anyway?"

"Tonight, he's coming straight from work, he's away on business for a week so I won't see him until next weekend."

Charlotte leant herself back against the counter waiting for Jess to finish.

"I'm seeing Harry again on the weekend."

Jess had been waiting for her to mention him, to be fair she'd restrained herself for longer than she had expected.

"Oh yeah, how did that go the other night?" she asked tentatively.

"Yeah, really good, we just had a couple of drinks at mine then he went home."

"Really?" Jess said raising her eyebrows.

Charlotte pulled a face.

"Yes really. I do have some self-control you know," she said giving her a playful kick, "have you guys got plans next weekend? We should go on a double date!"

Jess couldn't think of a worse idea, not just because William wasn't keen on Harry, but she didn't really like him either, despite the fact Charlotte hadn't actually been on a proper date with him herself yet. Given her track record, they might not even make it to next weekend.

"I think we're staying away for the weekend with a few of his friends."

"Oh, that sounds nice," Charlotte said trying to hide her disappointment, "where are you going, somewhere fancy?"

"The Mayhill Park Hotel I think it's called, its Buckinghamshire way, only about half an hour or so I think," Jess said, getting up and brushing the Kit Kat crumbs off her lap.

"Oh, that sounds lovely," Charlotte paused, "right, better get back to work then," she said as she tied her long hair up in a very efficient bun before heading to the storeroom.

The mother and the crazy children were sadly the only customers they had in all day. As she swept up the floor at four thirty Jess had the overwhelming feeling that her days at the pet shop were most definitely numbered, seven pounds twenty on cat wormer barely even covered the tea, coffee and biscuits they had consumed today.

Together Charlotte and Jess locked up before heading their separate ways, Charlotte had suggested a drink at the pub, but Jess wanted to get home and have a shower before William got there, or even better catch him as he arrived so they could have a shower together.

"See you on Friday," Jess called out as she got in her car.

Charlotte waved as she spun her golf around and drove straight out on to the road making Jess wince. It amazed her

Charlotte was still in one piece given the way she drove, as if everyone was going to just get out of her way.

Driving past the other houses and round the corner to her flat Jess saw William's Range Rover parked in her usual spot, good job she'd had a quick tidy up this morning, she thought to herself.

Climbing the stairs two at a time she took a deep breath, the smell of marijuana from the ground floor was being overpowered by whatever William was cooking up in her kitchen. Skipping down the hallway she saw him with his back to her by the oven, basting a part roasted chicken, still in his shirt and suit trousers.

She wrapped her arms around him, making him jump.

"Blimey," he said as he spun around and gave her a kiss, "shout next time."

Jess laughed and kissed him again, running her hands through his hair. She hadn't realised until now just how much she had missed him, it had only been three days, but it had felt more like three weeks.

"How was your day?" she asked between kisses.

He pulled her back and studied her face.

"It was great, how was your day?"

Jess kissed him once more before heading to the fridge.

"Yeah, mine was great too," she lied.

Pouring herself a large glass of white wine, she leant over and topped up William's.

"That smells amazing, I'm impressed," she said, looking at all the trimmings he was preparing in various trays and pans, thinking to herself how he couldn't possibly get any more attractive.

"It'll be ready in about half an hour," he said, carefully sliding the chicken back in the tiny oven.

"I might just pop next door and check on Janet, Paul said she wasn't feeling great," Jess said, planting a kiss on his cheek.

"Yeah of course," he nodded, his brow furrowed as he concentrated on making his cheese sauce.

Out in the hallway Jess knocked on Janet's door. She heard her shout loudly to Paul to go and see who it was. A few moments later Jess felt the floorboards move under her feet as Paul swung the door open.

"Oh, it's you," he said when he saw her.

"Hi Paul, I just wanted to check on Janet and see if you needed anything?" she said, squinting as her eyes adjusted to the heat.

"She's fine," he said firmly with a frown as he turned and walked back through the hallway, leaving the door open for Jess to follow him.

Jess walked through the hallway and peered around the living room door. She had been in their flat a few times when she had dropped off shopping, it was dated but always immaculate, never a spot of dust or an unvacuumed carpet in sight. Today it smelt stale, the old cushions on the sofa were all squashed and scattered, on the mantlepiece a vase of flowers sat parched, looking like they ran out of water a week ago. Across the entire coffee table were dirty plates and mugs, some scrunched up tissues scattered in the few spaces between them.

Over by the window Janet was sat in her usual spot in the worn out arm chair, her left hand holding on to the corner of the net curtain, ready to peer out at any sight of movement.

"Hi Janet."

She turned to look at Jess who was still stood in the doorway.

"Oh, hi Jess love."

Janet looked pale and tired, her eyes were set a little deeper in her skull than usual. Around her the carpet was littered with discarded tissues.

"How are you feeling?" Jess asked sympathetically,

"Oh, I'm fine," she waved her hand and coughed, "it's just a cold."

Behind her Jess heard Paul grunt as he came down the corridor, she stepped forwards, moving out of his way as he shuffled through the doorway and sat down on the sofa.

"I just wondered if there was anything you wanted me to get for you, any medication or shopping? Do you need any help around the house?" she asked, glancing at the mugs and plates on the coffee table.

"Oh no dear, you don't need to do that. It's good for Paul to get off his backside and go to the shops," she smiled at her.

Paul remained quiet as he clicked on the old television, ignoring his wife's insult.

Suddenly Janet's head spun around as she pulled the curtain back, staring out of the window.

"Lots of youths in hoods out today, I've seen a lot of them out just recently" she said quietly, gazing over the car park fence and out onto the road. On the far pavement a group of teenagers were walking along, there must have been half a dozen of them, all with their hoods up partially covering their faces. Jess watched as one of them shouted and threw an empty beer can at a passing car.

"Okay, well let me know if you need anything won't you."

"Yes dear, thank you."

Janet drew her eyes away from the window and gave Jess a little wave as she left.

Back in her flat William had changed in to a t-shirt and Canterbury tracksuit bottoms. Jess admired him from the door way, sitting on the sofa, his legs stretched out in front of him as he flicked through the tv channels.

"I'm just going to jump in the shower," she said, raising her eyebrows at him.

He looked over and smiled at her in response.

"That thing was not built for two people, I'll get dinner on the table," he said as he got up and made his way to the kitchen, kissing her as he went past.

Jess undressed in the bathroom, feeling mildly disappointed that William had turned down her suggestion. She quickly showered and washed her hair before padding across the hallway naked, hoping he might see her.

"Smells delicious," she said as she appeared in the kitchen a few minutes later, dressed in her softest loungewear, her wet hair wrapped up in a bun on the top of her head.

"Get it while it's hot," William said moving along the kitchen side, adding something from each pan or tray to their plates.

"Here you go," he said, placing the plates down on the

table whilst Jess topped up their wine glasses, "roast chicken with all the trimmings."

"Wow, thank you," she smiled, giving him a kiss of appreciation before sitting herself down.

"So how has your week been?" she asked, grinding salt and pepper onto her potatoes.

William sat down opposite her.

"Yeah, it's been good, just gearing up for this trip away tomorrow."

"Where are you off to again?"

"America. Chicago and Boston specifically, we've got meetings with marketing teams out there and big supermarket chains, it's exciting."

Jess smiled at the passion in his voice.

"So, how many of you are going?"

"There's six of us, myself and the marketing team, Francesca will be joining us too."

Jess hesitated, looking up at him.

"Francesca, your ex-wife?"

"Yeah, she doesn't get to do that much hands on stuff with the business, so she was keen to come," William said as he leant behind him to fork another potato out of the tray.

"Oh, I didn't realise she was that involved," Jess said quietly.

William paused and looked at her.

"Is that a problem for you?"

"No," she said quickly, pushing her carrots around her plate.

The thought of William staying in a hotel somewhere with his beautiful ex-wife felt very much like a problem to her, but she didn't want to seem unreasonable.

William took her hand across the table making her look up at him.

"She's my ex-wife for a reason. She's in my past, you're in my future."

He squeezed her hand and smiled.

Jess smiled back at him, relaxing a little as she took another big mouthful of wine.

After dinner they unwound on the sofa together. Jess lay with her legs across William's lap, his hand in hers as they sat quietly together watching an American rom com. Glancing across at him, Jess smiled to herself. To her this was a perfect moment, the two of them sat peacefully together in each other's company on a rainy Wednesday evening after sharing a lovely homecooked meal. If she could have this every night of the week, she would be a very happy woman.

Catching her gaze, he smiled back at her, his eyes dancing as if he was reading her mind.

Jess woke just after six the next morning. The room was still pitch dark and the road outside was quiet, only the occasional squawk of a bird breaking the silence. William was breathing deeply beside her, his arm in its usual place across her waist. Glancing down she saw she was still wearing the loungewear she had put on last night. She had been so tired she must have fallen asleep on the sofa and William had carried her to bed.

Quietly she slipped out of the covers and tiptoed to the bathroom, quickly brushing her teeth and undressing herself before making her way back into the bedroom. Climbing back in next to William, she pulled herself towards him, wrapping her arm across his chest.

In response to her touch, he rolled over towards her, his eyes still closed.

Jess turned herself over, pushing her back up against his chest, pulling his arms around her.

Slowly she began running her foot up and down his lower leg, pushing her body further back, closing in against him, feeling the heat of his skin against hers.

William stirred, his biceps flexing as he wrapped his arms more tightly around her.

Running her fingers gently up and down his arms she felt his breathing begin to quicken. Holding his hand in hers, she cupped it against her breast, her hand over the top of his, squeezing it gently.

William was definitely awake now, his breath hitting the back of her neck as he began kissing her softly.

Slowly she moved his hand down between her legs, hearing him groan quietly as he felt her.

Jess pushed her head back in satisfaction as his fingers found her, her skin trembling as he kissed her neck, his breathing deepening as she tried to reach around and take hold of him.

William intercepted her hand, showing he was back in control as he shifted her body fractionally up the bed and guided himself inside her.

They moved together, William holding on to her thigh, Jess gripping his hand tightly in hers, their fingers intertwined. After a minute William put an arm around her waist and pulled her up underneath him, so she was on all fours with him behind her.

Reaching for a pillow Jess buried her head in it, her hips flexing as far as they could go so William could reach the spot she needed.

With every minute his movement became harder and more powerful, the bed pounding vigorously against the wall behind it. The noise was shocking, Jess was sure the whole building would be able to hear them.

William climaxed quickly, Jess not quite making it as they collapsed together on the bed, their breathing heavy, sweat beginning to form on their skin.

Quickly William spun her over, his hand finding her, his fingers moving skilfully.

Jess gasped loudly and closed her eyes, running her fingers through his hair as his mouth found her nipples. After a few minutes she felt the climax coming, the familiar heat was rising in her face, she knew it was close.

Reading her response William picked up the pace as she arched her back, gripping his shoulder as she moaned, willing the orgasm to come.

It did, explosively, her body flexing forward as she released, still gripping on to William before falling back to the bed.

Lying there for a moment with her eyes closed, she relished in the feeling of endorphins surging around her body. William was still gazing down at her, watching her as she recovered. He waited for a moment before planting a long kiss on her lips and lying himself back down beside her, drawing her into his chest.

Finally, they pulled themselves from the sheets, conscious that Willam had a flight to catch, although Jess wouldn't have been too sad if he missed it. Quickly he showered and got dressed whilst she made some tea and bacon sandwiches.

"So, when do you fly home?" Jess asked over the breakfast table.

"I'll be back late next Thursday."

"That's a long business trip," she said with a frown, mopping up a dollop of ketchup on her plate with the last of her bacon sandwich.

"I know, but I have a lot of meetings to fit in. I don't want to have to travel back there for a while so I want to get as much done as I can," he explained.

Jess watched him gather his things and put on his jacket, thinking how handsome he looked in his grey, tailored suit.

"Right, I need to get going," he said, pulling her towards him.

She stuck out her bottom lip and gave him her saddest puppy eyes.

"Oh, stop it," he laughed, "I'll be back before you know it, whisking you away for a weekend in a hotel room."

His eyes danced with anticipation.

Jess smiled, "I can't wait."

She leant up and kissed him, holding on for a couple of seconds longer, her hands clutching his face.

He pulled back and gazed at her. There was the look again. She watched as something she didn't recognise flashed across his eyes as they stared down into hers.

"I'll call you when I land," he said as he headed for the

door, "oh and no flirting with those old men at the pub."

He turned and pointed a finger at her, grinning as he did.

Jess laughed, "I'll try not to," she called as he disappeared out of the front door and down the stairs.

Wandering into the living room she peeled back the curtain to watch him drive off.

Looking up at her in the window he waved and beeped the horn gently as he disappeared out of sight.

Jess sighed, thinking how long the next week was going to feel, wishing she was the one sharing a hotel with him, not his ex-wife.

Chapter Twenty

The car park at the care home was busy this morning, there was just one spot left in the corner under the cherry tree which Jess managed to squeeze her little car in to.

As she got out, she saw a woman walking from the building towards the carpark. She was crying, her husband had an arm wrapped around her, the other digging in his pocket for a tissue.

Jess watched them as she made her way across the car park, standing next to their car, the husband embracing his wife and she sobbed, trying to keep his own tears at bay.

There was another lady at the reception desk when Jess made her way in through the front door. Peering around her whilst she sanitised her hands she saw a very stressed looking Mrs Brown, she was sure she could see a glint of sweat on her brow. Patiently she waited her turn whilst the lady in front of her made quite a fuss about her father's meal plan, insisting that given the money she was paying her father should be eating fillet of beef and lobster every day, not cheese omelettes and pesto pasta.

Once Mrs Brown had finally reasoned with her and sent her down the hall she turned to Jess and smiled briefly.

"Oh, hello Jessica."

She almost seemed relieved to see her.

"Hello Mrs Brown, are you alright?" Jess asked, watching her wipe the sweat from her forehead with a handkerchief.

"Yes, it's just been one of those mornings," she said handing Jess the sign in sheet.

Jess signed her name next to her mother's.

"How is she today?"

"Not brilliant, there's been no improvement since we spoke in the week, the nurse we've got in is spending a lot of time monitoring her. That reminds me, I've actually got the new payment plan for you here."

Jess looked at her with confusion.

"What new payment plan?"

"For the extra care she's having," Mrs Brown said in a tone that suggested Jess should already be aware of this, "that comes at an extra cost Jessica, it's all in the contract you signed when she arrived."

Reaching to the desk behind her, she picked up a handful of papers all stapled together and handed them to Jess who flicked straight to the back page.

"An extra five hundred pounds a month!"

Jess stared wide eyed at Mrs Brown.

"I can't afford that!" she said, looking back down at the piece of paper to make sure she had read it correctly.

"Well, I'm sorry Jessica, but that's what her care is going to cost, I can't change that," Mrs Brown shrugged her shoulders as she spoke.

Jess's bottom lip began to quiver, the all too familiar feeling of oncoming tears was creeping up on her.

"Well, when does this come in to effect?" she asked, still staring at the total on the bottom of the page.

"The first payment was taken on Friday," Mrs Brown said as she tidied some other papers on her desk.

Jess looked at her and frowned.

"That's impossible, I don't have an extra five hundred pounds in my account. I can't believe you haven't told me about this before!"

Mrs Brown, unphased by Jess's outburst made a few clicks on her computer.

"It says here you're all paid up."

She paused for a moment before leaning forward, staring a little more closely at the screen.

"A new direct debit was set up with accounting last Friday, so I imagine it was taken from that."

"Wait, what?" Jess shook her head in confusion, "what new direct debit, I haven't set up a new direct debit."

She leant over the desk to try and look at the computer screen.

"Jessica please," Mrs Brown said taking a step back and waving her hand at her, indicating for her to get out of her personal space.

Jess obliged, reminding herself how the pandemic had permanently changed places like this.

"It says here on accounts that a new direct debit was set up for your mother in the name of a Mr William Archer, it says all her future care should be charged to him."

Jess took a step back, pausing for a moment as shock radiated through her body before lurching back across the desk.

"It says William Archer, are you *sure?*"

Mrs Brown rolled her eyes.

"Jessica please!"

Jess reluctantly moved back from the desk as Mrs Brown took a purposeful step forward.

"Yes, I am absolutely sure," she said, rereading the text in front of her and peering at Jess over the top of her glasses, "is there a problem?"

Jess hesitated as she tried to process this information.

"No" she said slowly, "no problem at all."

Sitting herself down on a chair halfway along the corridor, Jess took a moment to gather her thoughts. Sifting back through her memories she reached the one where William had seen the care home contact list stuck to her fridge a couple of weeks ago.

Jess could have cried with gratitude.

No matter what sort of work she did, it would have been a bloody struggle to afford that extra cost, if it wasn't for William her mother would have been moved somewhere else, somewhere unfamiliar with new surroundings and new people. Jess knew how hard that would have been, for both her and Audrey. She wanted to call him, to tell him how grateful she was, how much of a help this was going to be for her, but she needed to go and see her mum, she would call him when she came out.

Audrey was sat up in her bed, not by choice, she had been propped there it seemed, held up by large cushions stuffed all around her body. There were all sorts of new wires and contraptions surrounding her bed, a digital monitor that was keeping track of her heart rate and a drip held high up on trolley next to her, feeding into her vein through a tube. Her eyes were closed, her head hung limply from her neck like a leaf about to fall from a branch. The bruises on her right arm looked shocking, the dark purple colour running from her elbow right down to her wrist.

Jess clenched her jaw, trying not to cry as she sat quietly down next to her. Leaning forward, she gently stroked her mother's arm, her skin moving like tissue paper under her touch.

Behind her the door opened.

"Oh hello," a nurse whispered, "you must be Jess, Deloris said you would be visiting today."

It had only taken three years, but now Jess finally knew what Mrs Brown's name was.

"Hello," Jess said quietly over her shoulder.

Holding on to her mother's hand, she felt her pulse run slowly through her wrist, watching it correspond with the machine in front of her.

The nurse stood for a moment at the end of Audrey's bed, waiting for Jess to ask her a question.

She didn't, she just watched her mother, watched the

slow rise and fall of her bony chest as she breathed, the faint sound of air being drawn in and pushed out of her nostrils.

"She's very weak," the nurse began quietly, "but we've got her on fluids and are monitoring her vitals."

Jess didn't look round.

"Can she stay here?" she asked.

The nurse hesitated.

"For now" she replied, "we need to see how her condition develops, she may have to go into hospital."

Jess took a deep breath and swallowed back her tears. She didn't want her mum to be taken anywhere, she wanted to her stay here, cosy and safe in the room she now knew as her home.

"I'll leave you alone for a bit," the nurse said.

Jess glanced across to her, managing a small smile.

"Thank you for looking after her."

The nurse straightened up, holding her clipboard close to her chest.

"It's all in a day's work my dear," she said before quietly leaving the room, closing the door gently behind her.

"Mum," Jess leant forward, "mum, can you hear me?" she whispered holding her hand, willing her to respond.

"I miss you," she said as her eyes filled with tears.

She waited, holding her mother's hand, praying for some kind of response.

"I've met a man," she smiled through her tears, "he's wonderful mum, I know you'd really like him."

Jess paused, searching for something in her mother's face.

"His name is William," she paused, "and I think I love

him mum," she wiped her eyes and smiled, "and I think he loves me too."

"How was she?" Mrs Brown asked as Jess appeared back in reception.

"Quiet," Jess managed a small smile as she wiped the last of the tears and smudged mascara from her eyes.

Mrs Brown looked at her, Jess was sure it was compassion she could see in her eyes as she hopped down from her chair and walked around the reception desk. She stopped right in front of Jess and took a deep breath in before lunging forward, wrapping her little arms around her for split second before stepping back and exhaling.

"You're a brave young woman Jessica," she said, straightening her shirt before marching back round to her desk.

Jess stood in shock for a moment, not sure how to react to this completely uncharacteristic bout of affection.

"See you next weekend," Mrs Brown nodded at her, indicating for her to leave as more visitors made their way into the reception.

Once Jess was back in her car, she found William's contact number on her phone and clicked on the Facetime button. Quickly she glanced at her reflection in the rear view mirror, she wasn't looking great, her eyes were swollen and her makeup had washed away with her tears, but she didn't care.

William answered after four rings, his face was pixelated through the tiny screen and there was a delay on the sound.

"Hey, are you alright?" he asked.

It looked like he was walking down a street somewhere. Jess could see the sky above him and the sound of traffic in the background.

The connection was awful, they kept talking over each other, their conversation making no sense.

"Hang on, I'll call you back in a second," he said and hung up the phone.

A couple of minutes later Jess's phone buzzed in her hand, she answered straight away as William's face appeared on the screen much more clearly than before.

"Hey trouble," he said smiling at her, "can you hear me okay?"

Jess smiled back at him.

"Yeah that's much better."

It looked like he was sat in a bar, a waitress appeared next to him asking if he wanted a drink.

"Espresso please. Are you alright?" he asked, leaning into the camera, "you look upset."

"I've just been to see mum," Jess said through fresh tears, "thank you so much for what you've done."

Jess had hoped she wouldn't cry but she couldn't help it.

"Her payments have just gone up because of the extra care and there's no way I would have been able to afford it," she wailed as she wiped her cheeks.

"It's my pleasure," he said smiling, "I hope you don't think it was out of place, I knew you would have said no if I asked you. I just want you to not have to worry so much."

"It's so generous," she said through more tears.

"How is your mum?" William asked as his coffee appeared in front of him.

"She's not great, but she's comfortable and there's a lovely nurse here looking after her."

"That's good, so you're happy she's got the right care?" he said leaning into the camera, concern in his voice, "because we can get her more if she needs it."

"No, she's fine. Mrs Brown will let me know if there's anything else she needs," Jess shook her head, smiling at his kindness.

Someone appeared at William's side.

"William, we need to get going to meet with the Costco lot."

Jess couldn't see who it was, but it was definitely a woman's voice, with a very well spoken English accent.

William looked up.

"Sure, I'll meet you in the lobby."

The woman disappeared, Jess could hear the click of her heels fading in the distance through the speaker.

"I've got to go Jess, why don't I give you a call later on, are you at the pub tonight?"

Jess tried to hide her disappointment.

"Yeah, my shift starts at six but I'm around before then."

"Okay, I'll call you later on. Go and buy yourself a bottle of good wine and put your feet up for a bit," he said with a smile as he leant forward so his face was closer to the screen, "I miss you."

Jess beamed back at him, "I miss you too."

Under William's instructions Jess stopped at Marks and Spencer on her way home, with the extra money left in her account she decided to treat herself to some of the luxury items she would normally always avoid.

Inhaling the wonderful smells in the delicatessen section she picked herself a fresh loaf of olive bread and a huge chunk of brie. Strolling down the snack aisle, she filled up her basket with some chocolate chip shortbread and some fancy looking truffle crisps. All she needed now was some good wine.

Standing looking up at the wall of white wine in front of her, Jess scanned the bottles hoping to see one she recognised that William had served her over the last couple of weeks. There was a Chablis on the top shelf, she remembered having that in London at William's flat. It was an eyewatering eighteen pounds fifty, the most she had ever spent on a bottle of wine, so it had better be delicious she thought to herself as she added it to her already full basket.

As she drove home with her bags of treats for the weekend, she felt a sense of relief, that the huge weight she had been carrying around for so many years had been lifted and she could finally breathe.

It was just gone three by the time she had made it back to her flat. Sitting cross legged on the sofa she tucked into the still warm loaf of bread and creamy brie, washing it down with a little glass of wine to treat herself.

Scrolling through her phone she added a pair of jeans and some new trainers to her Asos shopping bag, the button had gone on her old pair and she'd been holding them together with a hairclip.

She was ten minutes into her second episode of The Kardashians and beginning to feel a bit sick after her cheese indulgence when her phone rang. William's face flashed up on the screen when she answered.

He smiled at the sight of her.

"Hello you, are you having a nice afternoon?"

"I am," Jess beamed, giving him a virtual cheers with her wine glass. It looked like he was in his hotel room, he was topless lying back on white bedsheets.

"How was your meeting?" she asked, wishing she was in the bed next to him.

"Yeah, it went really well, they loved the product so I think they'll definitely want to stock it."

"That's great."

"Yeah, I'm shattered now, I think I'm just going to order some room service and get some sleep."

"I wish I was there with you," she said with longing in her voice.

He gazed at her through his lashes, his eyes darkening slightly at her words.

"Oh, believe me, the things I would do to have you here in this hotel room."

Jess's whole body tingled with delight.

"I'll have to bring you with me next time," William said.

Jess smiled at the thought.

"I would love that, I've never travelled anywhere."

He frowned at her.

"Wait, you've never been abroad?"

Jess shook her head.

"No, I've never been anywhere."

He paused for a minute processing this information.

"God I've got so much to show you, we'll have to make a list when I'm back of all the countries we want to visit."

Jess beamed with excitement.

"Sounds like a great plan."

"Right, I'm going to get some food and some sleep, I'll call you tomorrow," he gazed at her through the camera, "I can't wait to see you."

"I can't wait either," Jess smiled, hanging up the phone.

Chapter Twenty One

The week had dragged on. Jess was counting down the hours until William landed back in the UK, he felt far enough away being in London during the week, let alone in America.

Her body ached for him, they had spoken every day that he had been gone and had even indulged in a bit of phone sex on Tuesday evening. She had never done it before, it had nothing on the real thing, but it was still very fun.

It was Thursday afternoon, Jess was in the pet shop repricing some dog collars which weren't selling as well as the supplier promised they would when she glanced out of the window to see Jeremy's old Land Rover park up outside. Watching him as he pulled his files and laptop out of the back seat and carry them under his arms, Jess strode up to the door and opened it for him.

"Thank you," Jeremy said, barely looking her in the eye.

"No problem," she replied, watching him make his way to the till. He looked extra small today, wearing his large wax coat with sleeves that came down over his hands, it was at least two sizes too big for him.

Pinging open the till, he grabbed the small handful of receipts and made his way into the break room.

Jess was busying herself in the shop, doing her third lap with the broom when Jeremy called through from the break room.

"Jess, would you mind coming in here?"

Her heart sank in her chest at the realisation of what was coming. Walking towards the break room, she kept the broom clutched in her hands as a final demonstration of how useful she was.

"Please sit down," Jeremy said, gesturing for her to sit on the small wooden chair next to the television that no one ever sat on.

Jess sat down as instructed, still clasping the broom in her hands.

He took a deep breath.

"Jess I'm afraid I'm going to have to let you go, our takings are plummeting, I just cannot afford to keep you."

Jess could hear the stress in his voice, he looked tired, his hair a bit more grey than it looked a few weeks ago.

"It's okay Jeremy," she said softly.

He looked up at her for the first time.

"Really?" he said, obviously expecting a confrontation.

If William hadn't taken it upon himself to cover Audrey's care bill then Jess would have put up one hell of a fight, but she would manage now with some extra shifts at the pub to cover her rent and other bills if she needed.

"I would keep you if I could," he looked down at the table in front of him, gesturing at the papers, "but all our bills are sky rocketing, I don't know if I'll be able to keep this place going at all at this rate."

He leant forwards and ran his hands through his thinning hair.

"Well, I hope you manage to," Jess said with a small smile, "it would be such a shame if this place had to close."

"I can pay you until the end of the month if that helps?" Jeremy said, flicking through some bank statements in front of him.

"Jeremy, it's fine," Jess said more firmly, "let's just call today my last day."

She leant forwards and put her hand on his arm, she was sure he was shaking a little.

"Okay, thank you. I really am sorry Jess, you've been a brilliant employee."

Jess smiled at him.

"Well, if I ever need a reference, I'll give you a call."

Jeremy straightened up.

"Of course," he said, "I'd be delighted to."

Jess took some pleasure out of making Jeremy feel okay about firing her, she knew he was up against it, it didn't take a genius to work out the shop was losing money.

On her drive home she called Gavin. He was absolutely

delighted that she was available for some lunchtime shifts, it wasn't quite the same hours as the pet shop but after totting up her bills in her head she had worked out she would still be fine. The lunch shift didn't start until eleven, which meant she could stay with William in London and then be back in time for work the next day. She smiled at the thought, it would be fun to spend more time with him there.

Back at her flat she had a very quick shower and made herself a cheese toastie with a large dollop of tomato ketchup. Sitting down at the table she pulled up the maps on her phone. Zooming out over the Atlantic Ocean she tried to guess where William's plane could be right now, he was due to land just after ten at Heathrow.

Suddenly unexpected goosebumps erupted on her arms, as if her body had gone into high alert, like it could sense him coming home.

As she continued to stare at the vast length of ocean between America and Europe a text pinged through on her phone from Charlotte.

I'm so sorry about you losing your job Jess, I really didn't want Jeremy to do that, but he said he had no choice.

Jess sent back a love heart. She didn't want to get into the details with her over a text message, but she also didn't want Charlotte to feel bad. Her phone pinged again a few seconds later.

I'll miss our coffee mornings, we'll have to actually go to a coffee shop together now! And we are going on that double date!

Jess smiled to herself, she had a feeling Charlotte was

going to hold her to that.

Before she left for work, Jess decided to pop her head into Janet and Paul's to see if they needed anything. Knocking loudly on their front door, she waited to hear Janet shout at Paul to go and see who it was, but there was nothing. Giving the handle a try she was surprised as the door just pushed open, swinging on its hinges as if it was inviting her in.

"Janet? Paul?" she called down the hallway.

"Who is it?" she heard Paul shout from the lounge, irritation in his voice.

"Oh, it's you," he said with a frown as he saw Jess appear in the doorway, "what do you want?"

"I was just checking in on Janet," Jess said glancing with confusion at the empty chair by the window, "where is she?"

Paul looked back at the television.

"She's in hospital," he said bluntly.

"What? What's happened?" Jess said loudly, stepping forward and standing in front of the screen.

Paul glared at her.

"She's got pneumonia," he said, waving at her to get out of the way, "ambulance took her in this morning."

Jess took a deep breath and stepped aside before Paul threw something at her.

Janet had been the closest thing Jess had to a mother figure in a long time. She always worried about her if she came home late and constantly pestered her about eating proper meals and putting some weight on. With everything that was happening with her actual mother, she wasn't sure she could cope if something happened to Janet as well.

Paul coughed loudly as he lunged forward and grabbed the tissue box that was sat on the coffee table.

"Is there anything you need Paul? Can I get you any food or help you with any housework?" Jess asked, surveying the mess which had increased significantly since she was last here.

"No, I'm fine," he said bluntly, keeping his eyes on the screen.

"Would you like me to take you to see her tomorrow?" she asked hopefully.

Paul hesitated for a moment before looking up at her.

"Would you?"

"Of course," Jess said with a smile, "I don't start work until eleven so we can go in the morning."

Jess wasn't sure, but she thought she saw a small glimmer of appreciation in his eyes when he looked at her.

"Thank you," he said before turning back to his programme.

The pub was busy this evening, there were six tables in and a group of local lads out having pre drinks before they headed to Oxford for the night. Jess didn't stand still until Gavin rang the bell for last orders at quarter to eleven. Taking a minute, she leant back on the worktop in the kitchen and began helping herself to a bowl of chips the skinny woman on table four hadn't touched.

"So how are you finding it?" asked Tony, the large chef, who turned out not to be so scary after the dinner shift had ended.

"Yeah, good I think, I quite like it when it's busy, time seems to just fly by," she said, stuffing another chip in her mouth.

"Do you want me to make you something?" he asked, gesturing at the nearly empty bowl in front of her.

"Oh no," Jess said, shaking her head as she wiped her hands on her jeans, "they're just too delicious."

Tony smiled at her as he tidied away the last of his pans.

"Fancy a drink after work? I usually convince Gavin to buy me one."

Jess paused, unsure what he meant by this. She had never stayed this late before, perhaps this was something all the staff did together when their shift ended. She had already clocked the gold wedding ring squeezed around his large finger, so she decided it was probably fine.

"Yeah, that sounds nice."

Once all the customers had paid up and made their way out into the car park Jess, Tony and Gavin sat at the bar with three pints of lager. Gavin had shouted up to his wife, Angela, to come down and join them. Jess had met her a couple of times, she would venture down when the pub was quiet, but seemed to keep out of the way when a busy service was in full swing.

The ceiling above them creaked as Angela made her way down the stairs that led straight behind the bar.

She glanced around the pub as she opened the door.

"Thank goodness that rabble have all gone," she said with a frown. Angela was in her fifties with short, dark hair and a quiet disposition. Gavin had told Jess that she was a retired nurse, given what Jess had seen on the news in the last few months about the state of the hospitals, it was no wonder Angela wanted a quiet retirement. It was what she had seen on the news that made her so worried about Janet being in hospital, and what desperately wanted her to prevent her mother from ending up in one.

Opening the fridge, Angela poured the remainder of an open pinot grigio bottle into her glass.

Glancing down the bar, she glared over at Gavin.

"Gav, did you ask Jess if she wanted wine, or did you just give her a beer?"

It was the later, but Jess didn't mind, she quite enjoyed a lager occasionally.

"Oh no this is what I wanted," Jess smiled at Angela.

She wasn't convinced as she continued to stare at her husband.

He kept his eyes down, looking into his glass as he sunk his pint.

"So, Jess, have you got a husband or a boyfriend?" Tony asked as he leant over and pulled a packet of pork scratchings from the box behind the bar.

"Erm well, I've actually just started seeing someone."

She felt a bit awkward saying this now, the answer was always so simple when it was 'no'.

"Oh nice, what's his story?" Tony asked, offering her a pork scratching.

Jess refused politely.

"His names William, he actually makes his own gin."

Tony nodded his head in admiration.

"That's awesome, what's the gin called?"

Jess thought for a moment.

"The Old Archer I think."

Angela paused for a moment before turning to the shelf behind her. Running her hand across the dozens of bottles she hesitated over one and pulled it from the shelf.

"Is this his gin?" she asked, handing the bottle to Jess.

"Yes!" she exclaimed, running her fingertips over the glass, thinking back to the one William had shown her at The Old Manor.

"That's one of our most popular ones," Gavin said, walking around the bar to pour himself another pint.

"He must be doing well," Angela said raising her eyebrows at Jess.

"Do either of you want another drink?" Gavin asked looking between Tony and Jess. Tony slid his glass across the bar to Gavin who began filling it up from the pump.

"No, I'm fine thanks," Jess said passing the gin bottle back to Angela, "I need to get home."

"I'll have a top up," Angela said handing her glass to her husband.

"So, we'll see you tomorrow at eleven," Gavin said nodding at Jess as she picked up her bag.

"Yep, see you all then," she smiled as she hopped off her stool and made her way to the door. As she walked around the corner she paused to fish out her car keys from the bottom of her bag.

"Such a nice girl," Angela said quietly, unaware Jess was still within ear shot, "did Gav tell you she's just been sacked from that sad little pet store on the other side of town?"

Jess heard the pop of a cork as Gavin opened another bottle of wine.

"Its such shame she's not really done anything with her life," Angela continued.

"Well, that's good for us," she heard Gavin say with a chuckle.

"I know Gav. I'm just saying what a waste, she seems to have too much going for her to end up here."

"Well sounds like she might be onto a winner with this gin bloke, he must be rolling it in. She'll be sorted if she can keep hold of him," Tony chimed in.

Jess had heard enough. Gently she opened the door and closed it silently behind her.

Driving home she thought about what Angela had said, she was right, she was heading towards her mid-thirties and what had she achieved in her life?

A sudden surge of anger washed over her.

She had hung on to the past for far too long, stayed put in this tiny town, never allowing herself the chance to move on with her life or achieve anything, just because Katie had lost the chance to. Katie's death was not her fault, so why did she still feel like it was?

Letting herself into her flat, the door banging hard against the wall as she kicked it open, she slung her keys on the table in the hallway before dumping her bag on the kitchen side. She was exhausted and pissed off, she'd also eaten so many chips she was beginning to feel a bit sick. Checking her phone for the tenth time, she saw there was still nothing from William, the two little ticks on the WhatsApp message she had sent hadn't gone blue yet, which meant he probably hadn't landed.

Getting herself ready for bed in the bathroom, Jess gazed

at her reflection in the mirror, closely inspecting the dark circles under her eyes, the faint crow's feet beginning to embed themselves in the skin beside them.

Shutting off all the lights except for the one in the hallway, she put her phone on silent and chucked it on the bedside table. Climbing into bed, she wrapped the duvet tightly around her as she tried to shut down her mind and drift off to sleep.

Chapter Twenty Two

The noise of Paul's television came blaring through the wall at half past seven on the dot. The disruption made Jess stir from a heavy sleep. Rubbing her eyes as they adjusted to the light seeping in through the cheap curtains, she stretched her arms before picking up her phone from the bedside table. There was a message from William at twenty past midnight.

Just landed, horrible delays in Chicago, can't wait to see you tomorrow! x

Jess pinged a quick message back to him before pulling the duvet up over her head in an attempt to block out the sound and light and get a few more minutes sleep.

It was no use, she was awake, no longer in the blissful ignorance of her subconscious.

Sitting up in bed for a minute, she tried to decipher what Paul was watching next door. The television was never on this loud when Janet was here, maybe that's why she was always hiding the remote, Jess smiled to herself at the thought.

Pulling herself out of the warmth of her bed and drawing the curtains, she noted how her mood had lifted in comparison to the night before, things always felt better in the morning. That was something her mum always used to say to her whenever she was upset.

In the kitchen she turned on the radio, cranking the volume up full blast to try and block out the sound of Paul's television. Dancing her way happily around the room to a Coldplay song, she made herself some tea and toast.

Once she had finished her breakfast, she went back to her bedroom. In an attempt to be organised she pulled out her overnight bag and made a start packing a few clothes for her night away tomorrow. Throwing open the wardrobe doors, forgetting about the broken one that fell off the top hinge, she began sifting through her options. Laying six different outfits on the bed she stood back, her hands on her hips, trying to make a decision when she noticed her phone vibrating on the bedside table, she'd forgotten it was still on silent.

Picking it up, expecting it to be William calling she saw it was the care home. Frantically she slid the answer button across on the third attempt.

"Hello?" she said anxiously.

"Good morning Jessica," Mrs Brown's voice came through the speaker, "sorry to call you so early."

"It's fine," Jess replied, "is mum alright?"

"Your mother's condition is the same as last weekend, she's not improved I'm afraid but that isn't why I am calling. I wanted to let you know that we've had three positive cases of Covid in the members of staff here this morning, therefore we are closing to all visitors."

"Oh," Jess said, disappointment in her voice, "so I can't come up tomorrow?"

"No, I'm afraid not. The infected staff have obviously left, we'll be testing everyone again tomorrow morning so I'll keep you updated," Mrs Brown said sternly, "as per our policy we have to close our doors, we must try to keep everyone safe Jessica."

"Yes, I understand," Jess said quietly.

"Okay, well I must get off, I have other families to call, all the best."

With that Mrs Brown hung up the phone.

Jess sat down on the edge of her bed questioning how many more visits she would have left to see her mum, she really didn't want to miss one, but it didn't seem like she had a choice.

Her phone began vibrating again in her hand making her jump, glancing down she saw William's name flash up on the screen.

"Hey, how are you?" Jess answered with a smile.

"Hello you, I'm good thanks, a bit shattered."

"Yeah I bet, you got in so late," Jess said, picking at a loose thread on her pyjamas.

"Yeah, I ended up getting home at one thirty, good job we've got a relaxing weekend ahead of us."

She could hear him smiling down the phone.

"I can't wait to see you," she said.

The thought of what they were going to get up to in that hotel room was already running through her mind.

"Don't," he said reading her thoughts, "I still have to wait twenty four hours to get my hands on you. What time do you think you'll get down from visiting your mum?"

Jess paused for a second.

"Actually, they've just called me. Some of the staff have tested positive so they're not letting anyone visit."

"Oh, that's a shame."

William hesitated.

"So, if you can't visit your mum, why don't you come to the hotel tonight?"

The idea had already crossed Jess's mind, but she didn't want to invite herself.

"Are you sure?"

"Absolutely, you're not at the pub tonight are you?"

"No."

"Well come down this afternoon then, there's a black tie dinner there tonight."

"Black tie!" Jess retorted, "what do I need to wear for that?"

"Just a dress of some sort, you'll look amazing whatever you wear, just get down there as soon as you can."

She laughed at his impatience, "okay, I'll head straight there after my shift later."

"Great. Listen I'm just heading into the office, let me

know when you're leaving."

"Will do," she said before hanging up the phone.

Frantically pulling dresses out of her wardrobe she concluded she had absolutely nothing acceptable for a black tie dinner. Grabbing her phone, she sent an SOS message to Charlotte who replied within seconds saying she would bring some dresses to work with her so Jess could pick them up on her way through. Jess sent her a thanks with a little angel emoji before pulling out some more clothes and shoes she might need for the weekend and chucking them in a bag.

It was ten to nine before Jess had packed and got herself ready. As she shut her front door behind her she turned to find Paul stood in the hallway, flat cap and coat on, walking stick in hand, ready to go.

"Sorry Paul, I didn't realise you were waiting out here," she said with a smile as she locked her door.

"It's fine," he said gruffly as he gestured for her to go down the stairs first.

Their visit to see Janet was awfully depressing. Jess hadn't realised how dismal hospitals really were, every nurse and doctor she laid her eyes on was running around like a headless chicken, dressed top to toe in masks, gloves and aprons, looking like they hadn't slept for at least a week. There were patients that had been sat on chairs in the hallways for hours on end, some luckier ones had a bed jammed down the side of the corridor, all being continually promised that they would soon be seen too. As she sat in dismay watching the chaos as it went by, Jess silently promised herself that she would take better care of her health to try and avoid ever being a burden to these people.

Janet had been in good spirits, she was still very weak and on oxygen to assist her breathing, but the doctors were confident she would be back home in the next couple of weeks.

Paul had taken her a bunch of flowers he had bought from the garage on their way there, Jess had suggested they stopped at the florist but he insisted, he said that would be a complete waste of money. Jess had taken her a pack of chocolate chip shortbread and some gardening magazines she had bought from the corner shop, sure Janet would appreciate them more than the two year old gossip magazines you usually found in hospitals.

Pulling up in the car park of their building, Paul flung open the door of her car and heaved himself out.

"I'm away this weekend Paul, will you be okay here on your own?"

He looked down at her and frowned.

"I'll be fine," he said sternly as he went to shut the door.

"I can take you to the hospital on Monday if you like?"

He paused, glancing back in the car.

"Thank you, I'd like that."

Jess smiled at him as he slammed the door, the side mirror shaking precariously as he did.

The pub was painfully quiet today. The only customers Jess had in were two middle aged women who were sat at the small table in the corner, deep in conversation, nursing the two coffees they had ordered over half an hour ago. Wiping down the bar for the tenth time that afternoon Jess heard the floorboards creak above her head. Moving quickly out of the way, she just managed to avoid being hit by the door as it swung open.

"Oh, hello Jess," Angela said, kicking the door shut behind her as she rummaged through her handbag.

"Hello," Jess said quietly, the things Angela had said about her last night still fresh in her mind.

"Ah got them," Angela said triumphantly as she pulled a large set of keys from the depths of her bag, "right, see you later."

She gave Jess a quick smile before tottering off out of the door.

Gavin appeared from the flat at four thirty looking like he had just woken up from a very long afternoon nap. Yawning, he tapped the till to see the takings for the day.

"Blimey it's been quiet," he said, raising his thick eyebrows until they nearly reached his hairline.

"Yeah, just those two over there, they're on their second coffee, I couldn't tempt them to any lunch," Jess said, nodding at the women in the corner who were still in deep discussion, one using some firm hand gestures, the other sat wide eyed listening to her. Jess wondered what on earth they were talking about, she was hopeless at lip reading.

"Right, you may as well get off then," Gavin said, already clocking her off on the till.

"Are you sure?" she asked, her eyes lighting up.

"Yeah, go on, off you go. We'll see you on Monday at eleven."

"See you then," Jess said as she took off her apron, picked up her bag and practically skipped out of the door.

Pulling up outside the pet shop, Jess could see Jeremy had increased his efforts to boost sales with several large, colourful discount signs slapped right across the windows.

Charlotte was sat behind the till eating a packet of crisps when the doorbell rang as Jess walked in. Looking up from her magazine she smiled as she saw her.

"Oh hi," she said getting herself up from the chair, stretching as if she had been sat there for a while, "let me just grab the dresses for you."

She disappeared into the break room and reappeared holding several dresses in long zip covers.

"Blimey Charlotte, you didn't need to bring this many."

"Oh, it's no bother," she said with a smile as she laid them across Jess's arms, "nice for them to get worn."

"Thanks so much, I'll drop them back to you next week."

"Oh whenever," Charlotte casually waved her hand, "here I'll get the door for you, unless you want a cuppa?" she asked raising her eyebrows hopefully.

She had never worked here alone before and she wasn't very good in her own company, Jess could imagine she was probably a bit bored and lonely already.

"Yeah, sorry I was going to get going, I want to try and miss the traffic."

"Sure, of course," Charlotte said, walking past her and holding the door open.

"Thanks again," Jess called, as she headed to her car.

"Pleasure, have fun," Charlotte yelled back with a grin.

Chapter Twenty Three

Jess's stomach was squirming with excitement at ten past five when she saw the sign for the Mayhill Park Hotel off the main road.

Pulling into the entrance, she turned down the radio which she had been blasting at full volume to drown out her tone deaf singing. Slowing the car right down she took in her surroundings. The grounds were spectacular, the driveway was at least half a mile long, lined with trees and little signposts directing you to the spa, the croquet lawn or the golf course.

Following the signs for the car park Jess found the main one was completely full, with rows of expensive cars lined up next to each other in the purpose built bays, gleaming in the autumn sunshine. Jess followed the sign for the overflow car park, which turned out to be a large area of gravel hardstanding behind a hedge, much more fitting for her old polo. Parking her car in the far corner, she dug her phone out of her handbag and rang William's number.

"Hey, I'm here," she sang as she heard him pick up.

"Great, I'll come and find you," he said before hanging up the phone.

Standing at the back of her car studying the contents of her boot, Jess wondered how on earth she was going to carry all the dresses up to the room when William strode up behind her.

"There she is," he said with a smile.

Jess let out a small squeal and spun around, running up to him and leaping into his arms.

"God, I missed you," he said between kisses.

She beamed at him.

"I missed you too."

Jess studied his face, he looked slightly more tanned and his hair was a little longer than it was a week ago. She didn't think it was possible, but he looked even more handsome today than he did then.

"Bloody hell," William exclaimed, putting her down and staring at the open boot of her car, "how long are you staying for?"

"Charlotte lent them to me, I haven't had a chance to try any on yet," Jess said, attempting to gather up the dresses.

"Here I'll take those for you," he said, scooping them all up effortlessly in his arms, "come on, let's get your stuff inside."

The hotel itself was once an enormous stately home, now occupying around a hundred and fifty guests with a spa and a golf course.

Walking through the building Jess gazed around in awe at the décor and furnishings. Long panelled walls led up to huge, elevated ceilings with detailed mouldings. Each surface was painstakingly decorated with hand painted wallpaper, large portraits hanging proudly on them, the occupier in the painting looking down on the people walking beneath them along the polished wooden floors.

Every corner Jess followed William around they were met by a member of staff dressed in black, holding open doors for them with a smile that seemed to be permanently etched on their face.

Following William up a ridiculously wide staircase to the first floor, Jess glanced out of the window at the view to the rear of the hotel. It was stunning. Huge, terraced gardens with little benches and chairs dotted around led down to a lake and acres of woodland beyond it.

"Wow, the grounds look amazing," Jess exclaimed.

William turned and followed her eyeline.

"Yeah, it's stunning here. There are some nice walking trails in the woods and little rowing boats you can take out on the lake."

Jess could see them moored up at the edge by the little jetty, slowly bobbing around, bumping into each other.

"We should take one out tomorrow," William suggested as he continued down the hallway.

Jess followed, drawing her gaze away from the window.

Coming to a halt in front of their door, William pulled a key card out of his pocket. As he pushed open the door another one opened just down from them.

"Hello Jess, how are you?" Tom said enthusiastically as he strode out of his room and embraced her in a hug.

"Hello," she smiled, "I'm well thanks."

"So great you could join us tonight. I'm just going to meet the others in the bar if you guys want to come down?"

"Yeah, we'll just get settled in," William said holding the door open for Jess, gesturing for her to go inside.

"Ah of course, see you later on," he winked as William shut the door on him.

Jess laughed as she threw her bags on the end of the enormous four poster bed and walked over to the balcony.

"This place is unbelievable," she said leaning on the metal railing, breathing in the fresh air, "thank you so much for inviting me."

William threw the dresses down on a chair and moved slowly up behind her. He wrapped his arms around her waist, his hand grazing her hip sending her nerves into overdrive.

"It's my pleasure," he whispered in her ear as his hand moved gently back and forth across the bare skin between her jeans and her top.

Jess flexed her hips fractionally, moving back into him, she was sure he was hard already as he continued running his fingers across her stomach, getting closer and closer the line of her jeans.

Jess could feel her need for him building as he swept her hair back, revealing the bare skin on top of her shoulder, placing kisses slowly down her neck. Taking her hand, he pulled her away from the balcony and walked her slowly back into the bedroom. He gazed down at her, his intentions clear as his mouth found hers, his impatience obvious as his hands moved quickly.

Within seconds he was pulling her top up over her head and unhooking her bra, throwing it on the floor behind him. William paused and looked down at her for a second, standing in front of him, topless, her long brown hair falling wildly down over one side of her chest.

Something animal like flashed across his face as he pushed her gently down on the bed. Moving forward, he braced himself over the top of her as the pace increased further, their kisses becoming more frantic, their breathing heavier as the passion between them skyrocketed.

Running his tongue down her chest he found her nipples. Jess gasped, her eyes closed, her hands above her head revelling in his touch.

William quickly took off his shirt, pulling it straight over the top of his head. Swiftly he removed his jeans and boxers as Jess leant forward and began to fumble for hers.

Taking control, he gently pushed her back down on the bed, his eyes wild and serious as he pulled her jeans down over her legs, chucking them on the floor. Taking another moment, he gazed down at her lying on the bed before leaning forward, kissing her thighs, moving up to her stomach and her chest before pulling down her black lace thong and moving on top of her.

Jess paused for a moment, running her eyes over his body, her hands moving up his arms to his shoulders.

He kissed her passionately as he slid his fingers inside her, her moan muffled by his mouth on hers. The foreplay was minimal today, William wasn't wasting any time as he held her hands above her head, watching her face as he moved into her.

Jess closed her eyes and arched her back in response to him, realising how long it felt since they had been together, hoping she would never have to wait this long again.

Bracing himself with one arm either side of her face, he picked up the pace, finding the rhythm he knew she wanted.

Wrapping her legs up around his torso Jess tilted her hips upwards. Opening her eyes she watched William's face for a moment, watched his muscles flex as he moved back and forth, thrusting harder with every movement.

Taking hold of both her legs, he placed them up on his shoulders, knowing exactly where to find her sweet spot.

Jess closed her eyes and focused as the familiar heat rose in her face, she held her breath, willing the orgasm to come. Her back arched as it did, erupting through her body as she grabbed hold of his hand, crying out loudly, every nerve inside her firing. A few seconds later William moaned as he came, his fingers still entwined with hers, his brow furrowed.

"Fuck, I have missed you," he said through laboured breathing, "what have you done to me Jess Taylor?"

"I missed you," Jess whispered taking hold of his face and looking into his eyes, "more than I've ever missed anyone."

He smiled at her and playfully nudged her nose with his.

"Like I said, you're coming with me next time. I'm never

spending that long away from you again."

Rolling over, their fingers still entwined, they lay for a minute enjoying the come down from their antics as their breathing gradually returned to normal.

"What time is it?" Jess asked.

William glanced at his watch.

"Twenty to six, time for a drink I reckon," he said, pushing himself up on the bed.

Picking up the phone on the bedside table he called reception and ordered a bottle of champagne to be brought up.

Jess stroked his back as she sat up next to him, happy that they were going to have a drink in the room rather than heading straight down to the bar with his friends.

"So, what time do I need to be ready?" she asked, looking at the huge pile of dresses stacked on the chair in the corner of the room.

"Drinks reception is at seven thirty I think," William said getting up from the bed and walking naked into the bathroom. Jess heard taps running as he appeared in the doorway wrapped in a white waffle dressing gown.

"Bath?" he asked with a sparkle in his eye.

Jess grinned at him.

"Champagne in the bath, what a start to a weekend."

They lay together in the hot bubbles, one at either end, their legs and bodies intertwined. Jess gazed through the steam at William who had his head leant back on the rim of the bath, his shoulders wedged between the porcelain with his eyes closed. She took another sip of her champagne from the shelf next to her, the condensation gathering on the cool glass as the warm air enveloped it.

Suddenly there was a loud knock on the door, too loud for housekeeping.

Slowly William opened his eyes, showing no intention of going to see who it was.

"Are you two finished yet?" Felix shouted through the door.

William smiled as he closed his eyes again.

"No," he yelled back making Jess laugh.

"Christ, they're still at it," Jess heard him say to his companion as he moved away from the door and down the hallway. Taking another mouthful of champagne, she leant her head back as far as she could risk without soaking her hair and closed her eyes.

Dozing in that lovely state of semi unconsciousness Jess felt William stir at his end of the bath. Leaning forward he pushed himself up, making the water level drop right down below her legs. Her skin has turned slightly red from the heat of the water and her hands had gone all wrinkly, like they used to when she was a child and spent too long in a swimming pool. Wrapping himself up in a dressing gown, William bent down and kissed her.

"Come on angel, let's get ready," he said as he passed her a towel.

Charlotte's choices of dress were far from what Jess would have chosen for a black tie dinner, not helped by the fact that Jess was three sizes smaller and six inches taller than her, meaning half the dresses either didn't fit or were so short she was in danger of displaying her bum cheeks if she didn't spend the whole evening standing bolt upright, hanging on to the hem of her dress as if her life depended on it.

Luckily Charlotte had packed a variety of styles and Jess finally decided on a dark red silk number. It was sleeveless with a deep neckline, a waistline she could tighten with a bow at the back and a long skirt with a split up one side. Curling her hair, she let it sit in Jessica Rabbit style waves down around her shoulders, using half a can of hair spray to try and keep it in place. She kept her makeup classic and put on the gold bracelet her mother had given her for her twenty first birthday.

Sitting on the edge of the bed, Jess was tying the strap on her black heels when William appeared from the hallway, carrying a selection of bow ties he had borrowed from Tom after realising he had forgotten his.

Standing up, Jess inspected her reflection in the free standing mirror sat the corner of the room.

"Wow," William exclaimed, stopping in his tracks as he took in her appearance, "you look incredible."

Jess turned to him and smiled.

"Thanks, so do you," she said admiring him, standing in front of her in his crisp white shirt and black trousers, his dark hair smoothed back, his eyes sparkling at her as he smiled.

"Which one do you think?" he asked, presenting her with a selection of ties.

Jess studied them before picking out the black velvet one.

"You can't go wrong with a classic," she said handing it to him. She in fact had no idea, she had never attended a black tie function in her life, but she was trying to play the part none the less.

William stood next to her in front of the mirror skilfully tying his bow tie.

Jess watched him intently, pulling his collar down for him when he finished. Turning him to face her, she straightened his tie at the front.

"Perfect," she said flashing him a smile.

There was that look again.

She met his gaze, trying to see into his soul in the way she was sure he was looking into hers.

"You're perfect," he said wrapping his arms around her waist, pulling her towards him and placing a long kiss on her lips.

Jess pulled away gently, wiping the dark lipstick from his mouth with her thumb.

"Come on, let's go downstairs before we end up getting back into bed," she laughed.

"If we have to," he said with a smile, giving her one last kiss on the lips before putting on his jacket. Reaching for her hand he led her out of the room and down the corridor.

They made their way down the staircase, three members of staff unnecessarily halting on their way up and moving well out of their way as they did.

Smiling at them as she went past, Jess had the overwhelming feeling that she had cheated the system somehow, that she should be the one delivering drinks and opening doors for guests.

Still holding her hand, William led her through to the main bar. As they passed through the large oak doorway, they were greeted by more staff stood to attention with trays of champagne, smiling from ear to ear, as if the more they smiled the more likely you would be to take a drink from their tray.

Glasses in hand they made their way over to William's friends. You could hear Tom before you saw him, sat on a bar stool laughing with Felix and Adam, Ben and a few others she recognised were beside them. Jess scanned the rest of the group, thanking her lucky stars that Stephen was nowhere to be seen.

To the left of the men stood Georgina and Elizabeth in deep conversation with another larger woman. Georgina was wearing a floor length green velvet dress, her hair pulled back in a tight headmistress style bun. Elizabeth stood leaning against the bar looking like she'd had a bit too much to drink already, her fringe falling down over her forehead, the strap on the left side of her gold sequin dress slipping off her shoulder. Spotting Jess as she approached, Elizabeth waved, gesturing for her to come and join them.

Jess let go of William who was making a beeline for the men, he looked round and winked at her as she broke off.

"Hi Jess!" Elizabeth exclaimed, embracing her in a hug.

Jess hung on to her as she stumbled on her heels before propping herself back up against the bar.

"Jess this is Lauren, Tom's wife," Elizabeth said through a hiccup, "Jess is William's girlfriend," she explained.

Lauren gave her a friendly smile, she too had opted for a slick back hair bun, showing off her very round freckled face, her rotund figure squeezed in a black satin dress that was a little too long for her.

"Hello, it's nice to meet you. Tom's told me all about you," Lauren smiled, "so glad you could make it tonight, we were a bit outnumbered last night with all the men!"

"Oh, Jess doesn't mind that," Georgina cut in as she leant forward to give Jess a hug, presenting her cheek on either side of her face.

"So, you all came down yesterday?" Jess asked, ignoring Georgina's jibe.

"Yeah, we have to leave tomorrow evening so we thought we would come down early and get two nights away from the kids," Lauren chuckled, her shoulders bouncing.

"Yes, Adam and I had a lovely evening last night, we ordered room service and never left the bedroom," Georgina interjected with a smirk.

"Ladies are you all okay for a drink?" Felix appeared behind them merging the two groups together.

"I could do with another one," Elizabeth said, raising her glass in the air.

Ignoring her, Felix turned to Jess and gave her a kiss on both cheeks.

"Hi Jess, so glad you could make it, you look stunning," he said, discreetly running his eyes over her.

"Oh, my pleasure, thank you for having me," she smiled back.

"Right, you can have another drink if you promise to put some big bids on at the auction," he said to Elizabeth, gesturing for a waitress to come over with a bottle.

"Go steady, she'll be asleep before the auction starts at this rate," Tom laughed.

Elizabeth playfully stuck her tongue out at him and smiled.

Jess watched the eye contact between them for a moment, Lauren had her head down fiddling with the bunch of bangles on her left arm as her cheeks filled with colour. Jess glanced over at William who had been watching them with a darkness in his face, raising his eyebrows at Jess as their eyes met.

Thankfully the awkwardness was broken by the front of house announcing that dinner was about to be served and everyone should make their way to the dining room.

There were around a hundred people in the bar area, all dressed up in their dinner jackets and long dresses who began filtering slowly through the large double doors into the dining room.

William appeared at Jess's side as the group began to move through, grabbing hold of her hand he gave it a squeeze.

"You alright?" he asked quietly.

"Yeah, I'm great," she said with a smile.

Their table was in the centre of the room, nine other beautifully dressed tables surrounded them with a stage area at the far end. Jess found her name card in between Tom and Elizabeth who were already seated. She glanced around seeing William sit himself down between Felix and Georgina.

"Red or white?" Tom asked, both his hands loaded with bottles.

"White please," Jess said offering up her glass.

Looking down she studied the cutlery in front of her, she

had never seen so many different knives, forks and spoons laid up. In the pub it was two sets at best, and often they were the same ones if the kitchen porter hadn't got his arse in gear and kept up with the washing up.

She glanced nervously up at William who gave her a comforting smile and raised his glass to her. Taking the hint, she picked up her glass and swallowed a large mouthful, and then another to help her loosen up.

"So Jess, how are things going with you and William?" Tom asked, topping up her glass with the last of the bottle he had dispensed around their side of the table.

"Thank you," she said sliding her glass towards her, "yeah really good," she smiled at him as her face flushed.

"I can tell," he said glancing over at William, "he's besotted."

William was watching them intently with narrowed eyes, almost as if he was trying to lip read their conversation.

Tom smiled mischievously at him.

"Just discussing whether you're really good enough for this young lady," he called across the table to him.

William smirked slightly.

"I'll be the first to admit that I definitely am not," he called back before turning to engage in conversation with Felix and Lauren.

"In all truthfulness," Tom turned back to her, "he's one of the best blokes I've ever met, fiercely loyal," he spun his wine glass around at the base as he spoke, "but break that trust and you'll be on the wrong side of him, that's not somewhere I ever want to be," he laughed.

Jess looked down at her own glass as he spoke, taking on board his warning.

"I can imagine," she said taking another gulp of her wine.

Their conversations were interrupted by the arrival of the first course, some sort of raw fish balanced on a few stacked leaves of spinach.

Pausing to make sure she used the correct cutlery, Jess followed Tom's lead and picked up the tiny knife and fork on the outside of her selection.

Tom inhaled his tiny portion in one mouthful before raising his hand to accost another waitress for more wine.

Jess watched the other women around the table carefully take their time dissecting their food into tiny mouthfuls, pausing between each one to make conversation or drink wine. She copied them as much as she felt she could, it seemed ridiculous to her to eat something so small so slowly.

Before their first course was finished another appeared, a line of waiters queued up whilst others frantically cleared the tables in front of them, apologising profusely as they went.

An hour and a half later, they were onto their final course. Jess was absolutely stuffed, her stomach full of small plates of rich food she hadn't particularly enjoyed. The cold glass of soup was the worst, closely followed by the whole fish she had to try and peel away from its skeleton whilst the animal stared at her though a charred eyeball. She exhaled, wishing she hadn't tied her dress up quite so tightly as a plate of chocolate torte was placed in front of her.

"I'm not sure I can eat this," she said, leaning back as the familiar feeling of heartburn churned away in her stomach, "I'm so full."

"Don't worry, I'll take it off your hands," Tom said between mouthfuls of his own dessert.

Next to Jess, Elizabeth mumbled something about Tom having too much cake and eating it. Her eyes were rolling slightly, her eyelids heavy as she slumped in her chair looking like she might nod off at any second.

Ignoring her completely, Tom swapped his plate with Jess's and began tucking into his second dessert portion.

"I'm just going to pop to the bathroom," Jess said pushing her chair back.

As she walked around the table William leant back and put his arm out, snaking it around her waist as she bent down and gave him a kiss.

"Are you alright?" he asked.

"Yeah, I'm great," she smiled, trying to hold in her bloated stomach.

"Jess don't be too long, the auction is about the start and there's some cracking stuff up for grabs," Felix said with an excited smile.

"Okay, I'll be back in a minute," she said slipping out of William's arm and making her way around the tables. She wasn't sure what sort of things were going to be sold here tonight, but she could near enough guarantee she wasn't going to be buying any.

In the bathroom she studied her reflection in the huge lit mirror on the wall. Applying a fresh layer of lipstick from her bag, she combed her hair which had flattened over the last couple of hours and quickly necked two heartburn pills. She was stuffing her makeup back in her bag when Lauren appeared from one of the cubicles. Her eyes were red and puffy, she was sniffing as she stood next to Jess and quickly washed her hands.

"Are you okay?" Jess asked, placing a hand on her arm.

Lauren forced a small smile, her eyes watering slightly.

"Yes, I'm fine," she nodded, "just a bit fed up and tired."

Jess paused, offering her an opportunity to talk.

"I'll see you back in there," Lauren said as she opened her own little clutch bag and fished out some mascara.

"Okay, see you in there," Jess said, giving her arm one last squeeze before she left.

Back in the dining room the auction had started, a man was stood up on the stage with a microphone shouting at the crowd. Jess didn't know what he was selling but the bidding was at seven thousand pounds already, with many guests still frantically shooting their arms in the air as the price soared higher and higher.

Back at the table, Elizabeth appeared to have come back from her near comatose state and had moved herself in to Jess's chair, her arm resting on Tom's shoulder as she whispered something in his ear.

Jess paused behind her seat for a moment, waiting for her to move.

Elizabeth glanced up at her briefly but made no indication she was going anywhere.

Sitting herself down in the empty chair, Jess clapped as the first sale of the auction came to a close at eight thousand and three hundred pounds. The crowd continued applauding as a balding man from a table near the stage stood up to receive an envelope from the auctioneer.

"What was that for?" Jess asked Adam who she was now sat next to.

"A day trip on a pucker sailing yacht," he said still clapping, "hi by the way, sorry I haven't had the chance to speak you."

"Yeah, sorry we didn't catch up earlier, how are you?" Jess asked, reaching for her wine glass before Elizabeth mistook it for hers.

"Yeah, I'm well thanks, busy, but busy is good. How are you? How's your mum doing? William said she wasn't very well."

Jess smiled gratefully at his concern.

"Yeah, she's deteriorating sadly and the home is closed down with Covid so I can't visit at the moment."

Adam frowned.

"Goodness that must be hard," he said placing a hand on her shoulder.

Jess glanced across the table and met Georgina's hawk like stare, Adam followed her eyeline and quickly removed his hand as the auctioneer started on the next bidding.

Lauren sat back down at the table next to Adam just as Tom had bought a weekend trip to Scotland for ten thousand pounds. Jess watched Elizabeth's hand sitting on his thigh, squeezing it every time he raised his hand to place a bid. As Tom made his way up to the stage she whistled and cheered, anyone looking on would have thought it was her that was going to be accompanying him, not his wife.

Jess couldn't face looking at Lauren, Elizabeth was

being so disrespectful it made her want to smack her right in her smirking face. As Tom sat back down, envelope in hand, Elizabeth snaked her arm around his shoulder, giving it a squeeze as he glanced at her and smiled, his eyes sparkling.

The auction rolled on, Jess sat with her arms folded over her lap trying to suppress a yawn as the final item was announced, a week in a luxury ski chalet in the French Alps with a chef and concierge. A hush spread around the room as eyebrows raised, guests whispering quietly between themselves, deciding what to bid. Under strict instructions from Felix the waiters made one last push at topping up wine glasses, in the hope that an extra half a glass might make the guests dig a little deeper in their pockets.

The bidding began at ten thousand pounds and was increasing rapidly. Jess was watching the auctioneer get more and more excited when William whistled across the table at her. She looked over at him as he leant forward and mouthed something to her, she leant forward as well, trying to make out what he was saying.

"Do you fancy a week skiing?" he mouthed with a smile as the auctioneer shouted twenty thousand pounds for the most recent bid.

Jess's eyes widened as she frantically shook her head.

"That's a crazy amount of money," she hissed back, "and I can't even ski!"

"I'll teach you," he said with a smile.

Jess stared at him, silently willing him to not raise his hand, but she knew there was no stopping him.

"Twenty five," he called across the room, casually

putting his hand in the air.

Jess held her hands up over her face, she couldn't watch.

"We have twenty thousand ladies and gentlemen!" the auctioneer exclaimed over the microphone, "do I have any more?"

The room went silent as all the guests looked around to see if anyone would match William's bid.

"No?" the auctioneer said after a pause, still looking around the room.

"Sold! To the very generous man on table six."

The crowd erupted in applause as the auctioneer jumped off the stage to hand deliver the envelope.

Felix slapped William on the back and shook his hand.

"Here you are sir," the auctioneer said as he reached their table, "are you not aware of how an auction works, that was a five grand jump."

"Well, it's all for a good cause isn't it," William said, raising his wine glass with Felix.

"Looks like you could be off skiing," Elizabeth whispered to Jess with a drunken smile.

Jess caught William's eye as he raised a glass to her and winked. She couldn't help but laugh as she took another mouthful of wine and shook her head at him, this really was a whole other world, she thought to herself.

It was quarter to twelve by the time they made their way to bed. Jess was sat at a table in the bar with Lauren, struggling to keep her eyes open when William finally managed to break away from the group and scoop her up.

"See you tomorrow," she smiled at Lauren, who also

picked up her bag.

"Yeah, I think I'll head up too," she said, standing up and looking over at Tom, who was sat up on a bar stool loudly ordering another round of shots, Elizabeth draped happily over his shoulder.

Jess and William watched as she walked cautiously over to the group and asked her husband if he was going to come up to the room with her. Tom, who had a boyish smile plastered all over his face, casually waved her off with an empty promise he would be up after this next drink.

"Good night," Lauren said to them as she scurried past and headed up the stairs.

Jess looked at William with a sad face.

"I feel so sorry for her."

William took her hand and led her out of the bar.

"I know," he said, "so do I."

Upstairs Jess collapsed on the bed fully clothed.

"I am so full, I'm not even sure I can have sex," she said as she shut her eyes.

William laughed as he began unbuttoning his shirt.

"That's okay, we've got plenty of time for that this weekend."

Jess heard taps running in the bathroom as she began drifting off to sleep. A few moments later she felt William pull her up on the bed.

"Come on, you need to get undressed and take your shoes off, you can't get into bed like that."

Jess made a half-hearted effort to sit up as William undid the straps on her heels and pulled her to her feet before slipping off her dress. Pulling back the covers he laid her down in the bed and tucked the duvet up under her arms.

"Thank you," she said sleepily as she rested her head down on the pillow.

"You're welcome angel," he said, placing a kiss on her forehead.

Jess was asleep within seconds, not even stirring as William climbed in beside her a few minutes later.

Chapter Twenty Four

Jess woke with a jump as shouting erupted in the room next to them. Sitting bolt upright, her heart pounding, she grabbed hold of William who was stirring in the darkness next to her.

"William," she shook his arm as he pushed himself up in the bed.

"Fuck sake," he whispered looking at the clock next to the bed which read 2.34am. They sat quietly for a minute hoping the shouting would subside, Jess couldn't quite make out what was being said, only Laurens high pitched wail followed by Tom's low voice which was gathering volume as the confrontation went on.

"I'll be back in a minute," William said as he got out of

bed and pulled on a dressing gown.

Jess went to follow but he stopped her.

"Stay here," he said firmly.

Jess did as she was told and pulled the covers back over her as the shouting intensified.

William quietly opened their bedroom door, Jess sat up against the headboard listening as hard as she could. She could make out William's voice as he entered their room, Tom spoke to him as Lauren let out another outburst before he had finished, something about where he'd been for the last two hours. Tom shouted something back at her but was quickly silenced by William's voice which matched his volume.

After a couple of minutes Jess heard doors opening and closing, moments later William appeared quietly back in their room.

"What happened?" she asked as he dropped his dressing gown and climbed back into bed.

"Tom's being a twat, I've told him to go and sleep in Felix's room," he said as he settled back down into bed, putting his arm around her waist.

"Is Lauren okay?" she whispered through the darkness.

"She'd be better off if she left him to be honest, but that has to be her decision," William whispered back as he closed his eyes and nudged her neck with his chin.

"Now go back to sleep," he said pulling her even closer into him, "you need lots of energy for lots of sex tomorrow."

Jess smiled to herself as she settled back down and closed her eyes.

Doors slamming down the hallway woke both William and Jess on Saturday morning.

"What a bloody racket," William moaned as he pulled a pillow over the top of his head.

It was half past seven, Jess sat up on the edge of the bed and looked out of the window. The sky was perfectly blue and clear, but a mist had settled over the top of the warm earth, blanketing the grounds and the lake in a grey cloud. There were people out walking already, Jess watched a couple disappear hand in hand along a mown path into the woods, someone else was out on a rowing boat amongst the mist making their way slowly from one side of the lake to the other.

Getting herself up, Jess took a long hot shower, washing off the makeup that she had neglected to take off the night before and combing the knots out of her long hair. Her stomach was still full, the thought of piling more breakfast on top of last night's dinner was making her feel a bit nauseous.

Rifling through her wash bag she tried to find some more heartburn tablets, she could feel it stirring threateningly at the bottom of her chest, she also needed some paracetamol, her head was beginning to thump thanks to the two bottles of wine Tom had forced upon her at dinner.

After searching for a minute or two she discovered her wash bag wasn't harbouring any useful pharmaceuticals, silently she cursed herself for not being more prepared, after her last meal out with William's friends she should have known this was going to happen. Pausing for a moment, she held on to the sink as the predicted wave of heartburn came over her. As it gradually subsided, she was sure she could hear movement in the bathroom next door, the sound of a loo flush and taps running.

Slipping on her dressing gown, Jess checked William had gone back to sleep before she stepped quietly out into the corridor. She knocked gently on Laurens door. There was no answer, so she knocked again, this time louder. After a few moments the door opened a crack, Lauren's pale, tired face peered around it.

"Oh hi," she said exhaling, opening the door further.

"I just wanted to check you were alright?" Jess said with a frown.

Lauren's eyes were bloodshot and even more swollen than they were in the bathroom last night, she looked like she hadn't slept a wink.

"Yeah, I'm okay. It's not the first time we've had a row about where he's disappeared off to, and I'm sure it won't be the last."

Following Lauren into her room, which was similar to theirs but with more of a green theme rather than a blue, Jess watched as she dropped down into the chair by the balcony, her legs splayed out in front of her, her hands rubbing her face emphasising her exhaustion.

Jess sat down on the seat opposite her and tightly crossed her legs, acutely aware that she was wearing nothing underneath her dressing gown.

"I thought his behaviour was pretty appalling," Jess admitted, "and hers wasn't much better."

Lauren looked up at her with half a smile of gratitude.

"Yeah, it's my own fault for staying with the bastard to

be honest, if it wasn't for the boys I would have packed my bags years ago. It's not so bad when we're at home together but when he goes off on these jolly weekends or nights out, I know what he gets up to," she said as she gazed out of the window.

Jess flexed forward as another bout of heartburn charged through her chest.

"Are you alright?" Lauren asked frowning at her.

Jess paused for a moment, waiting for it to pass.

"I'm fine, just all the food and wine has given me heartburn, you haven't got any tablets have you?" she asked, leaning back in her chair and exhaling.

"Sorry I haven't, but I need to nip into town today, I can pick you up some."

"Well, why don't I come with you?" Jess suggested with a smile. She liked Lauren and could only imagine she needed someone to confide in when her husband was being such an arse.

"Okay sure, we could pop in late morning," Lauren suggested as the door to her room opened gently.

In came Tom, shuffling through the doorway looking incredibly sheepish. His hair was ruffled at the back and he was still in the shirt and trousers he was wearing last night.

Jess got up quickly and scurried to the door.

"I'll see you later," she smiled back at Lauren who was laying a deathly stare on her husband.

"Morning Tom," she said quietly, struggling to smile at him as she rushed past.

Back in her room William was sat up in bed looking at his phone.

"Hello you, where have you been?" he asked dropping his phone down on the duvet in front of him.

"Just checking on Lauren," Jess said sitting down on the edge of the bed and planting a kiss on William's lips.

"Is she alright?"

"Yeah, I think so, Tom's just appeared back looking very sorry for himself. I'm going pop into town with her later on to get some bits," she said making her way to the bathroom.

"What do you need?" William asked getting out of bed and opening the door to the balcony.

"I've got such bad heartburn this morning from all that food so I'm going to get some tablets, do you need anything?"

"No, but I'm sure one of the staff could get that for you," he frowned as she appeared back in the room combing through her still wet hair.

"Well Lauren needs to go in anyway and I think she needs a friend," Jess said pulling the hairdryer out of the dressing table drawer.

Walking slowly over, William wrapped his arms around her.

"You're very kind aren't you," he said as he smiled lovingly down at her and gave her a kiss.

An hour later Jess and William were sat at a small round table in the dining room having breakfast. Jess hadn't managed to eat anything apart from a piece of dry toast and some green tea.

"Are you sure you're okay?" William asked with concern.

"I'm fine, my stomachs just not used to all this posh food," she joked, nodding at his eggs royale.

A few moments later Felix appeared in the doorway, William waved to him as he made his way over.

Felix was tall and always sharply dressed, his sandy hair styled over the side of his head and cut to within an inch of its life. This morning he looked as fresh as a daisy in blue jeans and a navy shirt.

"Morning guys," he smiled, "how did you sleep?"

"Yeah good, probably better than you with the roommate you ended up with," William said glancing at Jess.

Felix rolled his eyes.

"He's such a fucking nightmare when he's been drinking. I made him sleep on the sofa in my room, there was no way I was letting that mess in a bed with me," he joked. "A few of the others are heading off later but I've got a table booked for the rest of us tonight at eight, is that alright?" he asked, already looking around the room and catching the eye of some other people he knew.

"Yeah, sounds good mate," William said, "we'll catch up for a drink in the bar this afternoon or something."

"Yeah perfect, see you later," Felix flashed them a smile, his eyes lingering on Jess for a second too long before he strode off across the dining room to speak to another couple.

Jess leant back in her chair and took a large swig of her water, the talk of alcohol was beginning to make her feel a bit sick.

It was ten forty five by the time they had finished breakfast, the rest of the group apart from Tom and Lauren had all appeared in dribs and drabs. Adam and Georgina had Elizabeth in tow who looked even more nauseous about the breakfast presented to her than Jess did.

"I'm going to find Lauren," Jess said when they arrived back in their room.

"Okay, well I'll catch up with you when you get back," he said, giving her a quick kiss as she picked up her handbag.

"What are you going to do this morning?" she asked.

"Oh, I'm sure I'll be able to entertain myself."

He grinned at her as he sat down on one of the chairs by the balcony.

"Okay well don't have too much fun without me," she called as she left the room.

Tentatively she knocked on the door next to theirs, unsure who was inside. A few seconds later the door opened and Lauren appeared, bag in hand ready to go.

"Right, are we ready?" she said as she led the way down the corridor.

"Everything alright?" Jess asked cautiously as they descended the stairs side by side.

"Yes, all fine," she said with a forced smile as she picked up the pace down the last few steps.

Out in the car park Jess followed Lauren to her car.

"So, who has the twins this weekend?" she asked as she hauled herself up into Lauren's Audi Q7.

"They're with my parents, Tom's parents are almost as useless as he is with looking after them, so they nearly always go to mine."

Jess smiled awkwardly, not sure how to respond.

"Thanks for taking me to town."

"No problem, I was going to go in anyway. It's my parent's wedding anniversary tomorrow so I need to at least have a card to give them when we go and collect the boys tonight," she said, moving the seat forward so much her large breasts were resting on the steering wheel, yet her little feet could only just reach the pedals.

"I'm sorry we woke you last night," she said after a few moments of silence.

Jess looked across at her.

"Don't be silly, it's fine," she smiled in an attempt to make her feel better.

"I couldn't face coming to breakfast this morning, that woman winds we me up so much I think I could hit her," she spat, leaning even further forward in her seat as they came to the junction at the end of the driveway.

"Yeah, I can understand that," Jess said with a wry laugh.

They drove a few miles, eventually making their way right into the centre of Aylesbury. Lauren found the public car park and managed to squeeze her tank of a car into a corner parking space and just about get herself out of the driver's door without hitting the car next to her.

"Right, the post office is on the high street," she gestured to the left of the car park, "and Boots is down that way I think," she said, squinting down the right side of the street.

"Great," Jess said double checking her handbag had her purse in it, "I'll see you back here in fifteen minutes."

They both strode off on their separate agendas for the next quarter of an hour. Jess wandered down the busy street, still feeling a little uncomfortable as she dodged busy looking passers-by as they marched on their own missions of the morning.

The shop when she reached it was absolutely rammed. Jess made her way up the makeup aisle, snaking around a few middle aged women and past a group of teenage girls who seemed to be plastering every free sample they could find on their faces. In the next aisle she found some tablets for heartburn, she also picked up a couple of packets of paracetamol, certain in the knowledge she would have more alcohol forced upon her this evening.

Making her way back down the makeup aisle Jess passed a shop assistant, she was hovering near the group of teenagers with a watchful eye as she rearranged some bronzers.

The queue for the checkouts was long, winding its way around some stands filled with products on offer, a tactic used to lure queuing customers in to buying an extra item or two whilst they waited. Jess queued up behind an elderly lady with a basket full of talcum powder and soap as more people began queuing behind her.

Glancing towards the doors, Jess spotted the group of teenage girls skulking out of the shop, arms folded, dragging their feet as they went, the young assistant following them closely, ushering them out like a sheepdog driving a group of unruly adolescent lambs.

Running her eyes over the discounted products in front of her Jess could see how easy it was to be sucked in, amongst all the essentials like tampons and face wipes were bags of colourful sweets and chocolates, bringing a child in here would be a nightmare, she thought to herself.

Suddenly her mind went blank as her eyes darted back to the tampons on sale for half price. Frantically she tried to riffle through her memories to the last time she bought a pack.

Her heart rate began to skyrocket as she fumbled in her bag for her phone, quickly pulling up the app she used to track her cycle. As the pink screen loaded in front of her Jess realised her hands were shaking, silently she cursed herself for being so stupid, how could she not remember when her period was due.

The screen loaded with the calendar in the background. A lump formed in her throat as she read the words, 'One week late for period' written in grey bold font across the screen.

Jess clutched the phone to her pounding chest as if she was hiding a huge secret before glancing back at it again, hoping the words had gone away. They hadn't.

Jess glanced around at the queue of people waiting behind her.

"Excuse me," she said to the man stood beside her as she ran past him, almost knocking his basket out of his hands. Pushing her way backwards through the queue, her face a shade of crimson, Jess ran across the aisles looking down each one before she saw the sign for pregnancy tests hanging down from one of the shelves. There were so many, Jess had no idea what one she should choose. Scanning her hands down the shelves she went for the most expensive test she could see, firm in the knowledge it must be the most reliable one.

Holding the packet close to her chest so no one could see, she re-joined the queue, her heart racing, the feeling of vomit churning deep in her stomach. She thought back to all the times she had been with William, it was the most sex she had ever had in such a short time, but she hadn't even thought about falling pregnant. Granted, they hadn't used contraception, in the past she had always relied on her app to tell her when her fertile window was, but it had been so long she hadn't even thought about it. William admitting to her how he and Francesca had been unable to conceive had somehow subconsciously sat in the back of her mind, telling her it probably wasn't possible.

Taking some deep breaths, Jess tried to regain her composure as the queue crept forward. A few minutes later she was being called forward to a checkout by a young man who looked about fifteen. Sheepishly she placed her items on the till, glancing around her to see if anyone was watching.

"Would you like a bag?" the cashier asked, chewing gum as he slowly swiped her items through the till.

"Yes please," Jess said quickly.

She stuffed the pregnancy test in the small plastic bag followed by the paracetamol and heartburn tablets.

"Cash or—" he began to ask as Jess presented her card to the machine. It pinged through with a little approved message, a nanosecond later she was heading for the door. Shoving the carrier bag deep into her handbag, she held it tightly under her arm, aware of her secret looming inside as she marched back towards the car park.

Lauren hadn't returned yet, Jess took the opportunity to

dig out the carrier bag and quickly take some heartburn tablets and paracetamol before hiding it away again. Leaning against the car, glancing at the time on her phone every thirty seconds, she began to get more and more impatient, wondering to herself how on earth it could take this long to buy a card.

Five minutes later Lauren appeared around the corner from the road she had walked up no longer than twenty minutes before.

"Get what you needed?" she smiled at Jess as she unlocked the car for her.

"Yes, got some heartburn stuff," Jess smiled briefly, gesturing to her bag still clutched tightly under her arm.

"Great, let's head back then," Lauren said heaving herself up into the driving seat, "let's see if my husband has anything else to say for himself."

Jess ignored her comment and sat quietly gazing out of the window, pondering on her own possible situation.

They arrived back at the hotel as lunch was in full swing. The sun was shining, a number of guests had gathered on the terrace, being served drinks and tucking into large plates of food.

Jess strode quickly back through reception and towards the bar, in the hope of heading straight through it and up to the room.

Her hopes were dashed as she heard William calling her name. She looked around, the whole group except for Elizabeth were sat around a table in the bar with two open bottles of red wine and a platter of breads, cheeses and meats. Hesitating for a moment, Jess made her way over followed by Lauren, holding her handbag so tightly under her arm she was beginning to get pins and needles.

Tom got up and offered his wife his seat as she reluctantly allowed him to plant a kiss on her cheek.

"Get the bits you needed?" William asked as he stood up and offered Jess his chair, pulling up one for himself from the table next to them.

"Yeah, all good," she forced a small smile, "I was just going to pop and get changed," she gestured towards the door behind her that led to the staircase.

"You don't need to change," Georgina scoffed, "we're only having lunch," she gestured around the table as she rolled her eyes.

William ignored her.

"Come and eat, you barely had any breakfast this morning," he said pulling the chair back for her to sit down.

"Okay," Jess said, slightly annoyed but not wanting to make a scene as she rammed her handbag under the table, gripping it tightly between her calves.

Two hours passed. Jess forced herself to make polite conversation and managed to nibble on the plate of food William had put in front of her. Thankfully she was able to avoid any more wine, Tom wasn't quite as bold as he had been the night before and easily accepted defeat when she said she didn't want any.

William had just fetched her another lemonade when her phone rang. Diving under the table to pull it out, not wanting to risk revealing the other contents of her bag, she emerged and looked at the screen. It was the care home.

"Sorry," Jess said quickly as she answered, the rest of

the group barely noticing as they continued chatting amongst themselves.

"Hello," she said, holding her hand up to her other ear so she could hear better.

"Hello Jessica, it's Mrs Brown," she said in her usual tone.

"Is mum alright?" Jess asked with a frown.

"Yes, she's still the same. I just wanted to let you know that all the current staff and residents have tested negative, we'll continue with daily tests until Wednesday, if they're all clear we will open again to visitors. Given your mother's condition I'm happy for you to come any time from then."

Jess breathed a sigh of relief.

"Okay thanks for letting me know, maybe I'll come up on Thursday morning then."

"Yes, that will be fine, as I said I'll keep you updated," she said efficiently as she placed the phone down.

"Everything okay?" William asked placing his hand on her thigh.

"Yeah fine, they just wanted to let me know I can go and visit next week," she said, placing her phone down on the table in front of her.

"That's good, maybe I can come with you one day."

"Yeah, that would be nice," she said with a smile.

A ray of hope shot through Jess as a waitress came over to clear their plates and gather up any empty wine glasses.

"No, we're still going on the wine," Felix waved her off from across the table, "just bring us another bottle and top everyone up," he said bluntly, turning back to his conversation with Ben and Adam.

Jess sighed, wondering how long before she could make her excuses and head upstairs when she heard a female voice call her name from behind her.

"Jess?"

She spun around in her chair to see Charlotte and Harry stood at the bar.

"Charlotte?" she said in shock, watching her strut her way over to the table before leaning down and embracing her in a hug. Harry approached cautiously behind her, lingering a few feet back.

"What are you doing here?" Jess asked with confusion in her voice.

"Well, this place sounded so nice, we thought we would try it out," she said, standing back and wrapping an arm around Harry's back, placing her other hand on his chest.

Charlotte turned to William.

"And you must be the famous William Archer," she said a little too loudly, pushing her already visible cleavage a little further out of her low cut blouse.

Jess inwardly cringed, hoping the rest of the group weren't observing this conversation. Glancing quickly around the table she was thankful that Adam, Georgina and Ben had got up and left. Felix was taking no notice of them, now deep in conversation with Tom and Lauren.

Rising from of his chair, William stepped forward to give Charlotte a well-mannered kiss on both of her cheeks.

"So nice to meet you Charlotte, I've heard lots about you," he said with a smile.

"And this is Harry, he's actually one of Jess's old school friends," she said looking between the two of them, moving to the side so the men could shake hands.

"Harry," William said, his eyes darkening as took his outstretched hand, pulling it towards him slightly making Harry take a small step forward.

Jess watched as William's face closed in on Harry's until there was only six inches between them.

"It's good to meet you," he said in a low voice, his facial expression matching his tone not his words.

"You too," Harry said uncomfortably, pulling his hand from William's grasp, "hi Jess," he said glancing in her direction.

Jess gave him a sarcastic smile and a little wave over the back of her chair.

"Could you get us some drinks?" Charlotte said smiling at Harry.

Harry happily obliged and quickly strode off to the bar.

"Jess, could you show me where the loos are please?" Charlotte asked widening her eyes, indicating there was another reason she wanted her on her own.

Jess exhaled.

"I'll be back in a minute," she said, giving William a quick kiss before grabbing her handbag and leading Charlotte back through reception to the ladies' room.

Once the door had closed behind them Charlotte turned to her.

"Well that was pretty rude," she said pulling her lipstick out of her bag and frowning at Jess in the mirror, "I thought you'd be happy to see me and Harry, you two were old friends, weren't you?" she said with an accusing tone.

"Not really no," Jess said leaning against the wall, "why

did you come here without saying anything?"

"I thought it would be fun," Charlotte said with wide eyes as she puckered her lips together, "let's just all have a drink together later, honestly he's such a nice bloke and I really like him," she paused, "you're basically my best friend so it's important to me that you guys get on."

Jess frowned and inwardly rolled her eyes.

"Okay fine, we'll meet you for a drink later on," she said, defeated.

Charlotte let out a little squeal and clapped her hands.

"Great," she beamed, "I'll drop you a text when we head back down later. I might actually need to swing by your room and grab one of those dresses," she called as she headed out the door.

Finally, Jess thought to herself as she locked herself in one of the cubicles and pulled the test kit out of her bag. Sitting down on the loo she read through the instructions carefully before taking it, her hand shaking as she tried to focus. Placing the test face down on the ledge behind the loo she started the timer on her phone. She could hear her heart beating inside her chest as the door to the bathroom swung open making her jump, a few seconds later she heard a door shut and lock in one of the cubicles further down.

Thirty seconds to go. Taking a few deep breaths Jess closed her eyes and counted in her head. Glancing back at her phone she saw the two minutes was up.

With a shaking hand she turned the test over.

Unmistakeably obvious, clear as day, were two blue lines, exactly the same as the positive picture in the instructions she had just read.

Jess thought her knees were going to give way as she leant forward, bracing herself on the ledge behind the toilet as she tried to focus on her breathing. It felt like forever before she was able to compose herself. Eventually she picked up the test, checking it for the tenth time to make sure she had read it right before darting out of the cubicle and stuffing it quickly in the bin under the sinks.

Looking in the mirror she studied her reflection, she was pale and wide eyed, like anyone would be if they had just received this unexpected news, but somewhere deep inside her was a spark of excitement, an unplanned blessing that could change her life. As she walked back through reception she smiled to herself at the thought of telling William, she wasn't certain, but she was pretty sure he would be delighted.

Thankfully the spot where Harry was stood by the bar was now vacant, Jess glanced around to their table, surprised to see William was gone. Felix and Tom were the only ones left, still sat sharing the last of a bottle of wine.

"Is William in the loo?" Jess asked, interrupting their conversation.

Felix looked up at her.

"No, he took a phone call for you, I thought he left to go and find you," he said as he turned back to Tom.

Jess walked quickly through the bar and ran up the stairs two at a time, nearly knocking over a housekeeper as she rounded the corner to the corridor. Buzzing into their room with her key card, she opened the door to see William sat on the edge of the bed, his back to her, staring out of the window.

"Hey, I was looking for you downstairs," Jess said placing her handbag on the dressing table.

William didn't move.

"Are you okay?" she asked, rounding the bed to stand in front of him.

His face was stern, his jaw locked.

"What's wrong?" she asked as she went to touch his shoulder.

William stood up, recoiling from her hand.

He held out her phone and threw it to her, Jess fumbled as she caught it.

"The stripping agency called," his voice was cold as he stared into her eyes, searching for a reaction, "I thought it might have been the care home, so I answered it."

Jess's head spun in confusion as she glanced down at the phone in her hand.

"Why would the agency call me?" she said looking up at him, shaking her head.

"They wanted to confirm the booking you have for next weekend," he spat the words at her.

Jess could see the pain in his eyes that he was trying to hide.

"That's impossible, I don't have a booking next weekend," she stuttered, "or any weekend, you're the last person I did that for I swear!" Jess wailed.

She could hear the desperation in her voice.

"Stop making a fool of me Jess," he said, his voice full of anger as he looked down into her tear filled eyes, "I wanted to have everything with you, I thought I was falling—"

He stopped himself, Jess could hear a lump forming in his throat.

"But you still want to swan off and take your fucking clothes off for other men," he shouted as he stormed around the bed towards the door.

"William, I swear, I don't know anything about this," she pleaded, following him across the room.

He turned back to her, his eyes cold.

"I'm going for a walk, I want you gone before I get back," he said as he pulled open the door, slamming it behind him.

Jess fell to her knees, tears streaming down her cheeks as she cried, struggling for breath in between each wail, Tom's words of warning from last night ringing in her ears. The feeling of hope and happiness brimming inside her a few minutes ago had disappeared before her eyes and had been replaced with sheer panic and fear. How could William think she would do that, she asked herself.

Scrambling up off the floor she made a dash for the bathroom as vomit sailed up her throat. She cradled the loo whilst she retched and heaved, she didn't know if it was the shock of what just happened or the pregnancy.

After a few minutes she managed to calm herself down, it was all just a big mistake, she had to make William see that.

Standing in front of the bathroom mirror she took several deep breaths as she washed her face and wiped the smudged mascara from her eyes.

Back in the bedroom she looked out of the balcony door to see if she could spot William somewhere in the grounds.

It was six thirty and dusk was looming as the fog was setting in, Jess could make out a few figures heading out of the woods and some couples mooring up their rowing boats ready to head in for dinner. Pulling a hoodie on, she threw her key card and her phone in her handbag and headed out the door.

Walking quickly across the terrace towards the woods she wrapped her arms around herself, wishing she had brought a jacket as well. Heading around the left side of the lake she passed a couple walking slowly back to the hotel, laughing together as they wrapped their arms lovingly around each other. Jess kept her head down as she headed towards the mown trail leading into the woods, sure that if William had gone for a walk, he must have headed this way.

The woods were already dark, the last fading light of the sky blocked out by the towering trees looming above Jess's head. Pulling out her phone she lit up the torch, shining a light out on the ground in front of her.

The path was flat and easy to follow, every hundred yards or so there was a mown semi-circle off to the side with a little two man bench or a picnic table, it would be delightful on a summers day, Jess thought to herself as the last of the daylight disappeared above her and the darkness of the trees and the night sky merged into one.

She must have made it half way around the trail by now, she strained her eyes in front of her, praying to see William's figure in the dark. She began calling his name in the hope that hearing her own voice would at least comfort her as the surrounding darkness closed in.

A slight feeling of relief ran through her as the path

began to bend round to the right, indicating she was heading back towards the hotel. Looking around she saw another little bench sat on the side of the mown path with a jacket hanging on the back of it. A distant ray of hope shot through her as she ran up and grabbed it, praying it was the same one William was wearing when she found him sat in their room an hour before.

Holding it up in the light of her phone, she tried see if she recognised it. As she stood studying it, she heard what sounded like the snap of a twig close behind her making her jump.

Before she had time to spin around, she felt an arm wrap firmly around her neck, her knees suddenly buckled as something knocked into them from behind, collapsing her on to the ground.

Panic rose in her chest as a wet piece of fabric firmly covered her mouth and nose. She tried to scream but the noise was muffled and feeble. Behind her she felt a body, strong and steady, holding her tight, pulling her back so she was lying down. Quickly a pair of legs wrapped firmly around hers. Terror surged through her body as an arm went across her chest, holding her own arms helplessly at her side.

She was rolled over quickly, the left side of her face pushing hard against the wet grass underneath her. The feeling of dread had overtaken every inch of her body, her eyes were white with fear as she tried to struggle and scream, inhaling the chemical fumes from the soaked piece of cloth with every breath.

A couple of minutes went by, all her struggling was to

no avail. Whoever it was had her pinned, firmly holding her against the ground as her muscles wore themselves out, not moving an inch after all her efforts. She could hear her heart beating rapidly in her ears as her mind began to disconnect from her body, within a matter of seconds everything went dark.

Chapter Twenty Five

Regaining consciousness, Jess's heart began to pound. As she focused her eyes, trying to take in her surroundings, a shiver made its way around her whole body, goosebumps rose up on her arms as she realised how cold she was. Her hoodie had been taken off and her top was wet through, saturated with her cooling sweat.

It felt like she was in a car, she could hear the quiet rumble of the engine, her weight shifting around as it manoeuvred. She was face down, her cheek pushing against a wet cloth seat that she had been dribbling on. Her shoulders ached as she realised her hands had been tied behind her back, trying to move her legs she found the same had been done to her ankles.

Her brain kicked into action as a fresh wave of panic and adrenaline surged through her body. Straining her neck as much as she could she confirmed her suspicion, she was lying across the back seat of a car, but not just any car, it was her own car, she recognised the tracksuit bottoms and jumpers she had stuffed behind the driver seat. Straining round further she could see the red air freshener she had hanging from the rear view mirror.

As her heart pounded with fear, Jess struggled to get herself free, pulling her legs and hands apart as hard as she could, but it was no use, they had been tied too tightly. Letting out a wail of frustration she flung her body around, turning herself over on the seat.

"Oh, you've woken up," came the voice from the driving seat in front of her.

Jess froze. It was a male voice that sounded familiar, but she couldn't quite place it.

"Please," she begged through fear filled tears, "please let me go," she wailed, thinking of the tiny soul growing inside her, something that barely existed, yet the need to protect it had never felt so real.

"I can't do that I'm afraid, I need you," the voice said coldly as the car made a right turn.

Jess paused, replaying the words in her head.

He wasn't as well-spoken as before, but it was definitely him.

"Adam?" she exclaimed, voicing her shock.

There was a pause for a moment.

"That's what they call me, yes," he said slowly, "but that's not my real name."

Jess made another attempt to break free, wailing in frustration as her efforts failed again.

"Why are you doing this? Where are you taking me?" she yelled, before bursting into fresh tears and rolling against the back of the seat as the car accelerated.

"This was just part of the plan, so I can be free. They're asking questions you see, they've found new evidence and I can't take the blame," he said in a disturbingly placid voice, "I've come too far for that."

Jess's mind spun as she tried to make sense of what he was saying.

"What evidence? What are you talking about?" she shouted, trying again to pull her hands free.

"My sister," he paused, "they found the notes I wrote to her in the tree house that stupid man built for her and now I'm being investigated."

Jess felt like she had been hit by a bus.

Her brain was scrambling, trying to make sense of this information. As it did, as the enormity of what he had just said sunk in, all the air left her lungs.

After a moment she gasped for breath.

"You're Katie's brother?" she stuttered, trying to lean around and see him.

"Brother by blood, yes," he said, still unnervingly calm for someone who was in the middle of a kidnapping.

"But she had a very different life to me," he continued, "she was adopted by a family that gave her everything, I was left with nothing. Now how is that fair?" he asked her rhetorically.

Jess, still in a state of shock remained quiet, her mind reeling.

"I was pushed from care home to care home, no one wanted me. I had to beg, borrow and steal to get anything. It was only right she shared some of her fortune, why should she be given a decent life and not me?"

Jess closed her eyes.

"Did you kill her?" she asked quietly, a pit of terror opening in the bottom of her stomach as she waited for the answer that she already knew was coming.

He paused as he turned the car down another road.

"I had to," he said plainly.

Jess squeezed her eyes together as a lump formed in her throat. Taking a deep breath, she desperately tried to suppress the vomit that was threatening to make an appearance. Nearly half her life she had spent wondering what had happened to Katie that night, and now, here, in the middle of her own kidnapping, she was finally finding out the truth.

Taking another deep breath, Jess tried to focus, she knew she needed to keep him talking, it was the only way she might be able to manipulate him, to talk him out of whatever he was planning to do to her.

"So, you needed money?" she asked, blinking away her tears.

"Yes I needed money," he snapped back in a slightly raised voice.

Jess was sure she could hear the squeak of his gloved hands as they gripped the steering wheel.

"I had nothing, and she had everything. I was barely fed at the home, and then at eighteen I was practically thrown out, living in a friend's old car. I was homeless," he paused for a moment, taking a deep breath before he continued, "so I tracked down my dear sister. I remember seeing her trotting out of her huge house, dressed head to toe in fancy new clothes, a lunch bag all packed up for her," he spat the words.

"She helped me out for a while, told them she needed extra money for school trips and nights out. We used to spend quite a bit of time together the two of us."

He paused.

Jess remained quiet, holding her breath between tears.

"She told me all about you, how popular you were, how smart you were, how all the boys wanted to be with you. You made her feel so inferior, do you know that?"

He was taunting her.

Jess wailed as the wounds she spent so long trying to heal were severed open again.

"No," she cried through her tears, "I never made her feel like that."

"Oh, you did," he said with a smile, "she confided in me. I told her she was better off without you, that she didn't need you in her life."

Jess wanted to cover her ears, to scream so loud that she couldn't hear his words.

"Yes, we were getting along just fine for a while, but then she began getting resistant. She stopped answering the notes I used to leave her in the tree house, she wouldn't come out and meet me when I asked her to, said she couldn't get me any more money."

Jess closed her eyes and held her breath as she shed a silent tear at the thought of what Katie had gone through, no wonder she had a short temper, she was being emotionally blackmailed by a psychopath.

"I followed you both that night," he continued in a quieter tone.

Jess listened, trying to keep her tears at bay.

"I was there for her when she came running out of the gates of that house in hysterics. She told me how you shouted at her, how you tried to push her in the fire."

Jess could hear the venom in his voice.

"It was an accident," she managed in a quiet whisper.

"That's not what she said. I told her that I was right about you, that you weren't a real friend to her."

Jess's heart broke all over again, that these were the words Katie had been told on the last night of her life.

"I convinced her to get in my car, said I would drop her home. She was so upset with you, I said I didn't want her walking home, that it wasn't safe."

Jess coughed, choking on her tears.

"I dropped her a couple of roads from her house and then I followed you," he continued, "saw you running like a deranged little schoolgirl, crying out her name along the river," he paused, "you saw me ride right past you, but you would never have known it was me."

Jess could hear him smiling.

Her heart raced as another piece of the jigsaw fell into place.

"You were the boy on the skateboard?"

"Well done," he said sarcastically.

"But why drop her home if you wanted to kill her? And why were you following me?" Jess asked quietly, shuddering at the thought of him watching her that night.

"She agreed to meet me again half an hour later. She said she would go straight home and get the last bit of money I needed, but only on the condition that I got myself some help, that this was the last time, that I stopped asking her for money. She even threatened to tell her parents."

He hesitated.

"But I knew no one was going to help me, and I couldn't risk her telling anyone, so I had to make a plan."

Jess stayed silent as her whole body trembled with fear.

"Then I thought about you and how awful you had been to my sister, so after I dropped her home to get my money, I went to look for you, I knew you wouldn't be far. It didn't take long to find you with all that racket you were making, I just needed to know your whereabouts."

He paused as he indicated, turning the car around a corner.

"Katie met me half an hour later, she thought we were going for a little farewell drive."

Jess closed her eyes, her whole body shaking knowing what he was about to tell her.

"I told her what had to happen. She put up a quite a fight," he paused for a second, "it's not that easy holding someone under water, it takes a lot longer than you think."

Hot tears rolled down Jess's cheeks, her vision blurred under fresh ones emerging, struggling for breath as she cried uncontrollably.

"I loved her, she was my sister after all, but she couldn't be trusted. Telling the truth wouldn't have helped me," he scoffed, "I would have been locked away, them finding out that I had been stealing money would have been like opening a can of worms, do you understand?" he said to Jess in a raised voice, tilting the rear view mirror down so he could look at her.

"I was so sure you would have taken the blame. If it wasn't for that fucking security camera you would have done, I just know it," he said hitting his hand against the steering wheel.

"They would have linked your whereabouts to her death and that video of the two of you, well that would have been the icing on the cake. They'd seen you try to push her in a fire, pushing her in a river wouldn't have been a problem," he said with a small laugh.

"But then it all died down, the police did nothing and I just got on with my life. I managed to turn a corner somewhere and make something of myself, that would never have happened with a criminal record," he said trying to justify his actions.

"But then a few weeks ago they reared their ugly heads and started knocking on my door, saying they had new evidence, that the new owners of the house had found old notes in the treehouse that I had written to her. I mean, they don't prove anything, but I just couldn't take the risk, so that's when I went looking for you."

Jess closed her eyes letting more fresh tears roll down her face on to the wet patch on the seat.

"You were pretty easy to find," he continued, his tone

remaining calm and cold, "you hadn't gone anywhere."

Jess felt the car pull off a main road to a slower moving one. Fresh rain began beating against the windows, glistening against the glow of the streetlights outside.

"I found you on Facebook. It's a very useful tool for things like that, it led me straight to that pathetic little store. I thought the fat girl might give me some more information, so I asked her out on a date."

Jess reeled back through her memories before she reached the right one.

"The man Charlotte dated a few weeks ago, that ghosted her, that was you?"

"Yes, I had to endure three dates with that idiot before she revealed what you two got up to on a weekend, then it was easy, I just booked you for a random party and the let the plan fall into place. I thought I would let you do your little performance, then I could get you on your own, somewhere dark and quiet where no one would question it."

He paused again as he pulled out into a junction.

"Although it wasn't that easy because you and William couldn't keep your fucking hands off each other. He watches you like a besotted puppy, it's ridiculous," he spat as he changed down a gear.

"After that night I followed you some more. I realised you weren't that easy to get on your own, even at your flat, which is where I really needed you to be, that nosy fucking woman was always peering out of the window."

He went quiet for a moment.

"I swear she saw me once, then again the next time, I knew I couldn't get to you there, but then two days ago a miracle happened, the old bat got taken into hospital," he said with a laugh, "it was all too perfect."

He paused again and looked at her in the rear view mirror.

"It wasn't all quite so urgent until that tubby little girl showed up earlier, I had to leg it before she recognised me. And luckily my plan was already in motion when I found out you'd gone and got yourself knocked up, that would have really put a spanner in the works."

Jess who had remained quiet, silent tears falling down her cheeks let out a gasp at his last comment.

"That was you in the bathroom?" she exclaimed.

"Yes, it was me. It was also me that told William his precious new girlfriend was still a dirty little stripper. I had to improvise a bit on that one, I wasn't quite sure how I was going to play it, but then you left your phone right in front of him, it was just so easy," he said with satisfaction in his voice.

Fresh sweat glistened on her forehead, Jess had to close her eyes to try and concentrate on her breathing, the enormity of her situation was making her heart race so much she thought she might hyperventilate.

"I had to get him away from you and it was just in the nick of time, no one would believe your note if they thought you knew you were knocked up."

Jess opened her eyes.

"What note?"

He remained quiet.

"What note?" she demanded, trying to lift her head up.

"Right, we're nearly there," he said as he pulled over

abruptly on the side of the road.

Leaning over, he grabbed something from the passenger seat before flinging open the door.

Jess heard the door next to her open above her head as she strained to try and see out of it.

Adam's upper body appeared over the top of her, his eyes alight with adrenaline, the kind face he had been using as a mask to deceive everyone had been replaced with one of terror and lunacy. His eyes flashed as he looked down on her, like a hungry predator staring down on its prey. In a lightning fast movement, he grabbed hold of her face and squeezed it hard, Jess let out a scream as the inside of her cheeks dug into her teeth.

"Right, that's enough talking, I need you to be quiet now," he whispered viscously in her ear as he stuffed some sort of fabric so far in her mouth she retched. Moving fast, he ripped a length of industrial looking tape off a roll and stuck it firmly over her mouth.

She desperately tried to move her tongue to push it out, but it was no use. Lying back in defeat, she began to sob again as Adam closed the door above her head.

Quickly and quietly, he slunk back in the front seat and started driving again.

Chapter Twenty Six

Harry swirled the whisky around in his tumbler as he stared out of the bedroom window again, down towards the lake. He was sure he'd seen a woman that looked a lot like Jess wander down to the woods earlier, she was all alone, walking at speed with her long brown hair swinging in a ponytail behind her. Then that other man had followed not long after, the one sat at the table this afternoon that he sort of recognised, but he couldn't quite put his finger on where from. He turned as the bedroom door opened and Charlotte appeared carrying several dresses in her arms.

"Hey," she smiled, "how was your bath?"

"Yeah, lovely thanks," Harry said staring back out of the window.

"God, William was not in a good mood," Charlotte said throwing the dresses on the bed, "I asked if Jess would mind if I took them all back and he said he didn't care and that they wouldn't be joining us for a drink."

She rolled her eyes as she picked up her champagne glass, "I thought Jess said he was nice," she said as she took a swig.

"Did you recognise any of her friends earlier?" Harry asked, peeling his gaze from the window.

Charlotte frowned.

"They're not her friends, they're William's. Jess doesn't have a lot of friends, trust me," she said, topping up her glass from the bottle in the ice bucket.

Harry looked back out of the window again.

Darkness had descended upon the grounds so much so he couldn't tell where the trees finished and the sky began. The bright lights that surrounded the terrace had come on making the contrast into the woods even darker.

Padding into the bathroom, irritated that his memory was failing him, he picked up his aftershave and rubbed it on his neck as he looked in the mirror at his reflection.

He paused for a moment, slowly placing the small glass bottle down on the side of the sink, trying to unblur a memory as the realisation of what he had seen sunk in.

Suddenly he made a dash for the door, flinging it back against the wall.

"What do you think?" Charlotte asked, twirling around in front of the mirror, her curvy figure squeezed into a short black dress.

"Charlotte what number is William and Jess's room?" he

asked frantically, grabbing her by the shoulders.

"What?" she said looking at him with a mixture of shock and confusion.

"What room Charlotte?" Harry shouted, shaking her slightly.

"Erm, twenty three," she said as he released her and sprinted out of the room.

"Harry what's going on?" she shouted behind him as the door slammed shut.

Harry scaled the staircase three steps at a time to the floor below and ran along the corridor. Guests dressed up for dinner flattened themselves against the wall to get out of his way.

"Sorry," he called as he flew past them.

Grinding to a halt in front of William's door he banged on it with his fist.

"William!" he shouted, "I need to speak to you!"

There was no answer.

Gritting his teeth as he banged his fist harder against the door, he turned and saw a woman stood next to him in the hallway. Her eyes were swollen and wide, she looked like a very sad rabbit caught in the headlights.

As Harry studied her appearance momentarily the door in front of him swung back to reveal William, still in the clothes he was wearing earlier in the afternoon, a tumbler of whisky in his hand.

"What do you want?" he said coldly, eyeing Harry before glancing down the hallway.

"Georgina," he said quizzically, "what are you doing here?"

Chapter Twenty Seven

As the car slowed down Jess watched the street lights whizz past the window, giving her a small level of comfort. Her mind had been concocting all kinds of awful scenarios which involved her being dragged into a dark wood in the middle of nowhere. Street lights meant people, which in turn meant there was hope that someone might see them and intervene.

Adam slowed the car right down as Jess felt him turn a corner. The glow from the streetlights faded away slightly as the car pulled up against a curb, grinding the side of the wheel underneath her head.

Quietly he turned off the engine and opened the driver's door, sliding himself out.

Jess closed her eyes, bracing herself for him opening the door above her head, but he didn't. Instead the boot opened, Jess heard him pull something out before closing it gently. There was a pause for a minute whilst he surveyed the area he had parked in before the rear door opened.

Jess held her arms tightly against her side as he grabbed her, pulling her upright. She struggled as hard as she could, thrashing her body around, screaming through her gag, doing anything she could to resist him, but it was no use. For someone incredibly lean Adam had some strength to him, he pulled her easily up out of the car, his eyes wild, his head twitching with any sound that might indicate a person was nearby.

Jess frantically glanced around her looking for any sign of someone, or anything that might help her.

From what Adam had said she wasn't surprised at where they were, although she still couldn't understand why he wanted to bring her to her own flat.

Glancing up, Jess could see the glow of Paul's living room light behind the net curtains. She desperately wished for the familiar twitch of Janet glancing out, she would never have missed this happening right outside.

Her stomach flipped as Adam hauled her with ease over his shoulder, a few short strides and he was at her front porch, his bones digging into her stomach as she tried desperately to free herself, kicking him, digging her elbows in to his back with any remaining strength she had left. Like an expert stalker he grabbed the spare key from the ledge above the door and let himself in.

The familiar smell of marijuana oozed out of the ground

floor flat as Jess tried to bang on their door with her feet. She managed one quiet, dull knock before Adam sailed past it and up the stairs.

Placing the bag he had been carrying down, he pulled her car keys out of his pocket and opened up the front door. From where she was hanging behind him she could see his bag, it was zipped right up, concealing whatever it was he had inside.

Straining her blood filled head back, Jess could see the bottom of Paul's front door, she tried to shout his name, hoping he would hear something and come out, but she knew that was unlikely. Even if Paul did hear something, nothing would drag him off the sofa and away from the television at this time of night.

Kicking the door closed behind him, Adam made a left turn straight into the living room, slinging her back over his shoulder and down onto the sofa, her head flinging back and hitting the armrest.

As the blood began to drain from her head Jess tried to focus. Adam had his back to her pulling things out of his bag, chucking them on the armchair in front of him. Her heart was racing, she was trembling uncontrollably as more beads of cold sweat appeared on her skin. In desperation, she tried to stand up but the rope around her legs was too tight. She fell forwards, crashing on to the coffee table, sending a candle and vase of fake flowers clattering on to the floor beyond it.

Adam spun around.

"Don't do that," he said through a clenched jaw, "I need you to sit still!"

He pulled her up off the table as she flung her body around, screaming silently through her gag. Throwing her head forward she caught his lip with her forehead.

"Fuck!" Adam exclaimed, pushing her hard back onto the sofa. He put his hand to his face, dabbing at the small amount of dark red blood that was oozing from his lip.

"You bitch," he hissed quietly as he pulled the coffee table around and pushed it flush against the far wall.

Like a deranged animal he looked frantically around the room before grabbing her with his gloved hands, pulling her to the floor. Getting down on his knees, he straddled her, his whole weight pushing down on her stomach.

She tried to fight as much as she could, but he was too strong, too heavy. Jess sobbed as she gave up and dropped her head back against the carpet.

Adam moved himself down her body so his face was next to hers and reached his arms behind her.

Jess could smell his stale breath, gagging in repulsion as the hot air travelled up her nostrils.

Keeping a firm grip on both her hands, Adam untied them, bringing them round in front of her and retying them, carefully rewrapping a thick piece of fabric around them before knotting the rope over the top.

Jess looked down and frowned, realising she recognised the fabric he was using under the rope, it was the hoody she had been wearing earlier today, cut up into a long strip. Glancing down she noticed he had used it on her legs as well.

"Please, I need you to sit still," he said, his teeth grinding together as he shuffled his body forward so his crotch was nearly in her face. Pulling her arms right up above her head, he tied the end of the rope around the radiator pipe on the far wall. Shuffling back down her torso he spun around and quickly grabbed the rope around her legs, pulling it down before securing it to the pipe on the other side of the room.

Jess lay there, hot tears running down her face, snot dribbling from her nose, her body strung out in front of him as he returned to his bag, pulling more items from it.

Blinking her tears from her eyes, she looked around, trying to focus on what he was doing.

There was a long, thick rope piled in a loop on the armchair and a piece of paper folded in two on the arm.

She watched as he stood back and studied the living room door, swinging it back and forth quietly, assessing its height, tugging hard at the handle on the other side.

Suddenly Jess realised what was happening.

It was all so clear now, the note, the rope, the fabric around her wrists and ankles making sure there were no marks, no signs of a struggle.

He was going to stage her suicide.

She tried to make a sound through her gag, anything, she wanted to beg, plead with him to let her live. All she could think about was William and his unborn child inside of her, how could she die now when her life was only just about to begin.

Adam ignored her muffled noises as he grabbed the rope, tying one end around the handle on the far side of the door before throwing the remainder of it over the top.

Pausing for a moment, he looked over at Jess who froze under his stare.

He studied her body, running his eyes from her head down to her feet before turning back and creating a skull sized loop in the rope not that far from the top of the door.

"Now," he said quietly, "just a few more bits to put into place."

He began rummaging in his bag, after a second or two he pulled out what looked to Jess like an old mobile phone, nothing like the sleek new smartphones everyone had today, it was an older, bulkier one, deep enough for a chunky old age battery. As he held it up, Jess saw what looked like a flash of pink stuck to the back of it as her mind was taken on another terror filled trip down memory lane.

It was Katie's phone. The one that she had on her the night she died. The one the police never found or traced. The one they thought had been washed away in the river.

"I just need to hide this somewhere the police will find it," he glanced around before disappearing down the hallway into the bedroom.

Jess, whose ears were on high alert was sure she heard a bedside table drawer open and shut.

After a minute he reappeared with a disturbing smile on his face, the smile of a deranged person about to literally get away with murder.

"Now, this is for your dear William," he said picking up the folded piece of paper. He opened it and glanced over the scrawled writing.

"Don't worry," he stared at her for a second before returning his eyes to the page, "you've said some very nice things, but you just couldn't live with the guilt of what you had done any more. You couldn't live in true happiness knowing you had taken her life from her."

He smiled as he folded the paper and placed it carefully on the little table next to the armchair.

Jess wailed silently at the thought of William reading those words, at the grief he would feel, at the thought of him never knowing he could have been a father.

"Right," he paused, looking down at her trembling body. He glanced around the room once more before striding down the hall to the kitchen. He reappeared moments later with a chair from the dining table. Placing it in front of the door he stood back to gauge the distance between the seat and the rope at the top.

Jess squeezed her eyes together and said a silent prayer. A prayer that something, anything could be sent to help her. She began sobbing uncontrollably, struggling for air as her nose began to stream again.

"Shut up!"

Adam suddenly spun around, staring at the window that looked out on to the car park and the road beyond it. Like a burglar, he darted across the room, stepping over her before positioning himself by the window. Slowly, he pulled the curtain back an inch at the edge, peering behind it.

Jess strained her head around to see him as he pushed his ear to the glass, pulling the curtain back a little further. He looked around to the left, over the fence to the main road that led to her street.

"Oh fuck!" he exclaimed as he leapt across the room, catching Jess's knee with his foot.

Jess let out a silent scream of pain as Adam grabbed hold of his bag and spun around, looking back at the window, his face pale, his eyes wide, like an animal caught in the scope of a hunter.

Jess followed his gaze as she realised her prayer had been answered. The sound of sirens followed by the flash of blue lights shining through the curtains, getting brighter and louder. Within a matter of seconds, the whole room was glowing.

Jess heard the front door downstairs being kicked in, glancing across the room she caught sight of Adam, legging it out to the hallway as the door to her flat crashed open against the wall.

"Police!" a man shouted as he rounded the corner into the living room. He was in full uniform, a gun locked and loaded in his outstretched hands.

"Jesus," he said as he dropped to his knees in front of her, quickly ripping the tape from her mouth and pulling out the gag.

"He went down the hall," Jess shouted as she watched three other officers go past the door and disperse into the flat.

"He killed her, he killed Katie," she said in desperation to the man in front of her.

The officer looked into her eyes for a second, a mixture of sadness and anger in his face as he began untying her arms and legs.

"Are you alright ma'am?" he asked looking carefully into each of her eyes.

"Are you hurt?" he repeated when she didn't answer.

"No," Jess blubbed as she burst into fresh tears of relief.

"We've got him," she heard another officer shout down

the hallway from the kitchen.

"Lucy, come in here," the man in front of her called.

A female officer appeared in the doorway.

"Sit with her," he instructed as he strode into the hallway and down towards the kitchen.

Jess sat on the edge of the sofa, tears running down her cheeks, her whole body shaking as the lady next to her wrapped an arm around her shoulder.

"It'll be okay," she said in a calm voice.

Jess in a state of shock remained silent, staring at the wall opposite her.

She was listening to the first officer reel off an arrest statement in the kitchen when she heard another voice coming up the stairs.

"Where is she? Jess!"

Her head shot towards the door as William flew in the living room.

"Jess!" he exclaimed as he pulled her up in his arms.

He held her so tightly, she was sure she could feel his arms shaking as he wrapped them around her. After a moment her held her back out in front of him and studied her.

She could see the fear in his eyes.

"Are you okay?" his voice was wobbling slightly, his breathing rapid, the feeling of panic still with him.

Jess nodded as she grabbed hold of him, pulling herself back into his chest as she began to cry again.

"I'm sorry angel," he said kissing her head.

She could hear the lump in his throat, his voice racked with guilt remembering the final words he had spoken to her at the hotel.

"I'm so sorry," he said again.

Jess looked across the room as Harry and Georgina appeared in the doorway, both of them wide eyed and pale, afraid of what they were going to walk into.

"Christ," Harry exclaimed, taking in Jess's appearance before looking around at the ropes still attached to the radiator pipes.

Taking a step back, he stared in horror at the one hanging over the top of the door.

William followed his gaze, piecing together the scene in front of him.

"Is he here?" he said coldly to the woman who was now stood rubbing Jess's back.

"They're arresting him now," she said quietly.

"I'm going to fucking kill him!" William shouted as he let go of Jess and strode towards to door.

Harry leapt forwards, blocking his path.

"Don't!" he shouted as William tried to push past him.

"Don't!" he shouted again, using all his weight to keep him back.

"Look at her, just look at her! She needs you!"

Harry squared up to William, their foreheads touching as they braced against each other. William paused for a few seconds before dropping his head, Jess could see his shoulders shaking as he took a deep breath.

"He's not worth it," Harry said quietly, "he'll get what he deserves."

William let go of Harry's arm and turned to Jess who was still stood in the middle of the room watching him, her hand resting on her lower stomach.

"We need you."

She managed a small smile as she glanced down at her hand.

William frowned in confusion.

"We?" he said taking a step towards her, fresh tears gathering in his eyes.

Jess nodded.

"I'm pregnant," she whispered.

William paused for a moment before dropping to his knees in front of her, tears cascading down his cheeks.

Placing his hands on her hips her leant forward and kissed her stomach, his tears soaking into her shirt before getting to his feet and wrapping his arms around her.

"I'm sorry, I should have told you earlier," Jess whispered through her own tears.

William couldn't speak. He still had tears running down his face as he held her close to him, rocking her in his arms.

Suddenly there was frenzy of footsteps down the hallway. They all turned to see Adam being taken in handcuffs out the door, his face blank and empty, his eyes low.

The first officer appeared in the doorway.

"Miss Taylor, firstly we need to get you to a hospital to be checked over, an ambulance is on its way now."

William still had her in his arms, her head nestled in his chest.

"Okay," she said quietly.

"Right, I need to see the rest of you down at the station, now," he said turning to address Harry and Georgina, "and this flat is a crime scene, so no one touch anything," he said looking around the room.

"He hid her phone," Jess blurted out, pulling herself away from William's chest.

The officer looked at her blankly.

"Katie's phone, the one they never found, he had it," she said, her eyes wide, "I think it's in the bedroom somewhere."

The officer nodded slowly as he made a quick note of what she had told him.

"I'm going with her," William said firmly.

The officer looked up at him and sighed.

"Sir please, I need you at the station, I will have Lucy accompany Miss Tay—"

"I'm going with her," William interrupted him in the same tone.

The officer paused, clearly seeing how stubborn he was going to be.

"Fine, I'll see *you* tomorrow," he said, pointing his pen at William.

He then turned to Harry and Georgina.

"You two in the car now, we'll take you to the station and get your statements this evening."

They both nodded.

Georgina kept her eyes low as Harry put an arm around her and began to walk her into the hallway.

"Thank you," William said as they paused in the doorway, "both of you," he finished as they looked up and nodded at him.

Georgina still couldn't look at Jess, her eyes returned to

the floor as they left the room and made their way down the stairs.

The ambulance arrived within minutes. The whole neighbourhood was up and standing outside their houses, trying to get a glimpse of the commotion. As Jess and William made their way down the stairs, the young couple from the flat below stood in their doorway, watching for any action. Jess glared at them as she went past, resentful that none of her neighbours came to her rescue earlier.

The rain was coming down hard, but still dozens of people had made their way round to the side of Jess's building, some dressed in pyjamas and nightgowns, some had umbrellas in an attempt to stay dry as they watched them all leaving. A few police officers were stood at the edge of the car park keeping them at a sensible distance.

Jess watched as Harry and Georgina were escorted through the crowds in to the back of a police car, she watched as it pulled off in silence and made its way out on to the road.

"Come on," William said putting his arm around her, ushering her through the rain, aware of the public eyes on them as he held her hand, helping her step up into the back of the ambulance.

"Hello, Jessica Taylor?" a female paramedic gestured for her to sit on the bed that ran the length of the vehicle.

"Yes," she said quietly as she sat down.

"Are you hurt?" the woman asked with wide eyes.

"No, I don't think so," Jess said looking down at her body.

"Okay well try and sit comfortably, we'll get you to the

hospital as soon as we can."

William took a seat next to Jess and wrapped his arm around her shoulder. They sat in silence rocking back and forth as the ambulance wound its way around the streets of Witney and out on to the main road, heading towards the hospital.

"I think he used chloroform," Jess blurted out to the paramedic, "is that harmful?"

The lady looked at her with sadness in her eyes.

"It depends on the strength that was used my love, they'll do a blood test at the hospital."

"But I'm pregnant," Jess said anxiously, leaning forward over the edge of the bed, "could that have harmed the baby?"

William tightened his grip on her shoulders.

"There's obviously limited research into that sort of thing," the paramedic placed a hand on Jess's arm, "they'll do all the relevant tests when you get to the hospital, please just try and remain calm," she gave her a reassuring smile as she turned and continued filling in some paperwork.

It felt like an eternity before they reached the hospital. When they eventually did, they joined the long line of ambulances queuing to drop off patients.

The paramedic leaned forward and peered out of the window.

"Excuse me a minute," she smiled at them as she let herself out of the back door. They all watched as she marched down the pavement towards the building.

A few minutes later she reappeared with two members of hospital staff jogging behind her.

Jess got herself up as the rear door flung open.

"Jessica, these nurses are going to take you in," the paramedic said as she reached out her hand to help her down the steps.

"Thank you," William called to back her, pulling Jess in tightly towards him as they walked down the pavement and into the entrance of the hospital.

"Miss Taylor, please take a seat," one of the nurses gestured for her to sit in a wheelchair parked by the reception desk. It seemed a bit ridiculous to her, but Jess didn't argue and sat herself down as the other nurse pinged off the break, spun her around and wheeled her at pace down the hallway.

Behind them Jess could hear William's footsteps following closely as they headed further down the corridor. Abruptly the nurse slowed up and hung a left into an empty room with a narrow bed and a little plastic chair next to it.

Jess was sure the paramedic must have laid it on thick, she knew what it was like in this hospital, the fact that she had been seen to immediately and given her own room meant she was getting very special treatment.

"Right Miss Taylor, if I could get you to take off your clothes and put a hospital gown on, the doctor will be in to see you soon," the young nurse smiled at her as Jess sat up on to the bed.

"Can I get you anything to eat or drink?" she asked politely.

"A cup of tea would be amazing," Jess said managing a small smile.

"Of course," she nodded as she efficiently spun the

wheelchair around and headed out of the room.

William helped her get changed and got her up into the bed. Standing beside her, he ran his hand over her forehead smoothing the hair out of her face.

"I swear that call from the agency wasn't for me, it was him trying to get in between us," Jess whispered as her eyes filled with tears.

"I know," William said with a pained look, "I'm so sorry I didn't believe you."

"How did you find out it was him?" Jess asked, gripping his hand in hers as more hot tears ran down her cheeks.

"Harry came to see me, he said he recognised Adam from some party at school, something to do with Katie," William paused, a look of shame flashing across his face, "he said he'd seen him follow you into the woods, where you were looking for me, just like he planned."

Jess frowned, still focusing on the first piece of information.

"The boy at the party," she said to herself quietly, "that was him with Katie."

Closing her eyes, she took a deep breath, the extent of Adam's deception was completely overwhelming her.

"Why was Georgina there?" she opened her eyes, looking up at William.

"She heard him making the call to your phone. She said she'd found photos of you from the agency on his phone as well, she thought he had a thing for you and was trying to get in between us," William raised his eyebrows, "which he did, and was, but not like that."

"Jesus," Jess said as she exhaled, "he's a lunatic."

William sighed, “I know.”

He gripped her hand a little tighter.

“Jess, I’m so sorry for everything you’ve been through,” he paused as he fought back tears, “I promise I will keep you safe now, both of you. You are my everything, you two are the only things that matter now.”

He kissed the back of her hand, wiping a tear from his eye as he did.

Leaning back on the pillow, her own fresh tears cascading down her cheeks, Jess smiled back at him and closed her eyes for a second, it stung trying to keep them open. Her adrenaline levels had finally dropped and she was suddenly aware of how exhausted she was.

William was still stood next to her, holding her hand and gently stroking her hair.

She jumped slightly as the door opened and the nurse appeared with a cup of tea and two chocolate bourbons.

“Here we go,” she said placing them on the table next to the bed.

“Thank you,” William said with a grateful smile.

“I need to take these,” she said gathering up Jess’s clothes, “in case there’s any chemical on them.”

They both watched as she warily placed them in a clear plastic bag from the trolley by the door.

“The doctor will be in soon,” she gave them a brief smile as she closed the door.

Jess frowned, holding her hand on her stomach, her blinks becoming longer and longer as she struggled to keep her eyes open, as if the burden of the last thirteen years had finally been lifted.

As her mind began to drift off, the door to her room opened again making her sit up with a start.

William who had sat down next to her quickly got to his feet.

"Hello, I'm doctor Jenkins," said the short, balding man dressed in scrubs and a long white coat, "you must be Jessica Taylor," he said glancing down at her notes.

"Yes," Jess said quietly as he glanced between her William.

"It sounds like you've had quite the evening," he said with concern in his voice, "I'm sorry to hear that."

Slowly he bent down and took a close look in both of her eyes.

"Now the paramedic wrote in your notes that you're pregnant, is that correct?" he asked pulling back a page on his clipboard.

"Yes, well I mean, I've had a positive test," she said glancing at William who wrapped both his hands around hers.

"And how far along are you?" he asked still studying his notes.

"Oh, only a couple of weeks I think."

The doctor frowned slightly.

"Unfortunately, that's too early for us to scan you. Your pregnancy is dated from the first day of your last period, so you'll need to come back in six weeks from that date for a scan."

He paused, making sure she had understood.

"Right, let's take your blood pressure and heart rate. I'll take a small blood sample as well if that's alright?" he asked as he made his way round to the trolley on the other side of the room.

The doctor frowned as he strapped up her arm and pumped up the band.

"So, your blood pressure is a little high, which is understandable."

Pulling his stethoscope out, he pulled her gown down a fraction and placed it on her chest.

"Your heart rate is good, let me just get a sample."

Jess winced as he gently pushed the needle into her arm.

"Obviously you need to stay in tonight and I need you to have a shower, if there's any residue chloroform on you, I needs to be washed off. How long were you exposed to it, can you remember?" he paused, looking down at her.

Jess closed her eyes, trying to focus.

"A couple of minutes maybe, I can't remember," she frowned, shaking her head.

Next to her William remained quiet, his eyes closing as he gripped her hand a little tighter.

"It's okay," the doctor said, trying to reassure her, "the blood sample will tell us if there is any still in your system."

"Right," he said sticking a label onto the small tube of blood he had just extracted, "try and get some sleep, I expect the police will be in to see you in the morning."

"Okay, thank you," Jess said, laying her head back against the pillow.

William ran the shower for her, making sure it was warm enough before helping her out of her gown.

Jess stood in the tiny wet room, the hot water spraying

over her, the bright, white spotlight on the ceiling shining down into her eyes. Steam built up around her as she desperately scrubbed her whole body, paying extra attention to anywhere that Adam had touched her.

She washed her face five times, the memory of the chemical still strong in her nostrils, the soaked rag that was forced against her skin for what seemed like a lifetime.

Rubbing a small hole in the mirror she saw how red and sore her skin was, her eyes were swollen and blood shot and there was a small lump on her forehead where she had hit him in the chin. Grabbing the flannel, she winced at the pain as she rubbed her forehead, right on the lump, desperate to get any trace of him off of her.

Jess drifted in and out of consciousness over most of the night. Whenever her mind managed to find a peaceful place in her subconscious to float off to, visions of Adam would appear. The things he had planned to do to her, and in turn her unborn child. The things that he had done to Katie all those years ago that had gone unpunished for so long. Several times Jess woke up in a cold sweat, shrieking in fear as she sat bolt upright in bed before reality brought her back to where she was.

William stayed next to her the whole night, getting a few brief minutes of sleep when he allowed himself.

The buzz of the morning routine in the hospital was a welcome sound, even with William sat beside her, the darkness of the room and the quiet corridors were making Jess feel uneasy.

At seven thirty the doctor came around to do her vitals again, swiftly followed by a nurse who wheeled in a tray of breakfast food. Jess tried not to look too unenthusiastic as she was presented with a plate of cold buttered toast and very soggy scrambled eggs.

"Thanks," she said, trying to suppress the lump in her throat as she studied her breakfast. As the nurse left the room William whipped the tray off her lap as the colour drained from her face.

"Shall I see what they have in the shop downstairs?" he asked as he rubbed her back.

"Yes please. Nothing with eggs" she said, shaking her head.

"Okay, I'll be back as soon as I can."

William returned five minutes later with two fresh croissants and two cups of early grey.

"This is yours, it's decaf," he said, passing her a polystyrene cup.

"Thank you," she smiled as she began forcing down her croissant.

As they finished their teas there was a knock on the door.

Jess glanced up to see a man in a cheap looking suit enter the room, followed by the police officer that had been in charge when they arrested Adam in her flat last night.

The first man stretched out his hand to her.

"Jessica Taylor?"

"Yes," Jess said, taking his hand as William stood up next to her.

"I'm Detective Hill, I'm now in charge of the Katie Lockhart case," he said shaking her hand vigorously.

"We thought we would come and see you," he paused, gesturing behind him to his colleague, "we wanted to come and talk you through everything and see if you had any—"

"Where is he?" Jess interrupted him.

William took her hand in his, trying to give her some reassurance.

"He's in a cell, which is where he will stay for a very long time. I promise you," he said, nodding his head and placing his hands in his pockets, "as soon as William and Harry alerted us to who they thought he was, we traced your phone and followed your movements back to your flat. The Sergeant here rallied and team and got there as soon as he could, which was just in time by the sounds of it."

He frowned and glanced down at his feet.

"I did try and reach out to you a couple of weeks back. The house Katie used to live in changed hands recently, the new owners had a bit of remodel. They found notes from him buried under a floorboard in her old room, a few more had been hidden up in the treehouse. There was nothing there to convict him, but we were about to undergo an investigation."

Jess looked down at her lap.

"I did see the email, but I've had lots of those over the years. I just wanted to move on from it all," she said looking over at William who was still holding her hand.

"I can quite understand that," the detective said glancing between them.

"Adam," he said, making quotations with his fingers, "has pleaded guilty to everything which amongst other crimes amounts to one case of murder and one case of attempted murder."

Jess's breathing quickened as she began to cry, fresh

tears emerged thick and fast from her already swollen eyes.

Hearing the words spoken out loud seemed so surreal.

"I am so sorry for what you have been through," the detective said, "we have a specialist team that can provide support for you, it's important that you get the help you need to recover and then hopefully you can get some closure from all of this."

He leant forwards and placed a hand briefly on her shoulder.

"We will be in touch," he said, nodding at William as both him and the officer turned simultaneously to leave the room.

Pausing in the doorway, he turned back to them, a hint of a smile on his face.

"Oh, and congratulations."

Chapter Twenty Eight

The early autumn sunrise crept quietly over the treetops lining the driveway. The Old Manor glowed in its warmth as the house lit up.

Opening her eyes half an inch, Jess gauged the time by the level of sunlight sneaking in through the gap in the curtains. The room was quiet, beside her William lay in a deep sleep, his breathing slow and calm.

Glancing over, as she always did now as soon as she woke, Jess peeked into the white waffle lined bassinet sat to the side of the bed. Pushing herself up on her elbow, she smiled as she gazed at the perfect little face, still fast asleep, her nose twitching slightly as she dreamt.

Hope they had called her, Hope Audrey Archer.

Jess thought back to the day she was born. It was an early trip to the hospital after six hours of contractions at home. William was by her side for every one of them, making sure she was as comfortable as she could be, bringing her odd food requests and rubbing her back through the pain.

Hope was born four hours into their hospital visit. Jess remembered sitting back in the bed covered in blood, sweat and tears as she was handed her daughter. She remembered the look on William's face when he saw her, like his heart could burst with love. She thought hers might burst as she watched him hold her for the first time, this tiny little person wrapped up in his enormous arms, like he could have held her there forever.

Jess rolled over, gently stroking William's face as she kissed him on the cheek, feeling him stir under her touch.

Slowly he turned his head towards her.

"Happy birthday darling," she whispered before kissing him again, this time on the lips.

"Thank you," he smiled opening his eyes, "how are my girls?" he asked quietly as he propped himself up to look over at Hope.

"Still sleepy," Jess said following William's gaze, "she should be, she was up four times last night."

William yawned as he picked up the phone to order some tea.

"Good job she's so cute," he said, punching in a number to connect to Gwen.

Jess got up and quietly pulled back the curtains, letting the heat from the morning sun warm her face.

"What time are your family coming?" she asked as she

gazed out at the rolling hills in the distance.

"About twelve I think, I thought we could do some celebratory drinks in the garden," William suggested.

"That's a lovely idea," Jess said looking down at the diamond ring on her finger, sparkling in the sunlight.

William had proposed to her on their ski trip, although there was no skiing involved, Jess was four months pregnant at the time, but it was still the best week of her life.

They laid in every morning, making their way up the mountain around midday after Jess's daily bout of morning sickness to find a panoramic spot for lunch. On the way down they would stop in the local town and have a wander around, looking in shops and enjoying the vibrant bustle of the après ski bars. When dusk began to descend, the thousands of fairy lights that decorated the whole town would light up. Jess had never seen anything like it, it looked like every Christmas she had ever seen rolled into one.

On their final day they took the cable car up to the top of the glacier. The view was spectacular. A blanket of cloud sat below them in the valley, miles away in the distance they could see other mountain peaks, so mighty they had emerged through the cloud, perfectly white against the bright blue sky. The snow conditions on the only run down were less than ideal, aside from a couple of other walkers that had the same idea as them, they were pretty much alone.

It was there, whilst they were stood on top of the world, that William got down on one knee and asked her to spend the rest of her life with him.

Jess cried with happiness the whole ride back to the

chalet, where they spent the evening in front of the open fire, making plans for the rest of their lives together.

They hadn't seen all of William's family since the proposal, or since Hope had arrived. It was also the first time Jess was going to meet Matilda, so a celebration was certainly in order today.

Hope began to stir as William picked her up. Cradling her in his arms, he kissed her gently on the top of her head.

"Good morning my little angel," he whispered, pausing to inhale her scent.

There was a quiet knock on the door as it swung open.

"Morning," Gwen whispered, unsure if Hope was awake or not.

"Morning," Jess smiled as she took the tray of tea from her.

"Oh, how is the little darling today?" Gwen said as she crept across the room to get a closer look at Hope.

Jess smiled at her affection, catching William's eye as she did.

"Oh, and Happy Birthday," she looked up at William, "I nearly forgot," she said, stroking Hope gently on the forehead, her little wisp of dark hair pinging back up every time.

"And talk of forgetting," Gwen said, "the attorneys called yesterday about the trust left for you Jess, they want to meet with you next week to sign some forms."

"Okay thanks, I'll call them on Monday," Jess replied as Gwen gave Hope's hand a tiny squeeze before tottering out of the room and down the hallway.

Audrey had passed away three months before Hope was

born. She had lived longer than any of them expected her to, given her condition. The last six months of her life were spent sat in a bed being fed through a tube, it was absolutely heart breaking for Jess as she watched her mother's body being kept alive, whilst her brain just wanted her to slip away. In the end it was a relief. She hadn't recognised Jess for a long time, and although she had met William on several occasions, she never knew him properly and he never knew her.

As Jess watched William dressing Hope on the changing table by the window, she thought to herself the greatest shame of all was that Audrey never got to meet her granddaughter.

Around a month after the funeral, Jess was contacted by a firm of solicitors who informed her Audrey had been keeping a trust in her name.

It turned out her estranged father, a man called Albert, had died when she was ten and had left a considerable amount of money in a trust for Jess.

The sum of money wasn't the most shocking thing about the whole situation, it took a long time for Jess to accept the fact her mother knew about this connection with her father and had kept it from her all these years.

The large sum of money which ironically, she now didn't need, she planned to donate to the care home. It needed roof repairs and insulation. Mrs Brown was always desperately trying to put together coffee mornings or bake sales to raise some cash for the place. Jess couldn't think of a better use for it. She would tell Mrs Brown to get new carpets for the hallways and to splash out on a decent television.

"Right Mumma," William said handing Hope over to her, "she's hungry and I'm no good for that I'm afraid," he said as he kissed them both.

Jess smiled down at the perfect little face nestling into her and said a silent prayer of thanks for the second chance she had been given, for these two perfect souls who had made her whole again.

Want more from Jess and William?

The Wedding

Coming soon